a Dead Sin

Tracie Podger

Jeanette

Enjoy!

Tracie x

Cover designed by Margreet Asslebergs
Rebel Edit & Design
Cover Model – Jase Dean
Cover Model shot by – Wander Aguir
Formatting by Irish Ink – Formatting & Graphics

Acknowledgements

My heartfelt thanks to the best beta readers a girl could want, Karen Shenton, Alison Parkins, and Rebecca Sherwin - your input is invaluable.

Thank you to Margreet Asslebergs from Rebel Edit & Design for yet another wonderful cover, this makes our ninth collaboration!

I'd also like to give a huge thank you to my editor, Karen Hrdlicka, and proofreader, Joanne Thompson.

A big hug goes to the ladies in my team. These ladies give up their time to support and promote my books. Alison 'Awesome' Parkins, Karen Shenton, Karen Atkinson-Lingham, Marina Marinova, Ann Batty, Fran Brisland, Elaine Turner, Kerry-Ann Bell and Louise White, Catherine Bibby & Ellie Aspill, – otherwise known as the Twisted Angels.

To all the wonderful bloggers that have been involved in promoting my books and joining tours, thank you and I appreciate your support. There are too many to name individually – you know who you are.

If you wish to keep up to date with information on this series and future releases - and have the chance to enter monthly competitions, feel free to sign up for my newsletter. You can find the details on my web site:

www.TraciePodger.com

Success if not final, failure is not fatal: it is the courage to continue that counts.
Winston Churchill

Cover design – Rebel Edit & Design

Model – Jase Dean

Photographer – Wander Aguiar

Formatting – Irish Ink – Formatting & Graphics

Chapter 1

Capital Vices. Cardinal Sins. Which one is the worst? Is it pride, greed, or lust? Maybe it's envy, gluttony, or even wrath. As for sloth? What does that actually mean?

I guess we've all been guilty of these sins but no more than the man I have been watching for years. I know every thing he does. I know the time he leaves his house each morning. I know the speed he drives his car to work, the exact moment he will turn on the indicator when he makes that right turn into the parking lot.

I know the friends he meets with a slap to the back, a high five, or a shoulder bump. I know the women that fawn over him. He, they, made me feel sick to my stomach.

They don't know me; I doubt they've ever noticed me. They will, though, soon. I've waited a long time for this, a long time to turn his comfortable life on its head, to destroy him.

———

My palms were sweaty as I walked the stone floor corridor. My footsteps echoed, and in my head I could hear my heart beat a frantic rhythm. I took a few deep breaths as I reached the double oak doors, intricately carved with figures. I was thankful that the hand I reached out to turn the large brass handle, was steady. My other hand held a revolver down beside my thigh. I wasn't sure what I was going to be faced with when I gently turned the handle and slowly pushed the door open. It creaked as the old rusting hinges protested, reminding me of a scary movie.

Sunlight blazed into the empty room through a broken glass window. It picked out every speck of dust that floated around. Immediately, my senses were assaulted by a metallic tang, it filled my nostrils and coated my taste buds as I took a breath in through my mouth. Then I saw her.

Against the back wall was my missing girl. Crucified.

My stomach lurched; I swallowed down the bile that rose to burn my throat. I closed my eyes briefly. Casey Long: blonde-haired, cheerleader, straight A student, naked and covered in blood, was tied to a cross against the back wall.

"Fuck!" I whispered. "Fuck!"

For five days I'd been searching for her after her mother had called in a missing person's report. Five days of having no idea she was practically on my doorstep. I holstered my gun and made a call.

"Dean, she's in here," I said.

I took care to retreat only in the places I had already stepped. Making sure not to further disturb any forensic evidence, until I made my way back out of the room and gently closed the door behind me. There was no need to check for signs of life; Casey was very clearly dead.

Within seconds, the corridor was filled with activity. Dean, my partner for the past five years, strode toward me. His size ten feet clomped on the polished floor.

"Is it definitely her?" he asked. I nodded.

"Dead?" Again, I nodded.

"Fuck!" He echoed my sentiments.

"Detective?" I turned toward the voice behind me.

"Samuel, I think you best step outside," I said to the caretaker of Montford High School.

No matter how many times I'd told him to call me by my name, he never did. Samuel was an old guy; he'd been the caretaker when I'd been a student at Montford some years ago. He was as old as the school back then.

I watched as he nodded and backed down the corridor, wringing his hands together. I imagined the sight of what he'd discovered on his morning rounds would finish him where working at the school was concerned. How do you recover from seeing something like that? It was bad enough for me and Dean, and we'd seen our fair share of murder.

"I've called in the doc, she's on her way," Dean said.

"Okay, we need to seal this off, close this wing down. You want to call it in?"

Dean fished his mobile from his pocket and called through to the station. As he walked a little way down the corridor for a better reception, I took a deep breath, I knew at some point that day I'd be delivering the worst news possible to the parent of a missing child.

I'd always wanted to be a cop, ever since receiving a costume for Halloween one year. Despite growing out of it, I'd kept that badge for years. I loved my job, normally. I just hated knowing what I would have to do soon. I could send someone else, but I'd grown up in this town, I knew most of its occupants, and I wanted to be the one to break the news to Sally Long.

I scrubbed my hand over my face, feeling the two-day-old

stubble around my jaw. Dean would take a statement from Samuel while I waited for Doc, or Eddie, as she was called.

Our state medical examiner had, only a few hours prior, been naked in my bed after we'd spent the night fucking. Neither of us had gotten any sleep, but I knew that as soon as she arrived, there would be no evidence of that.

———

Within a few minutes of Dean calling the crime in, the parking lot was flooded with blue and red flashing lights. Groups of teens hung around, trying to find out why part of their school was closed the first day back from break. Teachers were questioning the sheriff, who I'd positioned at the front door, blocking the entrance. I decided to speak to the principal while I waited for Eddie to arrive.

"A death?" Mr. Turner asked.

"Yes, and until we can process the scene and remove the body, this wing is closed off," I replied.

I was standing just inside the main entrance with the principal of Montford School. I was reluctant to give too many details, but I imagined Samuel would soon be regaling his colleagues. I waved over one of the sheriff's deputies and instructed him to take Samuel to the station; we'd need to interview him formally, and rule him out as a suspect, of course.

"I need all the CCTV images you have, covering the last twelve hours. I'll ask one of my team to accompany you," I said.

Mr. Turner nodded his head. "Do you know who it is?"

"I'm not able to give any more details right now."

"Is it Casey?" His voice broke as he spoke.

I didn't answer and I guess that was confirmation enough. Tears welled in his eyes. He gently shook his head and placed his

8

hand on my shoulder.

"I don't envy you your job, Mich. You should have stayed with the FBI," he said.

"Wasn't solving crimes, Mr. Turner," I replied.

I'd left the FBI some months prior, exhausted by the bureaucracy and taken a backward, some might say, step to where I'd started and what I loved the most: solving crimes within the community I'd grown up in.

I motioned to an officer to accompany Mr. Turner and retrieve as much CCTV as he could. I had a team scouring the outside, looking for evidence. As I made my way outside, the medical examiner's black, unmarked van arrived. It reversed up close to the doors in preparation. A few seconds later, I heard the throaty roar of a large, black motorcycle as it joined us. Eddie was about the most unconventional medical examiner I'd come across. She killed the engine, unfastened her helmet, and hooked it over the handlebars before swinging a long, jean-clad leg over the seat. Despite the severity that had brought nearly twenty police officers and sheriff's deputies together, I watched as heads turned and lips curled into lustful smirks, following her as she walked toward me.

"Mich," she said, showing no recognition of the night we'd spent together.

"Eddie. She's in here."

Eddie stopped at the side of the van and slid open the door.

"Talk to me," she instructed, as she reached in for her box of tricks.

"Casey Long has been missing for five days. The caretaker found her crucified in the school hall, this morning."

Eddie pulled on white coveralls and threw some gloves and

plastic booties at me. At the same time, her two assistants exited from the front of the van. They donned the same clothing. One retrieved a camera and the other, another toolbox.

"Have you or the caretaker contaminated the body?" Eddie said, staring at me.

I raised an eyebrow at her in annoyance. "Of course not." She gave me a small nod.

Eddie wasn't just a medical examiner, she was also a forensic pathologist, and about the best I'd ever witnessed when it came to processing a crime scene.

"Where's the caretaker?"

"At the station, being fingerprinted and processed, of course."

Eddie nodded and I held out my arm, inviting her to walk ahead of me. We made our way to the hall. Before we entered, Dan, Eddie's assistant, took photographs of the corridor and the two oak doors, concentrating on the handles that would be dusted for prints by my forensic team.

I pulled the latex gloves on and covered my shoes with the plastic booties. I opened the door. The sun had shifted slightly. Instead of bathing the center of the room, a beam of light streaked across, highlighting Casey. Had it not been a real person on that wooden cross, we could have been forgiven for thinking there was something angelic or ethereal about the scene. I heard the whispered prayer that Eddie gave at every murder scene she and I had attended.

"Shit, Mich," she said. I heard her take a deep breath.

Casey Long had five obvious stab wounds on her. They mirrored the cross she'd been attached to. Somehow, and as ridiculous as it felt, I was pleased to see her wrists and ankles had been bound with rope and not nailed. Her head lolled to one side, and her eyes, wide open, stared down at us. Dan photographed her from every angle.

"You've detailed the broken window, I take it?" Eddie asked.

"Yes, my team has taken shots of it and are about to dust outside. I don't hold much hope for prints, it rained last night."

"Was the window broken before?"

"Not according to the caretaker. Although this room isn't used at the moment, it was closed off for renovations, something to do with varnishing the floor."

Eddie pivoted slowly, taking in every aspect of the room. It was empty, save for a bench on the opposite wall, beside the door. She stared at it.

"It's been moved," I said. She looked up at me.

"There's a couple of very faint scratch marks on the floor, they look fresh to me, as if the bench has been dragged in position."

"To sit and admire his work?" she asked.

"Possibly, and that's an assumption, Doctor," I said, with a smirk.

"Not an assumption, Detective. You'd need some strength to haul a cross with a body on it upright, stabilize and fix it into place. I think we're safe to assume a male perp. And she wasn't killed here."

Dan moved to the bench, having taken all the shots he needed. Eddie and I walked toward Casey.

"Not enough blood," she whispered, as she stared up at the young girl. "Let's get her down."

The cross was leaning against the back wall and just a little larger than Casey herself. It looked custom-made. Thick planks of a dark wood, possibly oak, seemed to have been expertly joined together. Someone had taken care to make that cross, its joints were dovetailed. Eddie's assistants stood on either side and gently lowered the cross to the floor, placing her to one side of her original position, and on a plastic tarp.

I stood back a little and watched as Eddie did her initial assessment. Most of her determination would be done back at her office. She spoke to Casey as if she were still alive, apologizing for the prodding as she felt her way around the body. I think that was one of the things that endeared Eddie to the folks of our town; she had the utmost respect for the dead, as well as the living.

While she tended to Casey, I strode around the room, absorbing the scene, hoping it would give up its secrets. I found myself back at the bench, and although I didn't sit, I stared at the wall where Casey had been. Something caught my eye, something so subtle I'd missed it at first. I walked toward it. Scratched very lightly, in the plaster above where the cross had stood, was one word. It took me a moment to understand; the letters were widely spaced.

L U S T

Chapter 2

Detective Mich Curtis, former FBI agent. Just his name, as it rolled off my tongue, brought goosebumps to my skin. He looked so sad; those fine lines across his forehead were deeper as he furrowed his brow, trying to make sense of the scene he'd found. I chuckled. The game had begun; the hunt was on. But who was the hunter, and who was the prey? Which one of us would be the winner? I could see him stare at the word, trying to work out its relationship to the crucifixion of the naughty girl. Lust. I'd love to get inside his head. Hopefully I will, although it wouldn't be in the psychological sense. You see, Mich Curtis ruined my life, and I intend to repay him for that.

As for her, I see her. I see the way she looks at him. They were fucking, that much was obvious. I wondered how he fucked her: hard, fast, slow, tenderly? I made a note to watch, to familiarize myself with her body, and how his hands traveled over it. I wanted to see her face when he made her come, when he brought her to the edge of such pleasure, her mind and body giving itself over to him. My mouth watered at the thought, my stomach knotted with desire for them both.

"What do you think that means?" Eddie asked, as she stood beside me.

"I have no idea yet. He lusted after her?"

I called Dan over to take a couple of pictures. Eddie wouldn't allow any of my team in the room until she had removed the body and handed the scene over to me. It was only our relationship, and my standing in the police force, that had me in there with her as it was. Not that our relationship was common knowledge, and not that we had a *relationship* beyond fucking, regularly.

"As soon as you're ready to move her, I can get my team in," I said, hoping that might speed things up a little.

"We're going to move her as is, I want to examine the cross as well. I've asked Dan to erect some tenting around the back of the van. I don't think we need the spectators to see this."

Although the students and teachers had been kept well enough away from the entrance to the school, they could still see across the parking lot. Dean stood at the open door, waiting for permission to come in. He had his protective clothing on. I pointed to the word on the wall and watched him squint as he tried to read it.

"Samuel is being interviewed," he called out.

"And the team outside?" I asked.

"A couple of footprints, no fingerprints as of yet. There's a tire track just across the way, we've taken molds." He consulted his notebook as he spoke. "CCTV is back at the station, waiting to be analyzed, I'll get someone on that straight away. Oh, the window? Smashed from the inside."

"Inside?" I asked.

"Yeah, shards of glass on the ground outside. So someone came in, and then smashed a window. Fuck knows why."

"To get her in?" Dan asked.

I looked at him. "If they came in, they'd have brought her with them. Why break in, then smash a window?"

"And that, my friend, is why you are my assistant and he is the detective," Eddie said. "Let's get her back to the office."

———

As slight as Eddie was in stature, it didn't stop her from helping to haul the cross onto a cart that had been brought into the room. She was a strong, powerful woman. My bruised body was testament to that sometimes. She kept fit, she rode a fucking Harley, and she refused to commit to a *normal* relationship with me. She pissed me off sometimes, most times. Then there were other days, like that day, when my admiration and respect for her were through the roof.

"I'll expect you at about three o'clock?" Eddie said, as they wheeled the cross, with Casey still attached, to the back of the van.

"Sure. We'll be there." Dean rolled his eyes at my statement; he hated attending autopsies about as much as I did.

A tunnel of plastic had been erected from the back of the van to the entrance of the school. I watched as the tarp-covered body was slid into the back, amazed that it actually fit. The doors were closed and the tenting removed. Eddie stripped off her coveralls and booties, threw the gloves into the side of the van, and without a backward glance, strode for her bike.

Once again, I watched as heads turned, following her every move. I wasn't scanning faces because I was jealous though. I was scanning to see if anyone gave any indication that they were more involved than helping to solve a crime. In my experience, it was often the case that the perpetrator turned up at a crime scene with some sick satisfaction at watching the police trying to decipher their handiwork. I knew everyone here, and there was not one person I'd have the slightest suspicion of.

Once Eddie and her team had gone, Dean and I headed back to the hall. We now had full access and met with our forensic guys at the door. I gave them my initial thoughts; dust the bench, the inside of the window, the wall. I wanted ultraviolet scans of the floor to see if we could pick up any specks of unobvious blood. Until I had a time of death, I would need to treat the hall as the murder scene. Eddie had thought Casey hadn't been murdered at the hall but elsewhere. That threw in way more complications than I was happy about. I'd need reinforcements to start a search. I hoped some clues would be given up on the body as to where I needed to start that search.

I stood in the middle of the room and tuned out. Once again, I tried to absorb every scent, every creak of wood; I allowed the crime scene to be soaked up by my mind. I wanted to be able to recall every crack, crevice, and corner without being there. I wanted to be able to stand in my office or my home, and perfectly picture the hall. I closed my eyes, seeing the room in my mind, satisfied that I'd met my objective.

Whereas Dean took copious notes, I had a picture perfect memory. I'd recall every word spoken and every detail, which I'd then write up when I got back to the station. I guessed it was one reason I'd been transferred to the FBI for a year. I'd learned a lot from my time with the Bureau, least of all, the ability to look beyond the obvious, to get inside the mind of a killer. Eddie thought I was fucked up by that, I believed she used that as an excuse not to get close.

"Mich?" Dean brought me out of my thoughts.

I checked my watch and noticed we'd been at the school over three hours. Dean and I headed to the parking lot and our car, leaving the rest of the team to carry on with forensics. I wanted to coordinate, but before I could do that, there was the matter of informing the parents. I didn't need them to make a formal identification; we had a recent photograph, there was no mistake that the girl on the cross was Casey Long.

I grabbed my phone and called for a family liaison officer to meet me. As much as I wanted to be the one to deliver the news, I also needed to get back to the station as quickly as possible.

"Oh, no. God, please, no!" Sally Long had her hands covering her mouth and tears streaming down her cheeks.

"I'm so sorry, Mrs. Long. I really wish I had better news for you."

The minute Sally opened the to door to me, I imagined the look on my face had given away that I wasn't coming with good news. She'd collapsed to her knees before I'd even spoken. I'd helped her to her feet and sat her on the couch. The liaison officer sat beside her. She'd peppered me with questions that I was unwilling to answer immediately. I explained that we needed to do further investigations before we could answer cause of death, but that I'd wanted her to hear from me before the rumor mill got to her door.

I sat for a further ten minutes before excusing myself and joining Dean in the car waiting outside.

"Shit part of the job, huh?" he said, as he turned the car around and we headed back to the station.

"Yep."

I rested back in the seat and closed my eyes for a moment. We continued the journey in silence with just the purr of the engine for company. I tried to calculate in my mind the number of murders I'd investigated. Thankfully it wasn't as many as I'd thought. Other than my time in the FBI, where I'd been on the trail of a cult that had decided to silence its ex-members, the sleepy town I lived in was pretty safe, or so I thought.

"Lust," I whispered.

"Huh?"

I opened my eyes and looked at Dean. "Lust. I wonder why he chose that word specifically."

"He wanted her, she wanted him?"

"Possibly, and I think that's what we're initially led to accept, but I don't believe he wants to make it easy for us. Casey Long, everyone's friend, nice girl, so why her?"

"Wrong place, wrong time?"

"No. My gut tells me she was selected for some reason. Right place, right time, we just need to know why."

The one thing I enjoyed the most about working with Dean was the bouncing of ideas. He asked the questions which prompted me to think hard and dig deep into my psyche. Transform myself from cop to killer. And that wasn't hard. Maybe that's what made me a great cop—I'd been a killer, too.

Chapter 3

I kept my attention on Mich as he watched all eyes follow the woman to her motorcycle. Jealousy. It should be added to our list of deadly sins. Maybe I should rewrite them, or add another. But I had a plan and there was no time to deviate from that plan. I was but a mere servant, there were far more important people waiting on my plan to come to fruition. I wanted to bounce on the balls of my feet, or clap my hands at the activity, the urgency, that surrounded me. I could smell their fear, their anxiety that a killer had invaded their small town. It excited me; it had my heart pumping fast. I'd watched the van take the girl away. I'd listened to the sobs of silly schoolgirls, who had no idea what had happened but wanted to be part of the fun, to gain some attention from the doped up jocks comforting them. Fucking idiots, the lot of them.

The station was a hive of activity. An incident room had been set up and I strode in, calling all available staff together. The chief was waiting for an update, but he usually left me alone in the first stages of an investigation. Patrick was waiting on retirement, I was supposed to be next in line, but being chief of police wasn't a job I was seeking. It reminded me of my FBI days: paper pushing, statistic balancing; reporting to senior officials, instead of doing my job, wasn't what I'd signed up for.

"People!" I shouted, to quiet down the hum.

I turned to the whiteboard that had a photograph of Casey, smiling in her cheerleader outfit, and next to it, a naked one, bloodied and dead. Underneath we had date, location, and what we had going on at that time. I checked my watch as colleagues took to seats.

Samantha handed me a coffee, black, strong, just as I liked it. I needed the kick start after so little sleep.

"Casey Long's mother has been informed, she has a liaison with her now, waiting on family to arrive and sit with her. Doc has the body, still attached to the cross. There were five wounds, most likely stab wounds, in the shape of a cross down her body. I'm not a medical examiner, but I don't see the stab wounds as cause of death, more symbolic." I studied the photograph as I spoke.

"There was a word scratched into the wall, faintly, above the cross. Lust. I also suspect our perp sat on a bench on the opposite side of the room to admire his handy work. When forensics come back, we'll have more details. There was a smashed window but we don't believe that to be our entry method. How are we getting on with CCTV?"

"We have vehicle lights that set off an outdoor motion sensor, all I can make out, at the moment, is it's a truck. The unfortunate thing is, that motion sensor was attached to some high-powered lighting, which distorts and blurs the recording."

I followed the voice to one of the newest members of the team, Pete. He was a young and very enthusiastic guy. I had high hopes for him. He happened to also be a shit hot computer wizard.

"Can you do anything with the images?" I asked.

"I'm going to see if I can run them through some programs to clean them up a little, but the glare pretty much wipes out anything useful at the moment."

"Fuck!"

"Makes me laugh. People spend all this fucking money on CCTV but then blind it with high-powered lighting. Anyway, the truck backs up to the edge of the parking lot and bounces up over the curb. I can't see into the back of the truck, but I can see an arm resting on the opened window, driver's side. I've zoomed in, and it's safe to say, unless our perp has some serious hormonal issues, it's a guy."

I didn't react to the snickering that followed Pete's statement. I accepted that, for some to cope with investigating the murder of a young woman, they had to inject some humor into it. It wasn't personal, it didn't mean they couldn't do their jobs or that they disrespected the dead, it was just their way.

"Tell me more," I said.

"Hairy arm and a strange tattoo that I'll need to enhance before I can get a decent image of it."

My heart raced a little and it wasn't from the coffee. A bare arm with a tattoo was fucking great news so early on in an investigation. But then Pete shattered my excitement.

"The bad news is, the truck doesn't hang around. I calculate that less than a minute later, it drives off."

A murmur spread around the room. "Okay, okay, quiet down. That doesn't mean this truck isn't involved. We don't know yet what time Casey was taken to the hall. He may have gotten spooked by the lights, just keep on that CCTV, right until the point you see us arriving, okay?"

"Samantha, I want you back at the school, I want to know any blind spots for those cameras. Could our man have come at a different angle? Dean, what do you have?"

Dean stood and walked toward the whiteboard. He picked up a pen and as he spoke, he wrote a synopsis.

"We have two footprints, one directly under the window and one a little further back, facing the opposite direction. It rained heavily during the night, so I'm not expecting fingerprinting on the outside to be successful."

"How did you get footprints if it rained?" The question came from the back of the room.

"The one under the window, he stood in a flower bed, mud in other words. And the one on the grassy area? Luckily for us, this part of the school is being renovated and grass replanted, by the looks of it. There was a bare patch. The soil around the school is mostly clay. Perfect molds," Dean said.

"Okay, here's what I need. Pete, you keep on that CCTV. Samantha, back to the school; check for blind spots. I want the forensics rushed through, no fucking me around. Call in favors, do whatever you have to. I want a house to house, see if anyone can remember seeing that truck, involved or not, it shouldn't have been on the premises at that time; Carl, you organize that. No talking outside this building, I hear one piece of information, and I'll fucking nail whoever shared it, understand?"

Heads nodded and chairs scraped against the tiled floor. The sound grated on me, it should be carpeted but budgets didn't allow for that kind of luxury.

"Dean, we need to head over to the doc's."

It was closing on three o'clock and I wanted to see the autopsy. I had no desire to watch Casey being cut open, organs removed and weighed, measurements taken, and discussions on her last meal. I wanted to know exactly what had killed her and if there was any indication of where.

I gestured for the car keys as we approached our vehicle. Dean threw them over the roof to me. It was often a battle as to who would drive. High speed was Dean's thing, but we weren't in a rush right then.

"You gonna take the job then?" Dean asked, as I started the car.

"The job?"

"Chief of Police."

"No, I don't think so."

"Who else would do it?"

"You? You're as qualified as me."

"No! Can you imagine me having to suck up to the mayor, and all that paperwork? No chance."

"Maybe they'll get someone in from outside."

"So, you and the doc? Any further on?"

We drove the short journey toward the Medical Examiner's office, stopping briefly at a set of lights and watched a TV newsroom van pull a U-turn. Hopefully they hadn't caught wind of our murder just yet.

"No, she likes us just the way we are."

Dean was the only one who knew about Eddie and me. He'd stumbled across us one night in a teenage make-out session in my car.

"And you don't?"

I looked over to him with raised eyebrows. "I like it just fine, but it might be nice to be a little more 'formal' I guess."

I might only be mid-thirties but I liked my traditional relationships. I wasn't about to turn away the 'fuck buddy,' but I felt something for Eddie. It was hard to form a relationship with the jobs that we had, so in my mind, we'd be perfect together. I guessed she just didn't feel the same way. She had commitment issues, for sure.

"Anyway, no time for that now. Let's get this over with," I added, as we pulled into the parking lot.

Eddie's bike was parked to one side, and the van would be around the back. I pushed the buzzer at the front door and waited to be granted entrance into a place not many of the living visited. We passed the administration office and I caught the wave Louise, Eddie's secretary, gave. I smiled back, not wanting to encourage any more. Louise had a *thing* for me. Many times I'd had to make an excuse as to why I couldn't go out with her. She was a nice woman, but I didn't do non-exclusive. Whatever it was that Eddie and I had, I stayed faithful to it.

I could see Eddie through the glass panel in the door. I knocked, waiting for her to look over. She nodded, that was her invitation to enter her sacred domain. She had already started and it looked to me like the worst part, the initial 'opening up' had already been done. Casey had been removed from the cross, which lay on its own table. To one side were the ropes that had bound her to it.

"She wasn't just tied to the cross," Eddie said, I guessed she's seen me looking.

"What do you mean?"

"She was impaled. I should have noticed that her body hadn't slumped, the weight of her hadn't been taken by the ropes alone."

Eddie rolled Casey over slightly to show me a fairly small hole in her back, between her shoulder blades. Sticking up from the cross was a crossbow bolt.

"Do you think he shot her through the wood?"

"I think he did, yes. And I think she was alive when he did that."

Eddie went on to explain the blood staining to prove her theory. As much as I didn't want to listen, I had no choice. It seemed the sick fuck had drilled a hole first, secured Casey to the cross then shot her.

"Did that cause her death?" Dean asked.

"No. I'm afraid it's worse than that. She died of internal bleeding; an object was inserted, roughly, and frequently inside her vagina. It ruptured her womb causing her to bleed out."

"Come again?" I asked.

"Do I need to?" she said.

"No, fuck!"

"There are splinters of wood inside her. It appears she had been repeatedly *raped,* both vaginally and anally."

"And this didn't happen at the school?" Dean asked.

"No way. There would have been an extensive amount of blood loss. If you look closely, she died on her back, not in an upright position."

I could see purple bruising that I knew was post-mortem lividity. Although faded, I wondered why I hadn't noticed it at the scene. However, I'd been concentrating on the room as a whole.

"Even though she was tied down, maybe to the cross, while some of this was happening. There's bruising and chaffing on her wrists and ankles. I suspect her legs were parted but she fought against her restraints. She has wood splinters under her fingernails and there are scratch marks on the cross."

"Please tell me there something else, DNA, anything to help us identify where this happened?" I said, knowing there was a level of desperation in my voice.

Eddie gently shook her head. "No DNA as yet. He didn't penetrate her at all. Whoever this is, he's a clever man. The wood splinters and the cross? Just a common oak. Could be bought anywhere that sells fencing, building materials even."

"Could even have been taken from the site," I said.

Dean frowned at me. "The school, it's having renovations isn't it? I bet they have a stack of wood ready for fencing or some other shit."

Dean stepped out of the room, I knew to make a call and ask.

Eddie snapped off her gloves and pulled off her apron, she gently stroked Casey's cheek before walking toward me. Dan would finish off. Once she'd scrubbed her hands, I followed to her office where she opened the top drawer of her desk and pulled out a bottle of whiskey. She grabbed two small glasses from a shelf behind her. I didn't particularly like whiskey, but I accepted the glass. The situation called for it.

Eddie sighed as she took a sip. "I'll have an initial report for you in the morning. Although I'm waiting on toxicology and bloods to come back."

She slid a folder over toward me, which contained a copy of photographs taken at the scene. Although my guys would have taken some, these concentrated on the body and the word on the wall.

"What do you know about Casey?" she asked.

"Not too much, cheerleader, grade A student, liked by everyone..."

"Drug user," she added, cutting me off.

"Drug user?"

"Yes, there were traces of cocaine under one fingernail. So I'm going out on a limb to say that was self-administered. I'll have it confirmed when her bloods come back, of course."

"Time of death?"

"Between eight and ten p.m. is my best assessment. She hadn't eaten that evening either."

"Because she couldn't?"

Eddie shrugged her shoulders. "That would be my assumption as well. She was held captive somewhere. But you say she was missing for five days? I'm wondering if she really wasn't *missing* but partying hard somewhere. Or she got real friendly with her captor to the extent that she accepted cocaine from him."

"Is there a way of aging the coke?" I asked.

"Not really. But I wouldn't expect it to stay under her fingernail for any real length of time."

"And there was no intercourse?"

"No. Even with a condom we'd see some sign, some residue of lubricant left. But nothing."

"So either we have a nice, wholesome girl who maybe isn't a nice, wholesome girl. Or we have a perp who forced her to take the coke."

"I can't answer that. The cocaine was under her fingernail; I'll add that I doubt it was the first time she'd taken it. There were signs of damage common with drug use in her nostrils."

I slumped back in my chair. "So, who really was Casey Long?"

We needed to go back to the beginning, reinterview her friends, her teachers, and her family.

Chapter 4

It had been two days since they had discovered Casey and two days of running around like headless chickens. The school hall was still closed off and it was laughable to see the candlelight vigils, the flowers laid by weeping students who had no idea who Casey was. I was having fun watching all the activities. I was having fun watching Mich and his love interest. Each night I sat outside the station, or his home, wanting to get my fix of him, desperate to see her sneak into his house when she thought no one knew about them.

I'd gotten a little distracted in my desire to see them together. I'd even walked around his house, checking for a way in. I had a plan, you see. A plan to set up a concealed camera. I'm not sure Mich would appreciate me standing at the end of his bed while he fucked her. But the desire to see them was becoming overwhelming. Maybe I needed to bring forward phase two.

I had enjoyed the media surrounding the beautiful, innocent Casey Long, though. If only they knew the truth. She was a slut, a dirty little whore who got exactly what she deserved.

I'd decided that we needed to reinterview Casey's classmates and teachers first. It was still too early to bring up our findings with the family. They'd been kept informed of course, and a viewing had been organized for them to see her. They had a right to all the details, but it was enough to discover their daughter had been murdered without knowing all the gory particulars.

The autopsy had thrown no new evidence as to where Casey had been murdered. All we had was the truck with an arm and a strange tattoo. Pete had managed to enlarge the image and was currently trying to match that tattoo to anything he could find on the Internet. It was symbol of some kind, my initial feeling was that it was something religious, tying in the crucifixion, but it bore no resemblance to anything we could find.

Dean and I pulled up in the parking lot of the school. We had decided to split classmates and teachers—he was to take the kids, and I would meet with Casey's teachers. In his own words, Dean was the more charming of the two of us, and thought he'd be able to coax information from Casey's friends. The reality was, I had one of those faces that the girls seemed to like. It was tiresome. I wasn't, and had never been, one for flirting, especially with girls half my age.

I headed to the staff room where a meeting had been called. Mr. Turner greeted me and introduced five of Casey's teachers. Ms. Parkins sat with a tissue, dabbing her eyes, as she spoke about what a wonderful girl Casey was. She offered nothing that we didn't already know. Casey had recently won an award, something to do with a cheerleading competition. She had been excited, kept talking about it to her classmates, according to Ms. Parkins.

"Such a shame, such a real shame," she said, as she shook her head.

Each of the teachers said the same thing, a nice girl, one of the 'in crowd,' studious with her studies—I was beginning to think she was a little too perfect.

Mr. Turner showed me her grades; she was pretty steady academically, never dropping below an A in any subject.

"What about after school activities? Did she do anything outside of her crowd of friends?" I asked.

"She was captain of the cheerleading squad, of course. Erm, I think she may have attended debate class, I know she spent a little time on the student newspaper, but I don't think that was really for her," he said.

"Maybe I could talk to whoever edits your newspaper?"

"Of course, we can head over there now."

Mr. Turner and I left the staff room and weaved our way through the throng of kids making their way from one class to the next. Mr. Turner looked through the glass window of a door before opening it. I followed him in.

"Helena, this is Detective Curtis, he wants to chat with you about Casey Long."

At the back of the room and hunched over a computer was a girl with short black hair, black-rimmed eyes, black lipstick, in fact, other than her pale skin, there was not one shred of color on her. She stared up at me with a scowl. I sighed, internally. There were some people that loved the opportunity to talk to the police, there were others, and I suspected Helena was one, that wanted nothing to do with us. I made a mental note to catch her surname and find out what the deal was.

"Mr. Turner, if it's okay with you, I'll catch up with you later," I said.

He nodded and left the room, closing the door behind us.

Helena hadn't spoken, but her face had changed from a scowl to one of amusement tinged with challenge. Her eyebrows were slightly raised and her lips formed a smirk.

"May I?" I asked, gesturing to a chair opposite her.

She shrugged her shoulders before dipping her head and focusing on her laptop.

"I wondered if you could tell me anything about Casey Long. I understand she spent some time working on the newspaper," I said.

It was the *humpff* and snort that had a slight pang of excitement run through me.

I didn't speak, and for a minute there was silence, other than the clack of keys as she continued to type.

"I'm just writing up her obituary," she said.

"And what does it say?"

"What everyone wants to hear."

"So not the truth then."

She looked sharply at me. "Casey Long was the epitome of the successful high school, all-American student. It is with great sadness that we report her loss today. Blah, blah, blah." She'd read from her screen.

"Does it kill you to have to write that shit?" I asked.

"Kill probably isn't the most appropriate word right now, don't you think?" she said. Her black-coated lips twitched into a smirk.

Take the crap off her face and she was a pretty girl. Goths, I think they called themselves. What the fuck a Goth was, I had no idea. She also came across as highly intelligent.

"Maybe not, but I get the impression that you don't believe a word you've typed. So, tell me, Helena, tell me who the real Casey was. I've had my fill of how wonderful she was, there's more, isn't there?"

Helena leaned back in her chair and studied me. "Do you know what it's like to be different? To have people mock your choices, tease you constantly because you aren't the American ideal, that you aren't interested in prancing around a football field, sucking up to the jocks? Casey spent her days doing that to anyone who wasn't in her circle. She was a brilliant student, selfish, self-centered, boastful, not willing to help anyone she felt below her."

"And you've been on the end of that, I take it?"

"Many times. She, her friends, made my life here hell for a while. It's why she didn't last long on the paper. She would have to answer to me and she didn't like that. She wanted makeup articles, dating tips, fashion columns. That's not what my paper is about, Detective."

"Did you enjoy the fact that you could get back at her?"

"No, because that's not the kind of person I am. In fact, it made life harder for a while. She was a bully, Detective. If you care to look close enough, you'll find many students at Montford who aren't mourning her."

"Why am I being told different?" I asked.

Helena fascinated me. Her body language was open, she was being honest, and nothing was concealed. She kept her focus on me, there was no shift in her eyes, her pupils stayed regular, and she sat still. Or she was one of the three percent that had the ability to fake their way through a lie detector test.

"I imagine it's because it doesn't do the school's reputation any good to know their homecoming queen, their spelling bee champion, their cheerleading captain actually wasn't a very nice person. Look around you. See that ad for the school? That's Casey

Long. She's held up as someone to aspire to, unless you've been on the end of her spitefulness."

"Why did you not come forward with this when I came here after she'd gone missing?"

"You never came and asked me. And why should I? I'm one person who'll be classed as jealous; the outcast who only ever wanted to be *down with the cool kids*. No one would have taken me seriously. I'm just bitter and twisted."

"Are you? Bitter and twisted?"

Helena snorted, again. "No, I pitied her. I tried hard to friend her but she wasn't having any of it."

"Outside of school, did you ever run into her?"

"Once or twice. At a party or the mall. The thing to know about Casey Long was there were two of them. In front of her peers she was a nasty, calculating, bitch. In front of her teachers, she was just a sweet girl."

"How did she behave at parties?" I asked.

"She got high, she slept around, a lot. Now, if you'll excuse me, I need to finish this article."

Helena shut down; she turned her attention to her laptop and continued to type. I smiled and, although she wouldn't have seen, gave a nod. I stood and left the room, picking up a copy of the student newspaper from a table by the door before I did.

So, Casey Long wasn't the wholesome girl we were being led to believe, maybe.

———

Dean was resting on the hood of the car as I walked out through the school doors. He looked over and raised his eyebrows, it was a look he had when he'd found out something interesting. I mirrored the look. We didn't speak as we climbed into the car and headed away.

"So?" I asked.

"Casey Long was a bit of a party girl by all accounts. Loved by her circle, hated by the rest."

"I got the same from a Helena..." I flipped open the school newspaper. "Johnson. Editor of this," I said, waving the newspaper in front of me.

We shared the information we'd managed to obtain, what Dean had learned pretty much confirmed what Helena had said. Casey Long was not the wholesome American cheerleader we were being led to believe. How that helped us though, we didn't know.

"Curtis!" I heard my name being called as we walked into the station. The chief stood just outside his door and was waving me over.

"Mich!" I said under my breath, as I strode toward him.

"The mayor is on my case for an update and the press wants a statement. What do you have for me?" he asked.

I hadn't taken one step into his office before he'd spoken. I gave him a rundown on what we'd found out so far, detailed Eddie's findings, and what we'd learned at the school.

"And the truck? That's our best lead at the moment," he said.

"Nothing as yet. We're doing a house to house, but it seems to be a blue Ford, thousands of them around. The tire track matches a standard Ford tire and we have no leads on the tattoo yet. One of the team has taken a photograph and is circulating it around the local tattoo parlors as we speak."

"We need to give something," he said.

"It's two days old, Chief. We have a lot of nothing written up on that board right now. Casey wasn't particularly liked, but I don't think that's something we need to publicize right now. What I want to do is a formal interview with her close circle of friends. They're all over the age of consent, but I'll speak to the parents first."

"Do you think this party thing is a factor? I mean, most girls her age are at it."

"I don't know yet. She had traces of cocaine under her fingernail, so I'm not convinced she was missing for the five days her mother thinks she was. I believe she was off somewhere, with someone who isn't talking."

"Anyone she was particularly close to? A boyfriend, maybe?"

"No boyfriend as such. She had a close circle; four or five friends that she hung out with regularly, two of those are star football players. It's those friends that I want to interview. We need to narrow down exactly how many days she was missing. It was school break, remember."

"Any social media accounts?"

"Yes, the normal, we've checked and didn't see anything unusual there. I have her laptop, we took that when the missing persons' was filed, but again, nothing to spark concern."

"Why are you so convinced she hadn't been held captive for the five days she was missing?"

"I just don't believe she was held all that time. I think she went out partying somewhere first. We know she died the evening previous to being discovered. I come back to the cocaine under the fingernail, I mean, how long would that have stayed there? I can't imagine it would be that long. The alternative, of course, is that her captor supplied her with the cocaine and she voluntarily took it. At the moment, my best guess is that she was partying with her killer."

"A classmate?" the chief asked.

"I doubt that, although I'm not ruling anyone out. Hence, the formal interviews."

"Okay, set them up."

I didn't need the chief's permission, those students were all over the age of consent but it helped to have him understand where I was going. There was just something that wouldn't let me believe Casey had been held captive for as long as she'd been missing.

———

The incident room was a hive of activity when I walked in. I went straight to the whiteboard and wrote up the names of the closest friends to Casey. Five names were listed, Vicky Bell, Alison Jenkins, Kay Davis, those three were cheerleaders. Then we had Dale Stewart and Louis Chapman, both football players.

I stared at the names; I wanted to know where they had all been the past few days. I turned to the team.

"Guys, I want you to take one of these names and interview them. These are the closest friends Casey had. One of them, at least, knows where she's been for the past few days, I'm sure of it. I want to know about parties, drugs, who is fucking who, everything."

Another cup of coffee was handed to me. I'd been surviving on caffeine, and little else, since we'd found Casey. I was exhausted, sleeping for an hour or so at a time on a cot in the station. I needed a shower, and I needed to shave. I ran my hand over my chin; the stubble scratched my palm.

"Why don't you head on home for a few hours?" Dean said.

"I think I will, I'll grab a shower and change of clothes, maybe get a couple of hours sleep, and then I'll be back."

As much as I wanted to be pounding the streets, I was better at organizing, at studying information and determining the course an investigation should take. I got a feel for the victim, for the scene, for the suspect even, but when I was tired, that all went to shit.

It was mid-afternoon when I left the station. I pulled my phone from my jeans pocket and sent a text to Eddie.

```
Heading home for a couple of hours sleep,
any results yet?
```

I didn't expect a reply immediately. I wasn't a priority when she was working and I didn't expect to be. She'd get back to me when she could.

I drove through the sleepy streets until I reached my house. I made a mental note that the yard needed mowing; the broken fence needed repairing and painting. The single story house, which had been left to me by my mother, was in need of some tender loving care.

———

I was in the shower, standing with my eyes closed, when I felt a small hand on my back. I kept my eyes closed as a naked body sidled behind me, wrapping two arms around my waist and planting a gentle kiss to my shoulder. In one hand, I noticed a small foil packet.

"Hey," I said, as I covered her hands with mine and slid them down my body. My cock twitched the closer she got.

"Hey, yourself," Eddie replied.

"I've missed you," I said, although it had only been two days. She didn't reply.

As the water from the showerhead cascaded down on us, Eddie walked around me. Facing me, she took my cock in her hand, gently sliding it up and down. I snaked one hand around the back of her head, pulling her closer. I wanted to feel her body against mine. She raised her head as I lowered mine. My hand tightened in her hair as our lips met. I heard myself growl a little as her teeth bit down on my lower one. She swiped her tongue over my lip before parting hers and allowing me in. Our kiss deepened the harder she gripped my cock, the faster she slid her hand up and down. I groaned as my stomach tightened and as the desire to fuck her hard increased.

Before she could make me come, I grabbed her thigh, raising her leg so she could wrap it around my waist. She had to hop a little as I forced her back against the tiled wall. Using my body to support her, I lifted her other leg, then cupped her ass. She reached between us, rolling the condom down my cock before positioning it at her entrance; without breaking our kiss I pushed into her.

I ground into her, slow and deep at first. She wrapped her arms around my shoulders, gripping the hair at the nape of my neck. She broke our kiss and her head rolled back, resting against the wall. Her moan was all the encouragement I needed to pick up the pace, to fuck her hard. Her tight pussy contracted around me, more so when I ran my tongue up the side of her neck, sucking her earlobe into my mouth. My biceps began to ache as I held her, pulling out until just the tip of my cock was inside her, then slamming back in and jolting her against the wall. She cried out and pulled hard on my hair, her fingernails dug into my skin.

"More, Mich," she said, between gasping for breaths.

Without pulling out, I elbowed open the shower door and walked her to the bedroom. My wet skin chilled in the cool room as I lowered us to the bed. Eddie wrapped her legs tighter around my waist, until she was on her back. I took her wrists, holding them above her head and gave her what she demanded.

I fucked her hard, fast, matching her breathy moans and feeling her stomach quiver with her impending orgasm. Her pussy pulsed as she arched her back. I lowered my head, taking a nipple between my teeth, and bit down hard as she screamed out my name. I fucking loved to hear that.

Eddie relaxed her legs, letting them fall to one side as she came down from her orgasm; I was nowhere near done with her though. I pulled out and held her hips, forcing her to roll to her front. I pulled on them until her ass was in the air and she brought her knees up. Fucking Eddie from behind was one of the things I liked to do the most. Maybe it was taking that little bit of control away from her that had my cock so hard that it was almost painful. I pushed her head to the pillow, leaving my hand between her shoulder blades forcing her down as I pushed, roughly, into her. I watched her hands grip the sheets as she gave herself to me, conceding for once.

Eddie exerted control over everything, everyone, but not in my bedroom. It was always a battle, one we both enjoyed; one I always won.

Eddie pushed her ass back toward me on every thrust, my balls slapped against her as I upped the pace. Every time we fucked it was fast and furious, we never made love, to do that would mean admitting some form of emotion, something she seemed incapable of doing.

I punished her, regularly, for that. I wanted to bring her to the utmost point of pleasure, of desire, of want and need. I wanted to hear her beg me to fuck her more, to get deeper, faster. I needed to hear that from her, and when I did, I stopped. I denied her the orgasm she so desperately wanted.

"Fuck me!" she screamed.

"No."

I stayed still, fighting my instinct to pump my cum into her. Battling with my desire to finish off.

"Mich," she whispered, rotating her hips, trying to fuck my cock.

I held her still. "What do you say?" I whispered back.

"Please. Please, Mich, make me come."

The hardness in her voice had gone. "You need me to make you come, don't you?" I said.

"Yes, you know I do."

I reached under her and very gently ran my fingertips over her opening, coating my finger with her juices. I circled her clitoris as I pulled my cock slightly out. She moaned. She cried out when I shoved two fingers inside her, joining my cock.

"Oh, God," she said, as she buried her face in the bedding.

My fingers slid against her wall and my cock, teasing us both at the same time. My heart rate picked up as her hot cunt contracted around me. I wrapped my free hand in her hair, forcing her head up, as I gave in to my need and allowed her to come. As my body rocked against her, as my fingers and cock teased harder; she came apart around me. She cried out, over and over.

My cock pulsed, my balls tightened, and I pulled my fingers from her to grip her hip. I needed to mark her; I dug my nails into her skin as I came. When I pulled out, as Eddie slumped to the bed, I watched her cum drip slowly from her.

After I'd removed the condom, I lowered myself to the bed; we lay on our sides, facing each other without touching. I'd given up wanting to hold her in my arms; she'd stiffen at the touch. At first, she had her eyes closed as she fought to control her breathing.

Eventually, she opened them at the same time as giving me a smile that brought a lump to my throat. Always, in that fleeting moment after sex, she dropped her guard and I saw the real Eddie.

Chapter 5

I didn't masturbate, normally. It was a sin to pleasure myself. However, as I stood outside the bedroom window, as I listened to the sound of skin on skin, of gentle moans escalating to screams of pleasure, I found my hand had slid under the waistband of the black joggers I wore. My cock was hard, it always felt alien to my touch, but as I listened, as I peered through the slightest gap in the sheer drapes, my body took on a will of its own. I didn't want to fight against it.

I wrapped my hand around my cock, feeling it in my palm, and stroked. I hated that I loved the sensations flowing through my body, the tingling over my skin as static coursed, and the fluttering in my stomach. I watched as Mich fucked her from behind. He took control. Just that action had my cock pulse in my hand and hot milky fluid spurt over my fingers.

I wanted him to do that to me; I wanted to fuck her. I wasn't gay; in fact I didn't know what I was. I'd never had 'real' sex. For years I'd had a plan, and once that plan was executed, I vowed I'd find a woman, or a man, and I'd do what I just witnessed.

I knew I'd be back later that day; Mich had left something that

I wanted in the trash.

———

Eddie closed down; her shield was up. I could hear her armor clink into place as she rose from the bed and headed back to the bathroom. Normally we'd fuck many times, but we were both on a tight schedule that day. As I lay with my hands behind my head and listened to her showering, I pushed away the thought that I should put a stop to whatever it was we had, or didn't have. Many times, over the past months, I'd tried to bring up a conversation about a relationship. Every time, Eddie would either silence me with a kiss or change the subject. I sighed as I checked my watch. My plan for a couple of hours sleep would go by the wayside as I slid my legs from the bed and stretched out my back.

I caught sight of movement outside the window and strode over. Maybe I'd imagined it, as I pulled the drapes open all I saw was a guy in workout gear jogging past. Sleep deprivation was about the one thing I hated the most when on a case, but I just couldn't do it. I couldn't go home at the end of my shift and act as if nothing had happened. Maybe if I had someone to go home to, things would be different.

Dean had Jo; they'd been married for years, childhood sweethearts who were still very much in love. It was easy for him. He could go home, and although like me, he didn't switch off, he had distractions. All I had was an empty house and piles of paperwork for cold cases, live cases, and dead people for company.

———

"There's coffee," Eddie said, as I joined her in the kitchen. I'd showered and slipped on a pair of jeans and a black t-shirt.

She was sat at my kitchen table with her laptop open, typing away. She hadn't looked up when she'd spoken.

"Thanks, I need it."

"How's the investigation going?" she asked.

"Nowhere just yet, well, I say nowhere. Casey wasn't the most popular student, that's about all we have right now. It's frustrating."

She hummed and I wondered if she was actually listening.

I sighed as I poured a coffee and took the seat beside her. I stared at a file on the table, an old case that I'd never been able to solve and one that I dipped into periodically. It annoyed me when a case went cold; it infuriated me when I couldn't solve it. It felt like I'd failed the deceased, their family. I had to work hard on not opening it though. Casey, at that moment, deserved all my attention and focus.

"Okay, that's the full report emailed to you, tox reports, internal damage, it's not pretty reading," Eddie said, then relaxed back in her chair.

She picked up her coffee with both hands, as if warming them.

"Anything different to what you've already told me?" I asked.

"No, cause of death is as stated already. Extreme blood loss after..." She didn't finish her sentence.

"Blood results?"

"Other than a small amount of cocaine, which suggests recreational use, nothing untoward."

"Anything that would give me a location?"

"Her body was exceptionally clean, which suggests she was washed prior to being moved to the school. And the wounds on her chest and stomach were done post-mortem, as you know. I believe those wounds were inflicted fairly soon after death, hence the small amount of blood."

"So, those wounds were done after she was washed?"

"Yes, I believe so. Maybe he didn't like how she looked on the cross."

Eddie snapped down the lid of her laptop and placed it in the bag at her feet. She stood and stretched her arms over her head, her shirt rose showing a toned midriff.

"I need to get back," she said, as she picked up her bag and headed for the kitchen door.

I nodded as I sipped my coffee. "Eddie..."

She turned her head to look at me. For a second, I saw a fleeting look of apprehension cross her face.

"Yes?"

There was a pause as I looked at her. "Nothing, call me later," I said.

That look of apprehension was replaced by one of relief.

When the case was over, if it was over, I would sit down with her and we would have the discussion I'd been trying to have for some time, whether she wanted to or not.

———

I grabbed my keys, phone, and a clean t-shirt then headed for the station. I'd had no missed calls or messages, so I knew there were no new developments on the case. I wanted to study the report Eddie had sent over. She'd never write her thoughts or even try to give an opinion in that document, it would be facts and nothing more. Those would be saved for a separate email.

I trusted Eddie's opinions, she'd seen more death than any of us, some natural, some not. She'd learned over the years to read a body and beg for the smallest of clues. At forty years old, she was one of the youngest medical examiners in our state, and I often thought the fact that she was older than me was one of her issues about us forming a normal relationship.

"Any news?" I asked, as I walked into the incident room.

Dean and a few of the team were sitting at some of the desks with photographs spread out.

"House to house is still going on, so far, nothing. I've faxed over details to all our neighboring forces to see if anyone had anything similar in the past year," Samantha said.

"Okay, widen the search area. I want to look more rural, somewhere that has, say, a barn or workshop for making the cross. Eddie believes the body was cleaned before it was brought to the school. Let's also look at industrial sites, somewhere clinical maybe. There was not a shred of evidence on her body, other than splinters from the cross, there's no fibers, nothing."

"Which suggests someone knew exactly what they were doing," Dean added.

"Yes. I don't believe this is his first kill, so I want someone to go through all databases we have access to and see if there is anything similar. Look at religious killings, rituals, that kind of thing."

"Can any of your *friends* help?" Pete asked.

"I'm on to that today."

I took a seat at a vacant desk and made a call to an old colleague in the FBI. I left a message for him to call me back when he didn't answer. I wasn't a profiler, although I'd started to build a picture and wanted some professional input in that.

"Curtis." I heard my name being called. "Mich," I hissed under my breath.

The chief was standing at the open door. I followed him after he'd turned and walked away to his office.

"Press release," he said, sliding a piece of paper toward me. I got on well with the chief but often got annoyed at his clipped tones, his two word sentences.

I scanned through, it was basic, which is what we wanted, and omitted some facts. We didn't need to give out all the information; we'd already had the usual call-ins from the local wannabe celebrities, claiming to be the murderer.

It was as I placed the piece of paper back on the desk that I heard the sound of running feet along the corridor.

"Mich, Mich, we've got another one!" I heard, from a breathless Dean.

I stood, abruptly enough to have the chair topple behind me.

"Where? What?" I asked once he'd gotten to the office door.

"Another kid, he was in a fucking dumpster, but... Shit, Mich, the garbage truck came..." Dean didn't seem to be able to finish his sentence. It didn't take a genius to understand what he was saying.

We ran to the parking lot and climbed into a car. Once again with lights blazing and sirens wailing, we headed to the diner.

The area was already cordoned off and the first sight that hit me was a man sitting on the curb, spattered with blood. His face was as pale as the white truck that stood in the middle of the road, and he shook, his whole body shook. Another sat beside him in blue overalls.

I made myself look inside the back of the truck. It was a warm day, and already the stench of rotting food caused my stomach to roil. The sight that greeted us had me want to physically throw up. The sides of the truck were splattered with blood and clumps of, well, flesh I guessed. There was a metal plate the size of the truck, which had started to compact the trash, it was halfway closed and I could see an arm. I had no idea if that arm was attached to a body though.

"It's a compactor truck," I heard. The man in the overalls had spoken.

"What's behind that plate?" I asked.

"Rotary blades."

There was silence, and then a sob as we contemplated what had happened.

"Fuck!" I heard; one of the sheriff's team was standing to the side of the truck.

"Don't touch that fucking dumpster," I said, as I caught sight of it.

A blue plastic industrial dumpster was left on the ground, after it had been unloaded into the back of the truck. On the front was the name of the diner that we were parked behind. Thankfully, we were on a service road, but I still wanted the whole area taped off. I fired off instructions.

"How does this open?" I called out to the man in the overalls.

He shook his head, not wanting to come forward but pointing to a panel of red buttons, just inside the truck on its metal wall.

Gears engaged, metal ground together as the mechanism went into reverse and the compactor panel rose. An arm rolled forward, and then, what remained of a body covered in waste food joined it.

I pushed another button to silence the blades and tried my hardest to breathe in deep through my mouth. I wanted to quell the nausea without inhaling the smell.

Dean was crouched in front of the two truck operators. I could hear one speaking, telling him how they loaded the dumpster onto the arms. It was only as the compactor panel started to close, and blood spurted, that they realized there was a body inside. Whether that body was still alive at the time, they had no idea.

A crowd had formed at the kitchen entrance to the diner. I instructed a deputy to move them back inside, get details of the owner, and any CCTV, although there didn't appear to be obvious cameras. I pulled my phone from my pocket, and as I dialed Eddie, I took a look around the dumpster. Scratched into the back was one word.

G L U T T O N Y

Chapter 6

    I wasn't at the scene so had no idea how Mich was doing. I could only hope my plan had come to fruition. I knew, of course, that he was there; I'd heard the call over the radio. I'd smiled at the panic in the voice that reported a body had been found. I'd had fun with that one. Dale Stewart, quarterback jock, piece of shit. It had been so easy, it often amazed me how dumb these kids were, how trusting. Hadn't they been taught anything? He was a greedy cunt, always wanting more. I held my hands over my mouth at my expletive. Mother wouldn't be pleased. "Cunt, cunt, cunt," I giggled as I said the words out loud. Mother would say, "Men don't giggle," but I didn't care what she said. Not anymore.

    I wondered if Mich would understand the reference, the little clue I'd left him. Casey was a slut, boasting about the men she'd slept with, sleeping around to get what she wanted. Lust was a sin. Dale was never satisfied, always wanting more, demanding, threatening; gluttony didn't just apply to food, you know. It was an overconsumption of food, drink, or luxury items to the point of extravagance or waste.

    Dale was garbage; it made perfect sense for him to be chopped up with the trash. Oh, that would make a mess! My stomach fluttered at the vision that popped into my head. I regretted my decision to not be at the scene when he was discovered, but I had to move on, time was running out, and people were getting restless. I had a plan to stick to, no more deviating. But I was having so much fun.

———

I watched the truck as it was loaded onto the back of a tow truck, there was no way Eddie, or any of us, could work the scene there. I had no desire to climb inside and pick out the pieces of whoever it was. I guessed a man simply from the clothing he wore, black pants and what looked like a blue t-shirt with some form of logo on the front. The shirt, however, was soaked through, darkened by blood, slashed in places. There wasn't much left of a face.

The dumpster was also removed for analysis, and I was about to sit down with the manager of the diner. I had a team searching every inch of the service road, looking for clues, hoping to find a footprint or something. One murder in our small town was bad enough; two would incite panic. We were unable to confirm publicly it was murder, of course, but those words scratched into the back of the plastic dumpster told me it was related.

"Can you tell me the last time an item was placed into the dumpster?" I asked the manager, an elderly man and one the town loved.

"It would have been closing time last night, about ten, I guess," Harry said. "It's the last job before we lock up."

"And who did that?"

"I did. I took the late shift because our regular cook didn't show. In fact, we still don't know where he is."

"And his name?"

"Dale Stewart, he's a senior this year. He did a couple of late-night shifts during the week."

My skin tingled at recognition of the name but I kept my features neutral.

"I know this seems an odd question, but talk me though exactly how you close up."

"Well, obviously I cash up first. If the receipts are large, I take it home, rather than leave it here in the safe. I clean down the kitchen, power down the grills, and the last job, as I leave, is to dump the trash. I should have looked, I didn't."

"What do you mean?"

"I open the lid and throw the garbage bags in, I don't hang about and look in the dumpster. Maybe I should have, he might have been in there, injured, or whatever."

"We don't know yet how long he was in there. If anything, I doubt it would have been while you were still around." I wanted to give Harry some form of reassurance; otherwise he'd be eaten up with guilt.

"Harry, will you give a formal statement to one of my colleagues?" I asked.

"Formal? Do you think I did it?"

"No, by formal I mean a written statement. Just so I have it all on paper."

"Sure, I've got nothing to hide," he said. I believed him; the guy was well into his seventies. I was surprised he'd even managed to lift a trash bag and throw it in the dumpster.

I left him in the care of one of the officers and went to find Dean. He'd had the truck drivers taken to the station, after a medic had checked them over, and was waiting on me.

"Dale Stewart is a cook at the diner, he didn't show for his shift last night. Dale Stewart is a friend of Casey Long's."

"Shit, do you think there's a connection?" Dean said, as we climbed in to the car.

"I don't know, but I don't believe in coincidences, either."

We drove back to the station and I was dismayed to see a small crowd of people in reception.

"What are you doing to catch the killer?" I was asked. A reporter blocked my entrance.

"We have a team of over thirty officers, deputies, and colleagues on this," I said, as I pushed through.

"Shouldn't you be out, pounding the street?" he asked. I bristled.

"As I said, I have over thirty people out there. My role is to coordinate; I can only do that when I get to my office. So, if you'll excuse me..."

As I passed the reception area, I motioned for the officer on duty to clear the area. We did not need a snarky reporter stirring up shit. Too often I'd curse at the local newspaper articles about police inefficiency. If only they realized, we didn't live in an episode of *CSI*, half of all detective work was often done from a desk, with a mountain of fucking paperwork.

"Prick," I mumbled, as we made our way to the incident room.

I went straight to the whiteboard and wrote up what I already knew, minus the victim's name of course. We'd need to formally identify before we knew it was Dale for sure.

"Lust. Gluttony," Dean said, watching me and having just returned from taking statements from the truck drivers.

"Two of the deadly sins," I replied. "Someone bring that up," I said, gesturing to a laptop.

"It says here, pride, gluttony, greed, lust, envy, wrath, and sloth, they're all sins, according to the Bible." Pete already had a page of information up on his laptop.

"Connect it here," I said, wanting the information on the second whiteboard used for presentations.

Within a minute a list was up and I stood back and studied it. "So, lust relates to Casey and gluttony to our man in the truck. Okay, I can get the gluttony, he was in a dumpster full of food waste, but lust...? What connects them?" I said, mostly to myself.

"Have we got a religious freak on our hands?" Dean asked.

I shrugged my shoulders. "I don't know. Pete, find me a priest or someone who can translate what they mean. Let's see if we can put them into some modern context. He wrote them for a reason, we need to find out what that reason is."

"Or he's just fucking with us," Dean said.

"Or he's just fucking with us," I replied.

I'd texted Eddie a couple of times, she hadn't replied and I guessed I hadn't expected her to. I needed identification on that body. His face was too damaged for obvious eye or hair color, but we'd have height, approximate age, build, and I wanted to know what that logo was on his shirt.

"Dean, how about you go to Dale Stewart's house, on the pretense that you want to talk to him about Casey? Find out if he's there. Harry, at the diner, said he didn't turn up for his shift." I turned back to the list of friends, the close circle surrounding Casey.

"And if he's there?"

"Ask him all the same questions we already have. What did she do out of school? Any friends she spoke about that he wasn't aware of? That kind of thing."

"Okay, on it now." He rose from the desk and left the room.

The phones rang, fingers clattered on keyboards as the civilian staff tasked to the team tried to come up with answers, clues. I'd asked for any similar crimes to be sought, any unsolved murders of high school children, and I wanted to find that damn pickup.

I hated waiting. I hated silence. I decided to head on over to the medical examiner's office and see what was going on. I had no desire to be around when the body was removed from the truck, but that should have happened already. Maybe I could get some answers to the million questions floating around my mind.

I was buzzed straight through when I'd arrived and walked the sterile corridor to where I hoped Eddie would be. I looked through the glass window in the door and saw her dressed in her coveralls, with a mask over her nose and mouth. I guessed she wasn't enjoying the stench of rotten food either. She looked over and gestured to the side, I understood what she meant. There was a second door beside the one I was looking through, it opened into an anteroom that housed the clothing and paraphernalia Eddie needed for this type of investigation. I was half tempted to shake my head and wait; but time wasn't on my side.

I pushed through the door and grabbed what I thought would fit. I pulled on white overalls and picked up a facemask. I held it to my face as I walked through a connecting door. The room was cold, the air conditioner and extractors were on full blast. Dan was busy hosing down the floor, so I understood the worst of the autopsy had already taken place. Silver trays were lined up on a counter, thankfully covered with blue paper towel.

"I really need to know who this guy is," I said.

"Well, the dead can't speak their names but he's male, young, I'd hazard a guess at between seventeen and nineteen. Fit and healthy, muscular beyond the norm for his age, so I'm guessing he's into sports of some kind. I have a call out for a dental match, but I'm afraid we can't do facial recognition. He has no distinctive marks. Brown-haired." Eddie reeled off some facts as she worked.

"Intensive injuries, as you can imagine, however, it wasn't rotary blades that killed him. See here? These wounds are more refined, if you look closer the edges of the skin is cleanly cut. The rotary blade cuts are wider and jagged."

"What caused them?"

"I'd go with some form of blade, a large blade. I should have something for you to work on later tonight. Mich, I've seen a similar wound before, a farmer, if I remember correctly, didn't quite angle his scythe the right way, cut his own leg off and died as a result of blood loss."

"So, he was dead before he ended up in the garbage truck?" I asked.

"I'll have that answer later but judging by that wound..." She pointed to a slash mark across his stomach. "I imagine so."

'He's a big guy, our perp must have struggled to have gotten him in a dumpster," I thought out loud.

"There's no way, with that injury alone, he'd have climbed in himself."

"Anything on the dumpster?"

"Dan is finished with that, you can send your guys over for fingerprinting."

I nodded my head and left through the anteroom, depositing the overalls and mask in a biohazard bin. I made a call as I walked to the front entrance, instructing the forensic team to make their way over. I didn't hold out much hope for prints. Well, I say prints, I imagine the dumpster would be covered in them, but narrowing them down to our killer was going to be a bitch.

"Dale Stewart didn't return home last night. Parents weren't overly concerned, seems it's the norm for him to take off to a party and return a day or so later. Last seen going out for a run the previous morning," Dean said, as I entered the incident room.

"Have we got a picture of him?"

Dean pointed to the whiteboard. A photograph of a smiling, brown-haired eighteen-year-old stood alongside his football teammates. Underneath someone had written some basic details, including height. He certainly matched our victim on everything other than looks.

"Okay, let's round up the friends. Get them in here. I also want some subtle, and I mean subtle, protection."

"Don't you think we should wait for identification?" Pete asked.

"No, the kid I saw over at the doc's is that kid, I'm sure of it. Whether our killer is targeting that group of friends, I don't know, but I'm not willing to take any chances. I want an update meeting here..." I consulted my watch. "Four o'clock. Let everyone know."

A very uneasy feeling started to settle in my stomach.

Chapter 7

I sighed; I hated crying. Why did girls cry? Crying made me angry. It wasn't going to save you, little girl. "It's a waste of energy," I told her. I tried to wipe her tears away, but she shook her head in disgust at my touch. That annoyed me. Didn't she see I was helping her? She was greedy, so very greedy. I told her that was a sin. She begged, of course, they all do. But Mother told me to ignore her words.

I was also angry that I'd had to take my eyes off Mich. I liked to look at him, to hear his voice; it gave me shivers. I had a photograph of him; it was pinned proudly to my wall, with the others. He was alive, the others weren't. I wondered what we'd do when we were finally together. Would he fuck me like he did the bitch? Or would he let me fuck him? I felt my cock stiffen at the thought. Oh, Mich, did you know what you do to me?

I picked up the crucifix that I'd made as a child. It was one that I'd been regularly punished with. I loved it. I licked it. It tasted of Casey. I prayed in front of it. Then I looked at my sinner, dressed in her designer clothes, with her gold earrings and necklace shimmering as the light from overhead reflected on them. I tutted, too much excess, too much love for money. Oh, Vicky, I warned you, I tried, but you never listened.

A very cocky Louis Chapman sat in an interview room, he rested back on two legs of the chair, and I hoped it would topple. The smirk on his face irritated me.

"Can you tell me about your relationship with Casey Long?" I asked, consulting the notes of our previous meeting to see if he said the same thing.

"We were friends, you know? Nothing serious."

"No, I don't know, how *friendly* were you?"

"Are you asking if I fucked her? Of course, so did many others." He openly laughed and I ground my jaw to keep the words from escaping.

"You don't seem overly concerned that one of your friends is dead."

At that his father, another obnoxious man, sat forward. "Is my son a suspect?" he asked.

"No, Mr. Chapman, not yet anyway. As you know, we are trying to find who killed your son's friend, who left her to be found in a school hall. I just find it odd that your son is amused by my questions."

"I'm fucking scared, okay? This shit is serious. I know that. I was with her just before..." Louis clamped his mouth shut as my, Dean's, and his father's heads turned toward him.

"When were you with her, Louis?"

He didn't reply. "Now is not the fucking time for withholding information," Dean added.

"We camped out, okay? All of us, she didn't tell her mom

because she was grounded."

"When, Louis?" I growled out my question.

"Just a couple of nights, last week."

"When, Louis, exactly when? After her mom reported her missing? After I came and spoke to you? During a missing persons' investigation, where I'd invested time and officers looking for her?"

He nodded his head. "I told her that her mom had reported her missing. She thought she'd go home and it would all be okay."

"Instead, she was murdered. Had they known where she was, maybe she might not have been," Mr. Chapman said.

Although the sentiment was on the tip of my tongue, I wouldn't have subjected the kid to the level of regret and guilt his father had just placed on him. Silence ensued.

"Where were you camping?" I asked.

"That old house, the derelict on Perry Street. We go there sometimes, see who can sleep inside without getting freaked."

I knew the house, it was run-down and for years the kids of the town would dare each other to go inside. Some said it was haunted. I didn't believe that, of course, but it provided hours of fun for them, and hours of not so much fun for the police in chasing them off.

Dean rose without me having to say anything. He'd send someone over to investigate. As he opened the door, Samantha was outside, she waved a piece of paper in her hand. Dean took it from her, read it, and then looked over to me. He motioned with his head for me to join him.

"Louis, you've wasted police time, withheld information, I could charge you for that. But right now I have something more important to worry about."

I rose; the meeting was over. I left Samantha to escort Louis and his father from the station.

"Dental match, our victim is Dale," Dean said.

"That was quick. Fuck! Forget sending someone to that house, I want us to go."

———

I heard the sigh and saw the shiver that ran up Dean's spine as we pulled up outside the house, I chuckled at his discomfort.

"Used to come here as a kid, never liked the place. I don't know why they don't tear it down," he said, as we exited the car.

"Who owns it now?"

"Not sure, I think the daughter of the family who lived here, she lives in Florida somewhere."

We walked to the front of the property, and I cupped my hands around my eyes to look through a window. I was staring into a living room with furniture covered in white, very dusty sheets. There were a few bottles of beer littering the floor. We made our way around the side of the property to the backyard. The grass was brown, burned from the heat of summer and as unkempt as the house. Overgrown bushes lined either side of what I assumed was the boundary, and toward the back was a patch of scorched earth. I walked over to it and crouched down. Someone had lit a fire there, ash and charred sticks sat in the center.

"At least they cleaned up," Dean said, walking toward a plastic bag full of bottles.

I had no real clue if visiting the house would add anything to our investigation, but it was the last known whereabouts of Casey's at least. I wanted to get in but procedure would be long-winded. I walked to the back of the house and stood by the door. It was ajar.

"Remind me again, we can enter if we think a burglary is in

process, can't we?" Dean said, not needing confirmation as he pushed open the door into a kitchen.

The house had clearly been empty for many years, occupied only by vermin and kids wanting to get their kicks. A layer of dust covered every surface and that showed up the handprints and small footprints of whatever animals had taken over.

We walked through the kitchen and into a hallway. There were four rooms off the hall, each contained furniture. Three of the four rooms had the furniture still covered over. The last one we entered, some kind of library or study, had chairs exposed and looked like it had recently been used.

The white sheets were piled in a heap in one corner and the chairs arranged in a semi-circle in front of an open fireplace. I checked out the grate, it looked as if it had been used. Like the bonfire outside, charred wood and ash were piled up.

It was a scrape of something against wood that had us reach for our guns, then still and listen. The sound had come from above. I glanced over to Dean, and as quietly as possible, we made our way up the stairs. I kept my back to the rail, facing toward the source of the sound as we ascended.

Like the floor below, there were four rooms off a central corridor. We crept to the one above the room we'd been in. The door was ajar and I motioned to Dean that I was going to push it fully open.

The door creaked and scraped against the floor as it sprang open. Both Dean and I swung our raised guns through the doorway at the same time. The room was empty, save for a bird trying to escape through a closed window.

"Fuck," Dean said, as he lowered his gun.

I holstered mine and walked over to the window. With a rattle of the pane it slid open and the bird was released. I turned to look around the empty room.

"How did it get in?" Dean asked.

"I don't know, might have got in downstairs and has been trying to find a way out."

I walked the perimeter of the small room, not entirely sure what I was looking for. It didn't appear that anyone had been in the room for a long time.

I shook my head. "Come on, there's nothing here."

After checking all the rooms, we left the house the same way we'd entered, and I made a call to a local contractor to board up the door. Whoever owned the house needed to be contacted and informed their property was being used as a party venue.

I stood in front of my colleagues in the incident room, after dispatching an officer to break the news to Mr. and Mrs. Stewart.

"Two teens, both friends, same school, what else do we have?" I asked.

"Both in the Philosophy Club," someone added.

"Philosophy Club?" Without being disrespectful to the dead, neither Casey nor Dale seemed the type to be interested in philosophy.

"Okay, who else is in that club?"

Their entire circle seemed to be budding philosophers. I circled the word philosophy after I'd added it to the whiteboard, simply because I found it a strange choice of subject for them.

"Anything else?"

"Doc won't have a report for a few days, but Dale's parents said when he left their house it was for a run. He wasn't wearing running gear in the back of the truck," Dean added.

"So he'd gotten changed somewhere, and that somewhere has a selection of his clothes perhaps. The diner? Do they have lockers?"

"There wasn't a staffroom, just an area outside, under an awning, where they could smoke or take a break," Pete added.

"Okay, but I still want you to check. Do we have anything from you guys?" I focused my attention on the civilian data techs.

"I've found a couple of unsolved murders in a small place called Millbrook, Texas. There are enough similarities for me to think you might want to take a look."

I was handed a green cardboard file. "How far away is Millbrook?"

"Only three hours away. It's a really, really small place, mainly rural."

"Give me an overview of what's in here," I said, as I placed the folder on a desk. I turned toward the whiteboard and drew a vertical line, sectioning off one area.

"It was a teenage couple that were murdered, found in a field, post-sex session, according to the medical examiner. They were positioned with arms outstretched, legs together, as if on a cross. That part stood out to me."

"You say post-sex, why?" I asked, while writing up what had been said.

"Well, they were naked and he still had a condom on."

"How did they die and when?"

"Five stab wounds across the chest and down the stomach. A little over a year ago."

"Not easy to kill two people by stabbing," Dean added. I agreed.

Maybe there was more in the medical examiner's report.

"But the clincher was, the word *sinners* was scraped into the ground above their heads."

My pen paused on the whiteboard. "I need to speak to the lead investigator on the phone," I said.

It was mention of a phone that reminded me I hadn't heard back from my old colleague in the FBI. I'd chase him up at the same time.

"Please, someone give me something on the truck or the tattoo. Pete, anything more on the CCTV at the school?"

"Nothing more than I've already reported. The image of the tattoo that we circulated didn't raise anything; one artist said he thought it looked more like a prison tat or certainly a backstreet job. It wasn't done professionally, he felt."

"Great! That leads us nowhere. Samantha, you checked out the blind spots at the school?"

"I did, as Pete can testify, their CCTV is shit. Mainly there for decoration, since it really has no function other than to focus on the front door, and in return that covers a part of the parking lot."

I wanted to punch the whiteboard; we had nothing other than two murders. Two teenagers who should be planning their lives were sitting on ice in the morgue.

"Let's go back to this religious element. These deadly sins, is there an order to them? Let's try to pre-empt him."

"Greed should be next." It was a quiet voice that offered that opinion. I looked to the back of the room.

"Greed? Are you sure?" I asked.

"Yes." A young man cleared his throat as he spoke.

"Can you expand on that?"

He stood, a slight man who had recently been recruited to deal with administrative duties, initially. If memory served me well, he had some exceptional computer skills and often helped Pete.

"Lust is the first sin, it's the excessive thoughts or desires of a sexual nature. Then there is gluttony, usually referred to overeating, but it really means overindulgence of anything. Greed comes next. Most believe its greed of money or material things. Sloth is the fourth, most people assume it means laziness, which it does in some Bibles, but it also means failure to love, God, especially."

"How do you know this?" Dean asked, interrupting him.

"I studied theology." The man came forward and I noticed his nervousness. I racked my brain for his name.

"I'm sorry, I'm Tim, I'm not sure I was supposed to be in your meeting, but I wanted to help," he said, holding out his hand to me. He saved me the embarrassment of not knowing him.

"Tim, I'm glad you're here." I shook his hand. "So what comes after sloth?"

"Wrath, which is the desire to seek revenge, then we have envy, I guess that's self-explanatory. Last we have the worst sin, the sin of pride. It's considered to be Lucifer's downfall."

"How can pride be a sin?" Samantha asked.

"The Catholic Encyclopaedia says it's the ultimate sin from which all the others arise. I don't claim to understand it, I just remember it," he said, with a smile.

"If our killer isn't finished, and he's following this pattern, we need to look at who fits the profile for greed then?" Dean asked.

"That's assuming he's targeting this group of friends and it's not coincidence, of course," I replied. I studied the list of names. "I have no fucking idea who would be next."

"Are we still rounding up the rest of the friends?" Pete asked.

"I think we have to. I'll have to run it past the chief though, it's not like we have a safe house or anything here. I need to make a couple of calls."

I headed to the chief's office first. I tapped on his door, noticing he was on the phone and didn't want to just barge through. He waved me in.

I sat at his desk while he finished his call, it was clear that I wasn't supposed to know what was being discussed; his answers were clipped and cryptic.

"What do we have?" he asked, once he'd replaced the receiver.

"Dale Stewart, friend of Casey Long. I think there is a pattern, following the seven deadly sins. I don't think Dale is the last one."

"Seven what?"

"Deadly sins, it's biblical. Casey was lust, Dale was gluttony, next up is greed. There are seven sins, six friends. I want to have them put in protection."

"Wait up! We don't have the facility for four friends, and their families, I imagine. This isn't the fucking city, Curtis."

"It's Mich, and we don't have a choice. The risk to them is too large."

"Give me something to connect the murders, other than coincidence. This is a small town, *Mich*; it's very probable that it is coincidence. We don't have the manpower, or the budget, to do that."

"Call the mayor, anyone. We must have some fucking senators or politicians running for something soon. Get them on the case, get the budget and the manpower."

I tried not to show the level of frustration that was building inside me.

"This isn't the FBI, things don't work that way here. You want them protected, take some of your team and have them patrol, park outside their homes."

"I've got every qualified man on the job. I've got eight civilians doing the job I need professionals doing. I can't spare my men."

"We have a mayoral election coming up, I'll see if I can get some support, but I wouldn't hold your breath. Get me something concrete, something that proves that this particular group of friends is being targeted."

"Isn't two deaths, two friends, concrete enough?"

"No, Curtis. No, it isn't."

I couldn't blame him; we were stretched normally, without having a potential serial killer on the loose.

Maybe it was time to do something outside the realm of the small town police force; something not strictly legal.

Chapter 8

Oh, Mich. Don't go, Mich. How exciting! He'd been so close that I could smell his aftershave. He walked so tall, so confidently. I envied his walk. Was that strange? To envy how someone walked? It won't be long, Mich, and you won't be so confident.

The silly girl tied and gagged to the chair struggled again. I slapped her face, then soothed her when I saw the redness creep over her skin. Her eyes were puffy; one was partially closed. I told her again how greed was going to be her downfall; maybe she'd listen now. It was time to give her another high, time to move her to a more suitable location; I chuckled at the thought.

The police had made their announcement, identified garbage man. I watched the press start to congregate outside the police station, demanding answers. I watched the streets become a little quieter, Harry at the diner complained about a drop in customers. People didn't want to be on the streets, how strange? Didn't they realize, it was safer now that the sinners were nearly gone?

———

"Arrest them," I said.

"Arrest them? For what?" Dean replied.

"Anything, traffic violations, I don't care. Arrest them; we'll have them in custody where we can keep an eye on them. The chief won't sanction moving them to a safe house just yet."

Dean and I stood just outside the station door. I'd hardly had any sleep in the past three days, I was running on adrenalin and caffeine, but it was when I had my best, or worst, ideas. If we arrested the remaining kids, we could keep them at the station. It wasn't ideal and it couldn't be long-term. Hopefully, for a few days, it would give us some breathing room to concentrate on finding the killer.

"Okay. Why not just invite them to come and stay for a while?" he said, shaking his head a little.

"Because then we'd have to tell them why and fuck knows what would happen then."

"Mich, we can't bring them in on a traffic violation. It's a ticketed offence, nothing more."

"So what can we bring them in for? Louis, for withholding evidence?"

"That's a fucking long shot, and you know it. I vote we get them together, with their parents, and give them the truth."

"What is the truth? Some lunatic is running around killing high school kids who may or may not be the same group of friends?" I sighed.

He was right of course, but we had to do something to ensure those kids were safe. "Call them in all together, at least," I said.

I ran my hand through my hair, closed my eyes, and raised my face to the sun. I was waiting on a call back from the detective in charge of the previous murders and while I did, I pulled my cell from my jeans pocket.

I dialed, for the second time, my old FBI friend.

"Mich, sorry, I was meaning to get back to you. How's things back in the good old police force?" Corey asked.

"Good, except I need some help on profiling," I said.

"What do you have?"

I ran through the details of the two murders, and my fears for the safety of the other kids.

"Shit, you guys don't do things halfway down there. I've got some leave coming up, need a hand?"

"Fuck yeah! I can't get my head around this one to be honest."

"I can be with you late tomorrow. Want to fax over what you have so far?"

"That would be fantastic, and sure, I'll get on to that now."

We said our goodbyes and I headed back into the station. Corey and I had worked together on several cases, but mainly one to bring down a nasty cult. That hadn't ended the way we'd expected it to, many died and the cult up and disappeared overnight. Tracking down the elders of that cult was one of my 'after hours' activities.

"Want the bad news or the bad news?" Dean said, as I made my back into the incident room.

"The bad news."

"Vicky Bell may be missing."

"What the fuck do you mean, *may* be missing?"

"She was supposed to be in school, according to her parents, she never arrived."

"Jesus. Fucking hell." I slammed my fist down on the desk.

If, and it was a big if, Vicky was the next victim, the speed at which our killer was operating at was unheard of. He had to have been planning them for a long time. It also left a seriously uneasy feeling in my gut. Were the killings a build up to something else?

"Her parents are on their way, as is Louis Chapman, Kay Davis, and their parents. And that's the other bad news, the chief knows his station is about to be invaded by all these people, and he's freaking about it," Dean added. I shrugged my shoulders.

"What about the other girl, Alison?"

"Parents are out of town, she's with them on an extended break, according to Mr. Turner."

"Okay, track them down, and I want every fucking building in this town searched. I want an immediate call out for help on the radio station, the newspaper, everywhere. Walk every street, look in every corner until we find her."

I could feel panic welling up inside me. I took some deep breaths to calm my pounding heart. I stared at Vicky's photograph, it was separated from Casey and Dale's and I prayed I wouldn't have to move it across to join them.

"What the fuck is going on?" I whispered.

"You have a call," I was told. I walked toward a desk and picked up the phone waiting for the caller to be transferred.

"Mich Curtis," I said, when I heard the click of a call connecting.

"Hi, Mich, I'm Detective Martin, from Millbrook County. I understand you wanted to speak about a case?"

"I did, thank you for returning our call. We have a couple of cases here that may have a religious element. I understand you were involved in a case with two teenagers some time ago". I fumbled around to find the file.

"The 'Sinners' case?"

"That may be what you called it. Two kids, naked, positioned in the shape of a cross?"

"Yeah. Sad one, that. Two great kids, high school sweethearts, prom king and queen, if I remember."

"What can you tell me?"

"Not much, to be honest. They had been at a party; parents weren't expecting them back that night. A dog walker stumbled across them the following morning. I can have the medical examiner's and our reports faxed over, if you like."

"That would be great. Were there any suspects?"

"Not officially. However, we kept a list of three residents that up and left in suspicious circumstances."

"What do you mean, suspicious circumstances?"

"Left without telling anyone. One was a bit of a transient anyway, a truck driver who would leave for periods of time, so whether he should be on the list, I don't know."

"Care to share their details?"

"I shouldn't in an official capacity but..."

The fact he left his sentence unfinished had me believing he would.

"If there is anything you can do to help, I don't believe our killer is finished and right now he's targeting a group of friends. Two are dead and one is missing. I really could do with anything you have, officially or not."

"I'll see what I can do."

We said our goodbyes after I gave him my personal email address. It may not be connected. It may be a total waste of time, which should be better spent elsewhere, but if Vicky Bell didn't show up alive, we were going to be getting pretty desperate.

"Mich, there's someone to see you," I heard. One of the admin staff had caught my attention.

"Who and where?"

"A priest, apparently you needed one? And in the interview room."

I nodded and popped my head through the doorway to the incident room and called for Dean. I checked in with Pete, to make sure this was the priest he had contacted; the last thing we needed was an imposter trying to gain information. Together we headed for the interview room.

As we entered, a man in slacks and a white polo shirt stood. I hesitated at the doorway, not expecting him to be dressed the way he was.

"I'm sorry, I guess you were expecting me in full uniform," he said with a smile. I imagined he'd seen the confusion cross my face.

"I was, sorry," I replied.

He chuckled before taking a step toward us and holding out his hand.

"David," he said.

I introduced Dean and myself, and we took our seats to one side of the small metal table, I gestured for him to sit.

"I was asked if I could shed some light on an investigation," he said.

I nodded as I flicked through the file I held in my hand. I retrieved just two photographs, the ones that showed the words scraped into the wall and on the back of the dumpster.

"It's kind of you to come in. I guess I don't have to tell you that what I'm about to share has to stay between us, Father..."

"Just call me David," he said, interrupting me.

"David. What can you tell me about the seven deadly sins?" I asked.

"Well, there are actually no real details of these sins, as we know them, in the Bible. However, there are precursors that reference them. The list has changed over time, of course. The sins that are the more recognized, the *current* sins for want of a better word were clarified by Pope Gregory, 590 AD, I believe."

"So, where does one learn about these sins?" Dean asked.

"A Catholic would be taught them at Bible study, in church as part of a sermon. I guess they could also self-study on line. Modern religion doesn't reference them so much, because their meanings have changed over time. Take gluttony for example. It's not necessarily related to overeating, it can relate to excess of any material form."

"If I had a group of people, could I attribute one of these sins to them easily?" I asked.

David shrugged his shoulders. "I guess so, but to be honest you'd need to know the ins and outs of their lifestyle, and who knows if one wouldn't fit two sins. The other thing to think about is whose version of the sins is your murderer working to. I'm assuming that's what we're really talking about here, isn't it?"

I leaned back in my chair. I would never normally divulge any aspects of a case to an outsider. Especially one I hadn't done a great deal of research on, but time was running out. We had a potentially missing girl and five more sins to worry about.

"He left words at each site, lust and gluttony. I'm making an exception here, David, in sharing this information with you. No one outside my team knows about that and all are under strict instruction, no, a promise, if this gets out, asses will be kicked, viciously."

David nodded his head in understanding. "Now, what do you mean, whose version?" I asked.

"The most famous version of the seven deadly sins is Dante's. His interpretation is slightly different to the church's. If you ask any student about them, most will immediately identify with Dante's."

"Dante, as in Dante's *Inferno*?" I said.

"Yes."

"But does that refer to the seven sins?"

"It does, in a roundabout way. If you think of the circles of hell, each represents one of them."

"There are nine circles of hell," Dean said, surprising me. I mentally slapped myself for that, but he didn't seem the type to know of Dante.

"There are, but the first is limbo, the entrance I guess you'd call it. I'm not suggesting your sins are a direct relation to *Inferno*, but Dante published his interpretation. It was just a thought. At the end of the day, no matter whose version, lust is lust, greed is greed. I have no idea how you'd apply those to the poor souls murdered, without knowing every intimate detail of their lives."

I sat upright. *Who knows every intimate detail of their lives?* I thought. Who had enough knowledge of those kids to apply a sin to them that wasn't outwardly obvious?

"I'm not sure I've been of any real help, but I can drop off some information you might find useful," David said.

"That would be good, thank you."

⸻

David left and Dean and I headed back to the incident room. I wanted an update on the search for Vicky.

"So, Dante, huh?" I said.

Dean shrugged his shoulders. "Had to learn it in high school, boring as fuck as I recall."

"What class?"

"Philosophy, I think."

His comment brought me up short. "Philosophy?"

He stared at me; I stared back. "Fuck!"

"Go find out where we're at with finding Vicky, I'll see who led their philosophy club," I said.

I rang the high school and was put on hold until the secretary could locate Mr. Turner. A few minutes later he was on the phone.

"Mr. Turner, can you tell me who led the Philosophy Club?" I asked, once pleasantries were exchanged.

"It was mainly student led, but James Thomas would advise, set reading assignments, that kind of thing, why?"

"It's just something that came up. Thank you, if I need to know more, I'll be in touch."

I went through my notes on the interviews we'd conducted. There was no Mr. Thomas listed. I brought up the schools website and scrolled through the list of teachers. Mr. Thomas was there, of course, and I guessed the reason we hadn't interviewed him was because our victims hadn't attended any of his classes. Although they had all been in Philosophy Club, not one of the friends had actually attended that as a class. I wanted to know why.

Chapter 9

I'd made a mess, who would have thought gold paint was not fucking easy to mop up? I sighed. Then I punched the slut in the face for making me late. She was begging me to die. I'd grant her wish, of course I would, I wasn't a sadist. Well, not entirely. I was angry, and I didn't like being angry, it was an emotion that caused slipups, fuckups.

I hadn't had my fix of Mich, my Michfix; I chuckled at my words. I needed to get rid of this girl, finish her off, and move on to the next.

The furnace was getting up to temperature, finally. Leaving the spilled paint on the floor I grabbed the gloves and slipped them on. She was whimpering and I looked down at her. I had her bound by her wrists, ankles, and throat to a gurney; I needed something on wheels for what I'd planned for her. She was naked, well, not quite. I'd covered her modesty with the gold paint. I should have used a spray can but the gentle stroke of the horsehair brush over her skin brought it to goosebumps. She was enjoying every second of my ministrations. I'd watched with fascination as her nipples had puckered. I placed the tips of my fingers against one nipple *feeling the hardness and the heat. The dirty slut obviously wanted me.*

Using tongs, I picked up the small smelting pot and placed it in the furnace. It would take a while, but Mother's gold had certainly come in handy. I smiled. Oh, Mich. I missed you this past day. Maybe I'll visit with you later.

───

"We've searched all abandoned buildings in the town and on the outskirts, so far, nothing," Pete said, as he consulted his notes.

"She has to be somewhere and I don't believe she's that far away."

I was getting frustrated. Where the fuck was Vicky Bell? Louis and Kay were being rounded up; they were due, with their families at the station shortly and we had officers with Vicky's parents. I wanted to speak with them before news of Vicky's disappearance hit the streets. I had no doubt in my mind the group of friends were being targeted and I needed to know why. If we could answer that, we might have something to go on.

I'd discussed voluntary DNA testing on all males residing in the town. The chief had balked at the logistics, more importantly the cost, but I had Dean consult with someone over at the local hospital to see if we could set up a dedicated unit to deal with it. Although our killer hadn't left any DNA, I was hopeful he would slip up at some point. It was a useful process of elimination, whoever didn't show, would be investigated further.

Coordinating that would be a nightmare, I knew. We'd need a list of all adult men registered as living in the town and there would be a couple of thousand of those. Then we had to persuade the townsfolk to take the test without the usual screams of invading their human rights! I've often wanted to write the dictionary meaning of the word 'voluntary' on a fucking billboard, but then I doubted most would still understand it.

"We've doubled patrols on the street, haven't we?" I asked. Dean nodded.

"All leave has been cancelled, and I suspect the chief will have a fucking heart attack at the overtime this month. And a rotation has been set up, so we have coverage twenty-four hours."

I stood in front of the whiteboard. I wanted to see if there was any pattern in when the murders occurred to when the bodies were discovered. It might give us an idea of how much time we had before...I didn't want to go down that train of thought.

We were notified that Louis and Kay had arrived, they were being kept in separate interview rooms, but I had no doubt they would have had a chance to talk. I decided to speak to Kay first.

———

A petite girl, dark hair pulled high into a ponytail and with her clasped hands in her lap, sat in one of the plastic chairs facing the Formica desk. A woman sat beside her, a man stood, leaning against the wall. All three turned their heads as I walked into the room.

"Thank you for coming down today," I said, as I took a seat opposite.

The woman introduced herself as Kay's mother and the man against the wall as her father. I already knew who they were. Kay stayed silent. I couldn't say it was a scowl on her lips, but she certainly didn't seem to be friendly. Not that sitting in a police station was anything to smile about, I guessed. I smiled, trying to put her at ease.

"I know you've spoken to one of my colleagues, but I wanted to go over some things, in the hope you can help, Kay. Is that all right with you?" I asked.

I kept my gaze on her. She shrugged at first, and then spoke. "Sure."

"Can you tell me about the last sleepover you had at the house on Perry Street?"

Her eyes darted to her mother and I wondered if, like Casey, she was supposed to be anywhere other than a derelict house with a group of friends.

"Erm, when?" she asked, a slight stammer was present in her voice.

I tried to relax my body, conscious of giving off the wrong vibe. "Would you prefer to speak to me alone? You are old enough to be interviewed without your parents. There is nothing formal here, we just need to ask you some questions to clarify some things that have come to light."

I saw her visibly swallow and her neck flushed a little. She shook her head. No matter what my professional training was, no matter that I hadn't taken the 'profilers' course, it was clear this girl was not comfortable and was about to withhold information.

"We used to camp out there every now and again, nothing to it. All the kids do."

"I understand that. But can you elaborate on the last time that you were all there? I know the dates, Kay, Louis has already confirmed those."

She blinked, rapidly.

"We went there, drank a little, told a few stories and that was it," she said.

I wanted for the sigh that threatened to leave my lips to be audible enough to display my frustration. Didn't these kids know this was fucking serious?

"Kay, two of your friends have been murdered. I'm not sure how seriously you're taking this. I would have thought you'd be bashing my door down to offer to help."

"I think she's taking it very seriously, Officer," her mother said. The father stayed silent.

"It's detective, and I don't think any of Casey or Dale's friends are. Something happened at that sleepover, which is why everyone is being a little tight-lipped about it. I want to know what it was." I turned my attention back to Kay. "Two kids have been murdered. I need to find the person who did that. You can help, or you can withhold information and live a life of guilt if our murderer strikes again, or is never caught."

I was beyond being nice. "Do you think he'll strike again?" she asked, quietly.

She'd said *he*. It was safe to assume most would suspect the murderer was a 'he.' It was extremely rare to have a female killer, but there was something about her body language that had me convinced she knew more.

"Yes, I do. Now, tell me about that sleepover."

It was time to put the fear of God into these kids. They may have no valuable information but even the smallest thing could lead the investigation in a different direction.

"It was Louis' idea. He'd scored some coke, we bought some beers, and Dale had brought sleeping bags. We were supposed to stay in the house, we'd done that before but I didn't want to, so I stayed outside for a while. We had already started a fire to keep warm, I sat by it and left them to it and after a while, I moved inside."

"Where did you sit, when you went inside," I asked, leaving the 'coke' comment aside for the moment. I was sure her parents would grill her on that.

"There's a room that has some chairs, in front of a fire. We sat there."

"All of you?"

She gently shook her head. "Casey and Louis, and Dale, would go off to...you know? Upstairs somewhere."

I nodded my head but kept quiet. I wanted her to carry on.

"We must have fallen asleep I guess, but then Louis, or Dale, started to mess around, trying to scare us."

"How?"

"Dumb stuff, you know? Saying they heard noises, scraping on wood, that kind of thing. Ali and I decided we didn't want to stay there anymore so we left."

"Where did you go?"

"To Ali's. Her parents were away, they're always away so we went back to her house."

"That's Alison Jenkins, right?" Kay nodded her head.

"Where did Louis score his coke, Kay?" I asked.

She gently shrugged her shoulders but wouldn't meet my eyes. "It might be important," I added.

"You'll have to ask him. I never took it," she said, looking at her mother as she spoke.

"But Casey and Louis did?"

"Yeah, frequently."

"Tell me about Philosophy Club," I asked. My question seemed to have completely thrown her. She looked up, her eyes wide.

"Phil...erm, we had to join some clubs. We thought it might be fun, it wasn't so we left."

"How long were you in the club?"

"A couple of meetings, no more. What has that got to do with...you know?"

"I don't know if it is related, but I thought it an odd club for you guys to be involved in."

"My daughter isn't the dumbass you think she is," her father said, finally pushing himself off the wall and adding to the conversation.

"I wasn't suggesting that she was, it just struck me as odd since she doesn't take the class."

"It wasn't for me, so I quit. Nothing more to it, really," Kay said.

Her pupils had dilated, her eyes flicked from side to side. She wrung her hands in her lap and fidgeted. She was lying.

"Is my daughter at risk?" he asked.

I looked over to her father. "Two of Kay's friends have been murdered. I don't believe our killer has finished yet, but I can't honestly answer that. Right now, I have two dead kids, who were friends, and one missing." I turned my attention back to Kay. "If you want to help me, then I'd sure appreciate that. You're not telling me the truth, or if you are, you're withholding information that might save another life. Right now, I can't force you to talk to me. I'll find a way though, Kay. I can promise you that."

I stood and, without a goodbye, left the room. It was time to play the bad cop card. What part of *your friends have been brutally murdered and you could be next* did these kids not fucking understand? I couldn't use those exact words but surely it didn't take a fucking genius to piece it together?

I'd taken a gamble in saying what I did. The two murders could have been random, coincidence, but my gut was telling me otherwise.

"You're not going to like this," Dean said, as I strode down the corridor toward the incidence room.

"What?"

"Vicky's mother is out on the streets, and I mean literally out on the street, trying to find her daughter. Telling all that will listen, we're not doing anything to find her and the killer has her."

"Fucking great!"

In one way, I was surprised it had taken as long as it had for that piece of information to get out. We had tried to keep her name out of public circulation, just for a few hours, to give us a head start. Without needing to ask, I knew the press would be congregating outside the station. One murder would certainly be front-page news. Two, we'd have a two-page spread but a possible third? It would be a frenzy out there.

I could hear shouting from the corridor. A voice that had my fucking fists itch with desire to throw a punch. The mayor had decided on an impromptu press conference in the station reception area. I refused to participate, despite hearing my name being called. I shook my head at the words *serial killer* and *what exactly are the police doing?*

"Don't even fucking ask," I said, as the chief walked into the room. "Every second spent speaking to those pricks is less time to find Vicky."

I watched as he perched on the edge of a desk. He'd aged, in just the few days since Casey had been found, his eyes had lost a little more of their spark, his temples had greyed further. Like me, he looked fucked. Yet I was operating on way less sleep.

"Give me something, please, Mich." A ring of desperation sounded in his voice.

I sighed. "We have a connection, we think, between the murders. That won't be disclosed to the press but it gives us some valuable information to work with. Tell them we've cancelled all leave, we've doubled the police force on the streets, and we're asking for all male residents to volunteer for DNA testing at St. Bart's. Maybe our killer will think he's left us a trace."

The chief nodded his head then disappeared. I silently thanked him for not pushing me to make a statement. I then made my way to the second interview room, and to Louis Chapman.

"I'm sorry to keep you waiting," I said, as I entered.

"We don't really appreciate being kept," Mr. Chapman said.

"Like I said, sorry to keep you waiting. Now, Louis, Vicky Bell is missing. I don't have time for bullshit. I have two questions. First, where do you buy your coke, and second, tell me about Philosophy Club."

I finished speaking just as I sat in the chair and then stared hard at him.

"What the fuck do you mean?" Mr. Chapman asked.

I ignored him and continued to stare at Louis.

"Is any of that relevant?" he asked.

"I don't know yet. But I need to know as much about Casey, Dale, and Vicky as possible."

I actually had no idea if I was clutching at straws, if a coke dealer or a philosophy club had any fucking relevance at all. I was getting desperate and trying hard not to show that.

"Dale got it from some dude at school, and as for the club, I quit that, wasn't my thing."

"Funny, Kay said the exact same thing. Name of dude, and why join the club if you're not even studying that subject."

"If you want the truth, I thought it might be interesting. I was wrong," he said.

"Mmm, Kay told me you were the one who supplied the coke."

"She was wrong, I guess."

"So you went to Perry Street, while Casey was supposed to be missing, I'll remind you, camped out, scared the shit out of the others, got high, and then left?"

"We didn't scare the shit out of anyone, there was a noise, and we all ran."

"What noise?"

"Scraping, like a wood against wood type thing, as if someone was trying to move a piece of furniture, I guess."

"Where?"

"A room upstairs, I didn't hang around long enough to find out."

"Do you think my son and his friends are targets?" Mr. Chapman asked.

"I don't know yet, which is why I need to get to know them all. Except, they appear to be stalling me."

"What do you need to know?" Mr. Chapman said.

"I'm going to be honest with you here. Casey, Dale, and possibly Vicky. Your friends. Murdered, or missing. Why? Why, your circle of friends, Louis?"

I could see tears forming in his eyes; he tried to subtly wipe them away. His shaking hand gave away how frightened he was.

"I don't know," he whispered.

"Someone knows a lot about you guys, he's leaving us clues that we just can't tie in yet. Answer me this, if you can. Why would anyone associate the word lust with Casey?"

"Lust?" He paused, and then shrugged.

"She slept around, a lot. I told her she had an addiction. Detective, she was so insecure she thought if someone fucked her, they liked her. And, yeah, I guess I took advantage of that, too. She used to brag a lot about how many men she'd had. She even said she'd had a couple of teachers, but I'm not sure if that's true."

"We think she was taken fairly soon after your campout. What happened there, where did she go?"

"I told you, we heard a noise and ran. I didn't wait for them, I should have," his voice trailed off to a whisper.

"Did she run?" I asked. He shook his head.

"She wasn't scared, like she sort of knew or was expecting the noise."

"Expecting it?"

"Yeah, she laughed, it seemed a strange thing to do."

"Louis, I'm concerned for you, Alison, and Kay. I can't get my chief to agree to placing you in a safe house, we don't have one but I think if you can all keep together, maybe in one house?" I finished my sentence looking at Mr. Chapman, who nodded.

"I'll have everyone at mine, the house is large enough and we have security gates."

"I'll post someone to patrol the grounds. I might be way off here, it might be coincidence but I don't believe so. And I'm asking one thing of you, this doesn't go any further than this room. I can't stress the importance of not leaking any information to the press, or anyone. I need to catch this person. I don't need for him to know what we are doing."

"By putting these kids together, is that not offering him bait?" Mr. Chapman asked.

It was a valid point and one that had crossed my mind for both good and bad reasons.

"I don't believe he'll come after all of them at the same time," I lied.

Mr. Chapman nodded, whether he was convinced, I wasn't sure. But what else could we do? At least if all the kids, and their families were together, they stood a better chance.

"Louis, if you think of anything, no matter how inconsequential, I need to know," I said.

"I think the dealer is a teacher," he said, quietly.

"A teacher?"

"Yeah. I don't know a name, just something Dale said, but then, he told a lot of lies."

"Where did he get the money from?" I was expecting Louis to tell me they all contributed.

"His family is wealthy. Dale liked to flash his cash around, waste his allowance on shit. Vicky was all over that. She liked him only because he had money."

"Okay, for now stay home, Louis. Mr. Chapman, thank you. Perhaps you can let me know when you have everyone together."

I left them and headed back to the incident room. I went straight to the whiteboard and wrote. Casey liked a lot of sex, hence the lust. Dale was wasteful, did that relate to gluttony? Vicky, if she was the next victim, was greed. Did her wanting Dale's money constitute greed? I scanned the room.

"Tim, I know it was theology you studied but what about Dante's version of these deadly sins?"

"I don't know, to be honest. You'd need to speak to someone else on that. Like I said, I just studied theology. My mom had an idea that I'd go into the clergy."

I picked up the notes I'd written and scanned through looking for the name Mr. Turner had given me.

"Dean, we need to head to the school," I said.

Chapter *10*

She looked so pretty, all sparkly. Now all she'd see is gold, the greedy girl. I had to leave her for a while; I needed my Michfix.

It felt wonderful to walk the streets with the autumn sun on my face. I smiled and bade a greeting to passersby. It was as I crossed the street that I saw him. I wandered into the school parking lot and watched him climb from his car. His sidekick dipped his head to speak to him and my hands curled into a fist. How dare he be so close! I bet he could smell him, I bet his stomach fluttered as his senses were assaulted by Mich. I kept to the shadows of the trees that lined the parking lot, moving slowly toward them. I wouldn't get close enough to hear their conversation though. I wondered what they were there for. Still clutching at straws, I bet.

Without thinking, my hand pressed against my pocket. I heard the comforting sound of folded paper as my fingers brushed over the newspaper clipping. Oh, Mich, if only you knew. One day I'll show him what's written on that piece of paper. A moment of conflict hit me. I should hate him for what he did, but I found myself so drawn to him that I couldn't distinguish between love and hate.

I guess they were so closely related it was natural.

I'll give you Vicky, tonight, I thought. There was a perfect location in town for her discovery, a very apt location.

I wondered how the investigation was going. I imagined he'd arranged something to get the friends together and into safety. Good boy, Mich, it would be a sensible thing to do. I mean, you'd hate for the murder of the other kids to be on your conscience because you didn't take measures now, wouldn't you?

"See you soon, Mich," I whispered, as I watched him head into the school.

———

"We'd like to speak with Mr. Thomas, the philosophy guy, if he's around," I asked Mr. Turner after being shown into his office.

"Of course, is there anything I need to know?" he said, as he picked up the phone from his desk.

"No, it's a question I'm hoping he can help answer, that's all."

Mr. Turner spoke to his secretary, asking on the whereabouts of James. Once he'd finished his conversation, he stood and beckoned us to follow him. We walked in silence along a corridor; occasionally Mr. Turner would nod or greet a student who eyed us suspiciously. We came to a halt outside a brown, wooden classroom door with a glass panel. I looked through to see a man sitting at his desk, marking papers I guessed. I thanked Mr. Turner and gently knocked on the door before opening it.

"Mr. Thomas?" I asked.

The man rose. He looked exactly as I would imagine a philosopher to look. If he'd had corduroy patches on his green chunky knit sweater that would have completed the look.

"How can I help?" he said, making his way out from behind his desk.

"I'm Detective Curtis and this is Detective Saunders, I wondered if we could have a moment of your time?"

"Of course, please take a seat. And call me James," he said.

"Thank you, James. I have a couple of things to speak with you about. First, I understand both Casey Long and Dale Stewart attended Philosophy Club for a little while, can you tell me about the club and their involvement?"

"Yes, of course. It's a student run club; they appoint a president, that kind of thing. My involvement is really only to supply material for them to read and discuss, perhaps answer a question or two, and occasionally to give a lecture. I don't think philosophy was really the best subject for Casey and her friend. Sadly, some students take these clubs because it looks good on any applications they need to send out. Such a shame really, because she was quite an intelligent girl, if I remember right."

"And Dale?" I noticed that he hadn't spoken that much about him.

"I got the feeling Dale only joined because Casey did, and their other friends, of course. I'd have to check with the president to see how long they lasted, but I don't think it was too long."

"And they didn't take philosophy, isn't that strange?"

"A little, but there are students who might join a club to see if the subject is something they might like, try before you buy kind of thing," he chuckled. I stared at him.

"I'm sorry, I guess that was a little inappropriate," he said.

"What were they like, as a group of friends?" Dean asked.

James leaned back into his chair, he sighed, rocking back on two legs.

"I think you'll find the pupils are divided where that group is concerned. I hate to speak ill of the dead, but they were the 'in crowd', the 'clique,' and therefore not overly liked by some. But other than the odd lecture in the club, I didn't really have a great deal to do with them. I wish I could help more."

"Okay, thank you. Before we leave, and this is unrelated, what would be the best reading material to learn a little more about Dante?"

"Dante? That's pretty heavy reading, Detective. I'm thrilled that you'd take an interest in him, of course. His work is one of my favorite things to study."

James became animated when he started speaking, giving me an overview of Dante, a history lesson, and a rather long synopsis of Dante's *Inferno, Purgatorio,* and his poetry.

"Consider your origin; you were not born to live like brutes, but to follow virtue and knowledge," he said, quoting Dante, I assumed.

He rose and headed to a bookcase. While he stood scanning the shelves, his finger trailing along the spines of old, dusty books, I took the opportunity to study him. He wasn't a particularly tall man, and it was noticeable that he wore clothes at least a size too large. His shoes were polished, which seemed at odds with the scruffiness of the faded at the knees corduroy pants, the checkered shirt with the frayed collar, and the green sweater, stretched as if it had been through a too hot wash. He was odd, but then I don't think I would expect a teacher of philosophy to be anything but.

"Ah, here we go," he said, sliding a book from the shelf. "This is really an overview of Dante's work. It might help you decide what you'd like to discover further."

I thanked him, took the book, and Dean and I left.

"Odd guy," Dean said, when we were away from the classroom and out of earshot.

"Yeah, he contradicted himself, saying Casey was an intelligent girl but then he didn't really know them. And his shoes...highly polished, but he didn't seem to take much care with the rest of his clothes," I said.

"He looked like an old-fashioned university lecturer to me," Dean said, with a laugh.

I got what he meant. James Thomas looked like he'd stepped out of a British TV show about college life.

We were at the most frustrating part of any investigation. We had a fair amount of information but nothing that led anywhere. The turnout for the voluntary DNA was better than I had expected, which meant we were backed up with getting the information on our database.

I had a file prepared for Corey's perusal when he finally arrived. The chief wouldn't sanction payment for his services, of course, but Corey was doing us a favor on this one. His profiling skills surpassed mine. I prayed that he'd be able to give us some clue as to who we should be looking for. I had my ideas, of course. I stood for ages, just looking at all the information written up on the whiteboard, trying to build a mental image. Our killer had to be strong but that didn't necessarily mean he had to be big. I suspected he was a loner; someone who kept to himself yet had knowledge of those kids.

I felt a hand on my shoulder and I turned to see Eddie standing behind me. I hadn't heard her walk into the room.

"I have the report for Dale, thought I'd bring it over in person," she said, handing me a large envelope.

"Thank you, got time for a coffee?" I asked.

"I do, although not the shit you have here. Come on, you could do with an hour of sunlight, you're turning pale."

I looked toward the window; the sun was setting so I wasn't sure about getting any sunlight. I called over to Dean, who looked as shattered as I did, to let him know I'd bring him back a coffee. He gave a thumbs up as he took a call.

"How are you doing?" Eddie asked.

"Getting very frustrated."

"I can imagine. Have you any leads?" she asked, as we crossed the street.

"We have a lot of information, we know the next one will have the word greed attached to it. That's assuming he's following the list."

"The list?"

"The seven deadly sins. Greed is next. We're scouring this fucking town inch by inch, Eddie, and we can't find her. I wanted the kids brought in, if I'd done that earlier she might still around."

Eddie placed her hand on my arm, a rare moment of affection from her, as I opened the diner's door.

"You can't know that, Mich."

We fell silent as we stood and looked for a booth. I spotted one and noticed the silence and looks as we headed toward it. I guessed the patrons weren't happy that I was taking an hour out of the investigation. Eddie slid across the black leather bench seat and I opted to sit beside her. A waitress came over and we ordered our coffees with one to go.

I rested my forearms on the table and my shoulders slumped. "If we could just find her," I said, quietly.

"I did a little research, I'm sure you've already thought of this, but there's a meat packing plant outside of town. That, in theory, would be a clinical environment."

"Been there. We've checked barns, empty houses…Shit!"

I stood, grabbing the coffees and slid from the booth.

"Mich?"

"Come with me."

I threw some dollars on the counter as I passed, not sure if it would cover the coffees and tried not to rush from the diner. I didn't want the patrons to notice.

"Mich?" Eddie said, again.

"Louis Chapman said something. When they camped out at the house on Perry Street, a noise, wood scraping against wood, spooked them. When Dean and I were there, we heard a similar noise, assumed it to be a bird trying to get out."

"But you checked all the rooms?"

We had crossed the street and were climbing the steps to the front door of the station.

"We did, or we thought we did. We didn't get into the attic."

"Let me come with you," she said, as we hurried to the incident room.

I called for Dean, leaving our mugs and his takeout container on a desk.

"We need to get back to the house on Perry Street."

We checked the glove compartment for flashlights before driving over to the house. Dean halted the car, leaving the headlights on and facing the front of the house. At first, once we'd exited the car, we stood, scanning each window.

"What exactly are we looking for?" Dean said, as we walked

around the side of the property.

"We heard a noise, assumed it was the bird. What if we were wrong? Louis said they heard a noise."

"We checked all the rooms," he said.

"We didn't check to see if there was an attic."

I was thankful that the backdoor hadn't already been boarded up; we had no time to get permission to enter. It stood slightly ajar, exactly as we'd left it. I used my foot to push it open, trying to remember if I'd touched the handle the last time we were there. Forensics would have my balls if I hadn't thought to put on gloves.

"Who owns this?" Eddie asked, as she stepped in behind me.

"The daughter of the previous owner, I have the name somewhere back at the station. We meant to contact her, tell her the place was being used as a playground," Dean said.

With the flashlight beams guiding us, we walked from room to room before standing at the bottom of the staircase. We fell silent. Other than the short breaths from Eddie, I couldn't hear anything.

We crept up the stairs, hesitating on every creaking floorboard and listening again. Once we hit the landing, I rotated my flashlight to scan the ceiling.

"Shit," I whispered. There was no obvious entrance to the attic. I had hoped to see a hatch.

I took the lead and walked into the nearest room. It would have been a bedroom at the back of the house, I imagined, although now empty. Keeping my shoulder as close to the wall as possible, I circled the room. I ran my hand over the wooden panelling. Nothing.

We crept to the room we'd discovered the bird in and I did the same. I placed my hand on the wall and walked around the perimeter, stopping at the back wall. Eddie had her flashlight trained upward, covering inch by inch the aged cream painted ceiling. I paused, and took a couple of steps back. I looked over to Dean and placed my fingers over my lips.

"What?" he mouthed. I motioned for him to join me.

I held my hand over a joint in the wood panel. I could feel a gentle breeze. Dean placed his hand alongside mine. I crouched, not wanting to use the flashlight in case it alerted anyone to our presence. I squinted, studying the joint. It was too narrow for me to get my fingers between and too dark on the other side for me to see through.

I felt Eddie place her hand on my shoulder, she gently squeezed as she crouched beside me. I moved to one side. Her small hands ran slowly down the seam, she'd pause every now and again, pushing on the wood.

"You've seen too many movies," I whispered, close to her ear. I heard her quiet chuckle. We wouldn't be so lucky as to find a secret catch that, once pushed, would have a door swing open.

Fuck me if we didn't hear a click.

I avoided the smug look I was sure I would get if I looked at her and watched as she forced her fingers into the small gap that had formed and pried a hinged panel open. At the same time, I heard the snap of his holster being released as Dean reached his gun. I placed my hand on Eddie, encouraging her to move out of the way. Once we'd exchanged places, I slowly ran my flashlight around the opening.

I ducked through and found myself in a very narrow hallway, high enough for me to stand and with a wooden staircase in front of me. I waved for the others to follow me as I tested my weight on the first step. It creaked and I hesitated, reaching inside my jacket for my gun as I did. I prayed there was no way out of the attic, because the noise our steps made would, no doubt, alert anyone up there we were on our way to join them.

At the top of the stairs was a door. I pulled my jacket down to cover my hand as I turned the handle, while trying to hold the flashlight at the same time. I raised my other hand, holding the gun steady as the door swung quickly open. I stepped into a room and swung the light left to right. At the same time, Dean was beside me. The room was empty of any living person, but our flashlights ended up on a wall of photographs.

We ignored the wall for the moment, focusing our search on the corners of the room. It was devoid of furniture, save for one wooden chair in the middle of the room, facing the wall. Satisfied we were not about to be ambushed, I lowered my gun.

"This isn't the whole attic," Eddie whispered, standing beside me.

"I know." The room wasn't large enough to cover the size of the house, but I guessed it to be about half.

Dean and I walked to the dividing wall. We repeated the process we'd done downstairs and felt every inch of what appeared to be a solid brick wall. It was cold to the touch, a little damp, the mortar between the bricks crumbled as I brushed my fingers over it.

"Mich," I heard. Eddie was standing in front of the wall of photographs. "Someone has the hots for you," she added.

The wall consisted of photographs taken from a distance, newspaper cuttings, and drawings. Mostly of me.

"What the...?"

I took a step closer and studied them. Most were recent but there were one or two older. One that I focused on was an old photograph when I'd been in the FBI. Corey stood beside me. If I remembered, that was about the time we'd been called in to a small town to handle the murder of cult members. The photograph was of us leaving the local sheriff's office.

The image that had my breath catch in my throat, that had my heart pound in my chest, was a very old newspaper clipping. I reached out for it, not wanting to alert Eddie or Dean to it and snatched it off the wall. I folded it quickly, not quick enough by all accounts. Eddie was staring at me, open-mouthed.

"Mich?" I shook my head, pleading with her to not say anymore.

Before she could, lights blazed above us. I spun on my heels. Dean stood by the doorway; he'd found a light switch.

"I thought the power was off," Eddie said.

"So did we. This is obviously hooked up to something separate from the house," he said.

The single overhead bulb highlighted the extent of the wall, and the amount of images. I took a step closer but was halted by a sharp intake of breath. Eddie pointed to a photograph partially hidden.

Casey Long sat on a wooden chair, not dissimilar to the one in the room. Her arms were bound behind her and her ankles to the front legs. She was naked with a rag stuffed into her mouth. Her eyes were wide and her cheeks stained with her tears.

"Call it in," I said to Dean.

"Don't touch anything else," she said, I raised my eyebrows at her.

Dean climbed down the stairs to get a better signal, Eddie slowly pivoted to face me.

"What did it say, Mich?" she asked.

"Not now."

"I saw the headline, what did it mean?"

"Eddie, please, not now."

"You're a cop."

"Yeah, I sort of know that. Later, okay? I promise, I'll tell you later."

I doubted very much that I'd tell her what that newspaper article was about. It was something from my very distant past, something I'd kept hidden, successfully, for many years. How the fuck did that newspaper article, from a local newspaper, from another fucking country, end up here?

I clamped my teeth together to stop the flurry of expletives that wanted to explode from me. This wall was about me, those photographs, images, fucking drawings even, spanned a few years. Yet interspersed we found more images of Casey and a couple of Dale.

"Look for Vicky," I said.

"I don't know what she looks like."

"You know that's Casey so any other female, okay? Look!"

I didn't want to snap at her, I wanted to take some deep breaths, slow my heart rate and get my focus back on track. But I'd been blindsided by that one piece of paper. My world was thrown off it's perfectly built, fake, axis. I breathed in deep through my nose, walking from one end of the wall to the other. Not wanting Eddie to see how stressed I felt.

"Team's on their way," Dean said, heading back up the staircase.

"Let's see if there's a way into the other side."

We didn't bother to conceal our voices. If there was someone behind that brick wall, we'd hear them trying to leave. We left the attic, descended the stairs, and crossed the room. We headed straight to the room on the opposite side of the hall and to the back wall. I hoped we'd find another false wall, another hidden panel, and access to the second half of the attic.

It was a scratch on the wooden floor, at the base of a sideboard that had my blood pumping. I dragged it away and a very obvious door was revealed. The fact the sideboard was there confirmed we were not likely to encounter anyone. Like before, I covered my hand with the sleeve of my jacket and pried the door open. A matching staircase took us straight to the attic room, no door on that one. It was a similar space and this time, not empty.

In one corner was an iron bedstead; a bare mattress that looked filthy, lay on top. Rope was coiled around the metal headboard. I didn't need forensics to confirm, I'd lay my salary that was the same rope used to bind Casey to the cross.

Shelves lined one wall. Each shelf contained books, neatly standing side by side, spines out, and without a speck of dust on them. Someone loved those books. I scanned the spines. Some were classics, there was certainly not much that I recognized, and all looked old with leather covers.

"Mich?" I heard Eddie calling from the hallway.

I left Dean to scout the room while I made my way back out. The cavalry had arrived. The road outside was lit up like a fucking parade. Blue and red flashing lights shone through the windows. Thankfully, the house was isolated, so we didn't have to contend with neighbors wanting to know what was going on.

"There's a bed up there, with rope. I bet it's the same rope used for Casey," I said, when I'd gotten to her.

The forensic team started to do their thing, we'd decided the whole property needed to be fingerprinted and we'd need the kids to be processed for elimination purposes. Eddie, Dean, and I were in the way, yet we didn't want to leave either. My heart raced with the anticipation that we'd find DNA on the mattress. It was heavily stained, clearly used, and even with the naked eye I could see hair. I watched as one of the guys pulled a few hairs, placing each one in small plastic bags. They then bagged up the mattress itself.

"I need you out of here," I heard. I knew we'd pushed our luck by being in the middle of the room for as long as we had and retreated to the downstairs.

A van was parked out front; it's rear doors open in preparation for the items that were being removed. Pieces of furniture were wrapped in plastic, similar to shrink-wrap, in the hope it would protect any evidence. Adrenalin and excitement began to course through my body. Not enough to quell the nausea that formed when the realization hit that we should have investigated the house a little more thoroughly before now, though.

That adrenalin spiked higher when an officer came running up the path, waving his radio.

"Mich, there's another one," he said, wheezing as he handed me the radio.

"What and where?" I said, into it.

Dispatch told me that a burglary had been reported, they thought a car had driven through the glass frontage of a small jeweler's. Turns out, it wasn't a car. The poor fucker who had gone to investigate had found a naked body on a gurney instead.

I shouted for Dean and Eddie before racing to the car. I wanted its engine running and ready to go as they piled in.

Eddie made a call, instructing her on-call team to meet us at the store. The area had already been taped off, but that was risen and we were waved through. Officers stood outside the shattered entrance waiting for us, and trying not to wince at the high-pitched wail of the alarm. They knew not to start until we'd arrived. Although nearly midnight, a small group of onlookers had formed. I asked for them to be pushed further back before we stepped through the smashed frontage.

In the center of the store was a grey metal gurney; similar to something we'd see used in a hospital. Strapped on top was a young woman, naked yet her genitalia was painted gold. I walked as close to her as Eddie would allow, bearing in mind I had no protective clothing on. Her breasts were covered with the same paint. But it was her face that nearly forced vomit to spew from my mouth. Her mouth was open in what would have been a scream, but full of...?

The small cabinet display lights that had been turned on picked out the shimmer of something gold. I took a slight step closer. Her mouth was full of a substance. I wanted to reach out and feel it; it was clearly a metal of some kind.

"What the fuck?" I whispered.

"Jesus," Dean said, as he stepped beside me, ignoring the wrath of Eddie for possibly contaminating her scene.

"Look at her eyes," I said.

Two gold orbs stared back at us. Gold streaked down the side of her temples, the skin around them was melted back to bone.

One hand was bloodied and palm face up. Letters were carved into each fingertip.

G R E E D

"Oh my God. I need..." Dean turned and walked out; I soon

105

followed him.

I couldn't even begin to comprehend the pain Vicky, and it clearly was Vicky, would have suffered. I silently prayed that she had been dead before being subjected to those horrors.

Eddie had donned her 'work clothes' and ushered everyone away from the body. Dan, her assistant, was busy erecting a tent; to not only shield the scene from onlookers, but to protect it.

At first we stood in silence, not sure what to actually say. The image of Vicky's face, the grotesque distortion of her mouth, the lack of lips, and bared teeth, was seared into my brain. And her eyes. What the fuck was that all about?

"Can someone shut that fucking alarm off?" Dean said.

One of the sheriff's deputies entered the store, within a couple of minutes there was silence and he returned holding a fuse.

A woman's scream echoed down the street, I looked over to see Vicky's mother running in nightwear toward us. She was held back by a couple of officers before she'd even gotten to the tape. I looked at Dean, I wasn't sure I could be the one to speak with her. And by his face, I was pretty sure Dean couldn't either. I cursed the onlookers for alerting her that quickly. I took a deep breath and strode over.

"Mrs. Bell, we need you to go home. Someone will escort you and keep you company."

"Is it Vicky? Please, tell me that," she said, sobbing and being visibly supported by an officer before she collapsed.

"Please, Mrs. Bell. Let us deal with the scene..."

"Is it my baby?" She reached out to grab my jacket in desperation.

I gently nodded my head. Before I could speak more, she'd

passed out. In one way, I was grateful for that. Not to save myself from any further disclosure but to ease her pain for a little while. One officer gently lowered her to the ground; he removed his jacket, placing it under her head and pulling down the nightdress that had risen to her thighs. I heard him on the radio calling for paramedics.

"I've got this," he said, looking up at me. I simply nodded my thanks.

It was the immeasurable pain I believed Vicky would have gone through that set her murder apart from the others. Her lips had literally melted from her face. There was no doubt in my mind that molten metal was poured into her mouth and over her eyes.

Vicky was removed from the store and the forensic team got to work. I had officers walk the street, like I had every other time, seeking out any CCTV, evidence, not that I expected to find any. The town's main street was a busy place during the day, although there were a couple of bars at one end, it was often pretty desolate at midnight. The late drinkers would be frequenting the bars on the outskirts of town.

"Dispatch said a call was made, do we have those details?" I asked Dean, as I joined him.

"Anonymous caller. It was a report of a suspected burglary. He hung up before giving any more details."

"Mmm, you thinking what I am?" I asked.

"Yep. Our killer called it in," Dean replied.

The townsfolk, in general, were law-abiding. I didn't think anyone other than our killer wouldn't want to leave details. It was possible, of course, they were up to no good themselves, but then why call in something that might just have been a break-in.

"He's making contact," I heard. Turning, I saw the smiling face of Corey. He'd arrived a day earlier that I had expected.

I stepped forward and shook his hand, introduced him to Dean, and my head of forensics, Joe.

"Good to have you here. So, he's making contact then?"

"If it can be confirmed that he was the one to call in the incident, then I'd say so."

"We have the call being analyzed, traced, but this guy is like a fucking ghost."

"He'll present himself soon, he'll get frustrated that you aren't close. No matter what the motive, all serial killers like recognition."

"Are we at serial killer status, then?" Dean asked.

"More than two murders by the same person, according to the FBI, is a serial killer," Corey replied.

We were given the nod that we could enter the store. The forensic team would be there for a while longer, but I guessed they had processed the main area. One of the officers was tracking down the owner of the store, but until we obtained a set of keys, we would have to step through the broken window.

"What do we have here?" Corey asked.

I explained about the house, what was found in the two attics and the call dispatch had received. I struggled through the details of what we then found when we arrived at the store.

"So we're looking for a blacksmith or someone with access to a smelting pot," he said.

"We've gone through every barn and agricultural building in this town and on the outskirts. Who are we looking for, Corey?"

"Having gone through what you sent me, I suspect we're looking for someone with the worst trait we want in a serial killer, Mr. Average Joe. Although these murders are gruesome, there's no showmanship involved. He's not displaying for praise. He's following a very rigid set of rules, in his mind—these seven sins thing."

"So are we looking at seven murders?" Dean asked.

"I'd say so, unless you catch him first. The thing is, I don't think these murders are his ultimate goal. He has a bigger plan."

Chapter 11

"Cunts. You fucking cunts," I shouted, as I watched a group of men in white cotton overalls remove items from my house. Tears streamed down my cheeks at the loss of my prized possession, my wall of art.

"Not now, Mother!" I said, hearing her fucking voice chastising me in my head.

She had been right, of course, the house was not the place to 'work' but I'd ignored her. I didn't attempt to brush the tears from my cheeks as I watched plastic bags of my photographs, my drawings, and newspaper clippings being loaded onto a white van. Why white? White overalls, white van—was that significant?

I didn't care for the furniture, that was years old and didn't belong to me. I cared only for my collection of images of Mich. It had taken me two years to build that up. Two fucking years: of stalking, of research, revelations, and heartache. All gone in the space of a couple of hours.

I slipped away, keeping to the boundary of the field alongside the house until I reached my truck. I was far enough away to not alert anyone to the sound of the engine starting, and I bumped *along the field road until I hit the main road. It was time to go and see how Vicky had fared.*

I parked some distance from the main street, opting to walk to where a small crowd of pajama-clad onlookers stood. There he was, something akin to grief etched into his face, my mood lifted somewhat. He'd been repulsed, I imagined, at the sight of Vicky. His sidekick seemed to be making endless notes on a pad and Mich was talking to a suited man, a man I knew well.

Corey Lowe, FBI agent and old partner of Mich's, stood close to him. I couldn't hear what was being said, of course, but Mich was certainly rattled to have called upon his friend. I had yet to decide if having Corey around was a good or bad thing. At least there'd be another person to mourn Mich's death, I guessed.

I watched for just a little while before slipping away. I placed a pre-paid cell in front of the wheel of my truck, climbed in, and rolled down the window. The cell I used to call in the suspected 'burglary' made a satisfying crunch as I slowly drove over it; then reversed before getting out and collecting all the pieces. No point leaving evidence, now, was there?

———

We had been informed that Mrs. Bell was in the local hospital; her sister had arrived to sit with her. I sent an officer to confirm the news, not because I didn't want to, but I needed to be back at the station. Eddie would, I hoped, have emailed me over photographs. She wouldn't autopsy Vicky that evening, or rather, that morning, but would wait until later in the day. I suspected she would have completed some initial paperwork then headed home.

I wanted to call her, or text at least, but after a quick glance at my watch and seeing it was just past three a.m., I decided against it.

Corey, Dean, and I headed back to the station; there'd be no sleep for us.

Corey walked to the whiteboard, he spent a while reading all the notes that had been written up.

"I don't believe our guy is religious, but he is a member of the community. He fits in here, doesn't stand out. Non-descript, if you want. He will likely be a white male, intelligent, comes from a dysfunctional family, and I'd bet there is a history of abuse. He's rigid in his thinking, if you couple that with high intelligence, it's likely our guy will be on the autistism spectrum. Because of that, it's also likely he's a loner. How many single white guys, perhaps in their early thirties, fit, and maybe no family known, do you have?"

"Fuck knows," was my honest answer. However it gave us the opportunity to narrow down the 'volunteers' we needed for the DNA testing.

"Is he likely to come forward to offer up a DNA test?" Dean asked.

"I'd say it's likely. He hasn't left any evidence, and he's confident you're not going to catch him. I wouldn't be surprised if he didn't make contact, not because he wants to showboat, or throw himself into the limelight, more because he wants to get close to you, Mich."

"Does he view me as a target?" I asked.

"He's clearly fixated on you. It might make life a lot easier if you could figure out why."

"I think I might know," I said, quietly.

Dean and Corey turned to look at me. I sighed as I sat on the edge of a desk. No one spoke for a moment.

"This was pinned to the wall," I said, reaching into my pocket and pulling out the newspaper clipping.

I unfolded it before handing it to Corey first. I watched as he read the article, his lips moving silently, and his eyes widening as he absorbed the information.

"This is you?" he asked, handing the paper back to me.

I nodded my head before sliding it over to Dean. I wasn't sure of the implication of my 'confession,' but the fact that this article was pinned to the wall meant one thing. The killer knew I was a killer, too.

"Fuck, Mich," Dean said.

"It was a long time ago."

"It doesn't matter how long ago it was, what was the outcome?" I knew where he was leading.

"I was arrested for murder in the second degree. It never got to trial."

"Because you were innocent?" Dean asked.

"Because I had a shit hot lawyer." It was neither an admission of guilt nor confirmation of my innocence.

"Who knows about this?" Corey asked.

"No one. This happened in Canada. I've never had to disclose this."

"Our killer knows."

"Appears so."

"Then we need to find a link between you and him, and this might be the key."

"Why is he killing these kids if he has an issue with me?" I asked.

"Because he can. Because he wants to. Because, somewhere in his mind, he's close to you. You're seeking him out, whereas for years he's been looking for you," Corey said.

"Why?" Dean asked.

"Because I really did kill that man," I said, quietly.

———

The incident room quickly became a hive of activity as those that had taken some time to head home for sleep were called back in. I stood at the front and fired off instructions. Was there a hospital missing a gurney? How was metal liquefied? Did we have a blacksmith in town? The list went on for a good twenty minutes as my brain whirled. I asked Samantha to isolate the DNA results we already had of white males, up to mid-thirties, in a separate document. We needed to work through those first. My cell vibrated in my pocket, I pulled it out and noticed that I'd received an email from Eddie. All it contained were two photographs that she'd copied over to me.

"This is what we're dealing with," I said, as I grabbed a laptop, logged in and projected the images to the second whiteboard.

Gasps could be heard as the first shot appeared. It was a close up of Vicky's face. The gold over her eyes reflected the flash of a camera. The closeness of the shot picked out every burnt and exposed charred bone as the gold had run down the sides of her face. What had previously been lips now appeared to be a mass of dried, cracked, discolored wax. There were no other words to describe it. Her teeth, or the stubs that were left, were gold, the same substance filled her mouth.

I heard a sob. Samantha rushed from the room; her hand covered her mouth. The image moved on. The second one was a full body shot showing the paint covering Vicky's breasts and vagina. It resembled an exotic bikini. Straps crossed over her chest, her stomach and her legs. Her wrists were bound to the sides of the gurney.

"Sick fuck!" Pete said, his voice cracking on each word.

"Before we continue, I'd like to introduce Corey Lowe. We worked together at the FBI and I've asked him to help with profiling. Listen to him, write it down, remember it, whatever, but this is the man we're after."

Corey gave his thoughts, describing the killer, as he believed he'd be. Although I hadn't worked that long with Corey, I'd never known him to be wrong. I trusted him and was grateful for any help he could give us.

My eyes stung with tiredness, my throat felt scratchy from talking so much, my stomach grumbled with hunger. No matter how shitty I was starting to feel, I took my place back at the front of the room and we began to formulate a new plan.

Somehow, I was the key. I knew I'd have to come clean at some point. Right then, I wanted to be the one to bring the sick fuck to justice—or did I? Jail time was actually a luxury I didn't want our killer to be afforded.

"We may also have riled our killer now," I heard Corey say. I focused my attention back on him.

"As you know, a wall of photographs, predominantly of Mich, was found. He would have treasured those photographs, maybe even masturbated over them. His fixation on Mich may manifest itself in a sexual way, but I don't believe he's gay, or bisexual, even. It's more a case of his attraction to Mich being misconstrued. He can't distinguish between love, lust, and hate, so, like primitive man, or an animal, the sexual aspect is more of a *conquering* thing. As we know, although Casey was *raped* with an object, there is no evidence of physical penetration from our killer."

"I wonder if I can add something," Tim said, from the back of the room.

"By all means," Corey replied.

Tim made his way to the front. "I've been thinking about this sins things. We assume, with Casey, lust was because either she wanted him, or he wanted her, right? We know she slept around so the *rape* thing..." he swallowed hard, uncomfortable with the thoughts that I imagined were running through his head. "Was that to destroy the very *equipment* that allows her to...you know?" he finished.

"I imagine so," I said.

"So, Vicky. She's wearing gold earrings, a necklace, and bracelet. Her clothes are designer. Greed of material things, and perhaps the reason for carving the letters onto her fingertips is because we use our hands to grab things."

"What's next on the list?" I asked. Tim frowned at me.

"What is the next deadly sin?"

"Sloth."

"Do we know exactly what that means?" Dean asked.

"Most people will assume it means laziness, but according to our friend, Dante, it's an absence or inadequacy of love," I said, picking up the book James had given me.

"Who fits that profile?" he asked, as he studied the board.

"Louis Chapman," I replied.

He looked at me. "Think about it. When we interviewed him he showed no sadness for the loss of his friends. Yeah, he shed some tears but that was mainly because he was scared for himself. He loves himself, for sure, but he joked about fucking Casey, showed no respect for her at all. Is that an inadequacy to love?" I said, looking toward Corey.

"Mmm, possibly," he said, nodding his head.

"But we still need to know where you come in," Dean said.

"Our killer has an ultimate goal. All these…" Corey waved his arm toward the whiteboard, "…are a lead up. Maybe there's a connection between Mich and these kids, maybe he's using these murders to draw you out, get close to you, or maybe he's just having some fun at your expense."

"I can't think of any connection between me and them. I didn't know them, never arrested any of them, or their parents," I said.

Although neither Corey nor Dean spoke, I knew what was running through their heads. They wanted a more detailed explanation of what that newspaper article was about, why it was on his wall, and how it connected me to the killer—trouble was, I had no immediate answer to those questions.

———

The sun was beginning to rise when my cell bleeped to let me know I had a text message.

I've pushed Vicky to the top of my list today, starting in an hour. Eddie

I'd long since ignored the lack of affection in any of Eddie's messages and, fair enough, in this circumstance, it didn't warrant any. I replied.

I appreciate that. We think we know the next target and we have a profile of our killer. I'll come on over later.

"Dean, Corey, let's go make some coffee," I said.

It was time for me to relive a part of my past that I'd hidden for the longest of times. A time that I didn't want to revisit but knew I had to.

I shut the kitchen door, leaning against it to stop any unwanted intruders. As Dean grabbed some mugs from a cupboard, I spoke.

"I killed a man. A man that had killed my father in front of my mom and me. I was just sixteen at the time. I was arrested, as you know. That photograph in the newspaper was me leaving the station with my lawyer. Some of the locals were not happy that the case against me was dropped.

"This happened when we were in a small town, north of Toronto. My dad was a logger; we stayed there, with his mother, so he could work. I don't know why my dad was killed, just that some guy came, late at night, and dragged him from his bed. He forced him to his knees in the yard and shot him in the back of the head."

"Fuck, Mich. You've never mentioned this," Dean said.

"It's not a conversation I ever wanted to have. It's not a memory I want to recall. Anyway, I'd heard my mother's screams, I went to my window and I witnessed it. We moved back home, and then, over time, I watched my mother fall apart afterwards. She killed herself, I took revenge." I wanted to shrug my shoulders.

At the time, taking revenge was the natural thing to do. It was all I could focus on for a long while.

"I knew the man, my dad worked for him so, one day, I hitchhiked back to my grandma's. I took my dad's hunting rifle that was kept there, I found him in the forest, and I shot him. I panicked, dropped the gun and ran. Leaving the gun was, obviously, my biggest mistake."

"Were there any witnesses?" Corey asked.

"No, and that was one reason the case fell apart. My fingerprints were all over the gun, I had motive, but no one saw me."

"But if your fingerprints were on the gun, and it's found at the murder scene, how?"

"Because I often used it. I was photographed holding it many times. Not only were my fingerprints found on it, so were the man's that I'd killed. I wrapped his hands around it. My lawyer argued that he could have taken the gun when he came for my dad. And I had an alibi, a false one."

"A false one?" Corey said.

"My grandma told the police I had been asleep at her house that evening."

"I don't know what to say," Dean said.

"There's nothing to say. I did wrong; I know that. When I was interviewed about my dad's murder, I should have told them who it was. I should have let the law deal with him, but he was an influential man. For some reason, my grandma didn't want us to, we had to deny we saw anything. Then when my mom died, I guess, for a little while, I lost it."

"What was his name?" Dean asked.

"I knew him as Tommy, Tommy Jameson."

"Well, it won't be hard to find out more and that's something we need to make a priority," Corey said.

I scrubbed my hands over my face; two-day-old stubble scratched my palms.

"Why don't you head on over to my place and grab some sleep," I said to Corey.

"Sleep? Who needs it? Let's get to work. Find that connection, we find your killer."

Chapter 12

I paced, I cried, I shouted, and punched the sides of my head, knowing I'd be bruised. My photographs, my pictures, my drawings!

"Shut the fuck up, Mother!" I screamed, hearing her mocking me.

I walked toward her, she was upright in her chair, and wearing the clothes she should have been buried in. A real Miss Havisham! I punched her face, some of her bones shattered under the force, crumbling, creating dust and a mess. The force of my punch had dislodged her skull. I cursed.

"Now look, I have to clean this mess up!" I shouted.

Her headless body sat mocking me. I heard her laugh, as if losing her head meant nothing to her. I cried. I picked up what remained of her decomposed head and tried to fix it back to her spine. I'd repinned her bones many times over the years. I smoothed down her dress, noting that it needed a cleaning; the ejaculate had stiffened part of the material. I grabbed a comb from the sideboard. Her hair had come lose from the bun I'd fixed for her.

"I'm sorry, Mother, so sorry," I said. "I have a pretty gift for you, do you want to see?" I held out the bloodied cardboard box to show her.

"We'll sort those out later for you."

I straightened her up, hating that my punch had caused her to sag. She was a proud woman, not that I'd known her. That cunt had taken all of her time: I'd only had her once she was dead.

Corey and I sat at a desk with two laptops. I Googled the shooting, bringing up as many old articles as I could find. It hadn't been national news but was certainly covered in the local press. Corey used his login to the FBI's database to see if Tommy's murder had been recorded anywhere, other than on the local police computer system. In theory, it should be a cold case, a file still held somewhere as an unsolved crime.

The second thing I did was to fire off an email to the lawyer that had represented me. I could remember that he'd been the duty lawyer on call that day and I Googled his name. His company was operational but whether he still practiced was another matter. I'd have to wait and see if he replied. I needed to be reminded of all the details of the case.

"I'm heading over to the doc's, want to come?" I said, looking toward Corey and Dean.

We arrived at the medical examiner's office and instead of joining Eddie in her examination room; we opted to enter the viewing gallery. Corey wasn't particularly great at watching the dead being examined. I was never entirely sure why there had to be a viewing gallery, other than to guess it was so a witness could be present in a high profile case. Not that our town had ever had any, until now. The murders had become national news, with CNN and Fox running endless reports and calling in so-called experts to give opinions on how the case should be handled.

Eddie looked over, having been alerted to our presence. She picked up a small earpiece with a microphone attached and placed it around her ear. She pointed toward us, gently waving her finger to the left. On the wall inside the room was a small panel of buttons, next to the glass window. I flicked a switch so we could communicate.

"Good morning," she said.

We listened to her as she circled the body. She confirmed Vicky's name, date of birth, and her initial observations. All of which would have been recorded. Dan was laying out trays and instruments on a table beside Vicky. Eddie continued with her external examination, scanning every inch of the body for evidence while Dan photographed her.

When she was done, Dan washed and weighed Vicky ready for Eddie to perform her Y shaped incision and start the removal of organs. The whole procedure took a couple of hours.

The very last thing that they worked on, and the one thing that we wanted to witness, was the removal of the gold substance.

In normal circumstances, Eddie would have to ensure the body would be suitable for an open casket funeral, in Vicky's case that was not going to be possible. We watched as Eddie gently chipped away at the gold that had hardened on the side of Vicky's face beside one eye. Small pieces were weighed and bagged.

She studied the substance and then turned to look at us.

"I'd need to have it confirmed, but I think this is real gold," she said.

"Real gold? Fuck!" Corey said.

It was about five or so minutes later when I heard Eddie whisper, "Her eye is missing."

"Her what?" I said.

Eddie ignored me and moved to the other side of Vicky. She chipped away at the other eye socket.

"Her eyes are missing," she said, looking up at us.

"Like, her eyeballs?" Dean asked.

"Yes, this gold was poured into empty eye sockets."

"Fucking hell! He took her eyes!" Corey said, his face screwed with disgust.

We watched some more, opting to leave at the point Eddie started to remove the larynx for investigation.

"Why the fuck would someone use real gold and not some other metal, colored to look like gold? And where the fuck are her eyes?" Dean asked.

"Because he's a perfectionist. He wanted the gold to symbolize the greed, he wouldn't use anything less. As for why he took her eyes, I can only assume as a trophy," Corey answered.

"How much gold would be needed?" I asked.

"I have no idea. He poured it into her mouth, I guess that would have cooked her from the inside out," Corey said.

I shuddered at the thought. Bile rose to my throat and the slight burn gave me a fraction of whatever Vicky would have felt at that moment.

"Who's on patrol at the Chapmans," I asked. Dean consulted his watch.

"Four patrol officers right now, they should be parked outside and will take turns to walk around the house. Although there should be a shift change shortly."

I nodded as we climbed into the car and headed back to the station.

A large group of reporters had congregated outside, and we were met with microphones shoved in our faces and a barrage of questions, none of which we answered.

I left the two guys to carry on to the incident room while I diverted to the restrooms. After taking a piss, I leaned on the sink, looking at my reflection in the mirror above it.

My skin was pale, dark circles were obvious under my eyes. My hair was a mess and I couldn't actually remember the last time I combed it. I could smell the faint odor of sweat born from fear, tiredness, and spikes of adrenalin. The black t-shirt that I wore was wrinkled. I picked up my badge that hung on a chain around my neck and tucked it in the neck of the t-shirt, while I splashed cool water over my face. I needed something other than coffee to revive me. I pulled a paper towel from the dispenser and held it over my face.

"You okay?" I heard. The chief had entered the room.

I pulled the towel away and looked at him in the mirror. "Yeah," I said, as I crumpled the towel and threw it in the trash.

"You got time for an update?" he asked. His question had me frowning. He didn't normally ask, but demanded.

"Sure, let me grab some notes," I said, leaving him lowering his zipper and stepping up to the urinal.

"I'm going to update the chief," I said, when I caught up with Corey and Dean.

"You gonna tell him about that newspaper article?" Dean asked.

I paused before answering. "I don't know, to be honest. I guess I have to at some point, but I want to be sure there is a connection before I do."

It could be nothing more than our killer had spent some time scouring the Internet and stumbled across that article. It was nearly twenty years ago. I grabbed a file from the desk; a file that Dean had kept updated and walked toward the chief's office.

I took a seat in front of his desk, opened the file and took out the two photographs that Eddie had sent and Dean had printed off. I heard the sharp intake of breath.

"Jesus. So how does this fit in?"

I told him our theory on greed, explaining that Vicky had the letters carved into her fingertips. I also told him that Mr. Chapman had rounded up the rest of the kids and whether we had the budget or not, I'd instructed a twenty-four hour armed patrol around his house. The chief nodded, finally accepting our killer was targeting those kids.

"There's another thing. The wall in the attic? Most of the pictures were of me. Corey believes he's fixated on me and that these killings are a build up to something else."

"How many sins left, Mich?" the chief asked. His use of my first name surprised me.

"Four, and three friends. So, I haven't voiced my concerns yet, but maybe one of those sins is going to be allocated to me."

"Then we need to get you some protection."

"I have all the protection I need. To be honest, I'm sort of hoping I'm right and I'm next. At least that way he has to come out of hiding."

Bait. If I put myself out on show, leave myself in a vulnerable position; perhaps I could draw him out. I had an idea.

"Call another press meeting. Let's appeal directly to him. I'll speak, see if I can make a connection with him," I said.

"Mich..."

"You got a better idea?"

The truth was, there was not one officer in that station, myself included, that had any idea how to move this forward, how to catch the bastard.

The chief shook his head. "Go home, get presentable. I don't want him seeing you dishevelled. He'll know he has you riled."

I'd coached enough parents of missing children in the past to fully understand where the chief was coming from. Our killer could not see any emotion from me, nothing that would allow him to feed off that, to get off on that.

"Okay, I'll be back in a half hour," I said, then rose and left his office.

I caught up with Dean and Corey and informed them of the plan. Corey opted to accompany me back to the house, and we took his car, leaving mine at the station.

"You know how to play this, yes?" he asked, as we drove.

"I do. I'm going to appeal to him directly. We've done all the 'witnesses come forward' bit, so if I can speak to him, encourage him to come forward, he might make contact."

We arrived at my house and left the car in the driveway. I fished out the key from my jean pocket. As soon as I walked through the door, a sense that someone had been in my house hit me. I raised my hand as I came to a halt. Corey understood and stood quiet as we listened. When I was satisfied that I couldn't hear anything, we slowly walked to the kitchen. I scanned each room quickly as we passed. The back door and windows were closed. I rattled the handle on the back door, finding it still locked. It was as I slowly turned around that I noticed it.

Sitting on the table was the green cardboard file that held the last case I'd worked on while in the FBI. Corey took a step toward it.

"Not sure you should have that," he said, quietly.

"I got permission. But that file wasn't open the last time I was in this room."

I specifically remember sitting with Eddie and having coffee, looking at the closed file in the center of the table.

"You think...?"

"I do. He's been in here," I replied.

We took a walk around the small house, checking all the rooms, rattling windows to see if one slid open. All were locked.

"Let's take a look outside," Corey said.

We rounded the house, looking for footprints or disturbance of the grass and bushes. Again, nothing was found. I started to doubt myself. Had I opened that file? I was tired, agitated. I remembered back to that morning, I'd wanted to speak to Eddie but she was preoccupied with her reporting. But I couldn't shake off the sense that someone had been in my house.

I left Corey in the kitchen, flicking through the file, while I took a shower. With just a towel around my waist, I walked into the bedroom. The bed was still unmade and I threw the duvet over it, straightening it as best I could. Housework and I weren't natural companions. I grabbed a white shirt and dark pants, some underwear, and then dressed. I wouldn't wear a suit because I didn't want to come across as official.

Before we left, I checked all the windows and doors again. I also collected up the cold files and took them with me.

"You want to get the locks changed?" Corey said, as we climbed back into his car.

"I will, I'll give someone a call. Maybe it's me; imagining something that wasn't there."

I shook my head of the doubt before I allowed it to creep too far into my brain. Someone had been in my house, that folder had been closed when I'd last seen it.

I didn't have time to wait for the locksmith before the press conference but made a call anyway. I'd ask Frank to call in at the station and collect my keys. He was someone I'd known for a long time, and we'd used him in the past when we'd needed to gain access to a property.

———

Reporters were still waiting around outside the station; they had been informed that I wanted to make a statement. Corey and I pushed past with a promise that I'd be back out in a few minutes. I checked in with the team to see if there were any developments before I made my way back out.

I held my hand up halting the questions that flew at me as soon as I stepped back out of the station door. We didn't have the room inside to hold a press conference.

"I'd like to appeal to the public to come forward with any information, no matter how small or insignificant you feel it is. We know a blue Ford pickup was seen at Montford School, the evening of the seventeenth. We'd like all owners to come forward and help us speed up the process of listing those vehicles registered, and we thank those that have so far volunteered with the DNA testing.

"Now I want to appeal directly to the perpetrator." I kept the tone of my voice soft and even. "I believe you want to make contact with me, and I'd like to hear from you. I understand the message you're trying to send, and I want to give you the chance to come to me first. You know that we found your wall. You also know you left me a very distinctive clue, so it's in your interest to come forward now. The net is getting smaller, come in and talk to me."

I didn't thank the press for attending; I ignored the questions and refused to speak anymore. I simply nodded and walked back into the station. I wanted the killer to know I had that newspaper article, I couldn't say that directly but I hoped I'd given him enough of a cryptic clue to understand. Now we would be back to the waiting game.

One of two things would happen. The one I was hoping for was that he would make contact. The one I was dreading was he'd go after one of the kids. I instructed Dean to organize upping the patrols around the Chapman house. I knew Mr. Chapman had called into the station, wanting an update when Vicky had been found. I hadn't had a chance to speak directly with him; he'd spoken to Samantha instead. She'd reassured him that we were doing all we could; we had no news to share with him but that we still considered Louis and Kay at risk. He was getting agitated, wanting to move to a more secure and secret location. Our problem was, if they moved out of town we wouldn't be able to control their protection.

As for Alison, we'd tracked down her parents. Thankfully they were still abroad and had extended their vacation. They had chosen not to tell Alison until it was safe for them to return. I had no doubt she'd be thrilled at the prospect of an extended break.

"You have a call," I heard. Dean was standing at the incident room door.

My heart started to pound and I quickened my pace.

"Before you get all excited, it wasn't him, but the lawyer you left the message for."

"Okay, I'll take it over here." I moved to one corner of the office for a little privacy.

"Mich Curtis," I said, as the call was connected.

"Good afternoon, Mr. Curtis. My name is Ralph Cooper, although I'm retired now, I took over from Mr. Webster. He was the one who represented you."

"I was hoping to be able to speak to Mr. Webster," I said.

"I'm afraid that won't be possible. Mr. Webster died some time ago."

"Shit," I muttered under my breath. Then a thought hit me.

"Can you tell me how he died?"

"Sadly, he was murdered, some months now."

Chapter *13*

So you want to talk to me now, do you? Now, after all this time you want to sit down and have a nice cozy chat? Over a coffee, perhaps? Maybe we'll head to the diner and grab dinner as well! Although my cock was hard and throbbing at the sound of his voice and the sight of him, acid boiled in the pit of my stomach with hatred. I didn't give a fuck he'd revealed details of my truck, it wasn't even registered to me. I didn't give a fuck about his DNA testing, the name I used was false, obviously. Well, not completely false. I chuckled. Oh, Mich, you have such a shock coming to you. I wondered how he'd fare when he discovered the truth. I knew we were close to the end. Mother would finally be proud of me.

She had a role to play and the time for that was soon. She'd gone beyond stinking and weeping all over the floor. I looked at her. Her skin resembled old, cracked, shrivelled leather. The hair on her head was patchy and grey, brittle to the touch. I'd tried to wash it but gave up after clumps attached to pieces of scalp would come away in my hand. She was held together with bolts and pieces of wire. I picked up the small bag of makeup I'd bought. I wanted Mother to look pretty.

I brushed some rouge on what should have been cheekbones. One side of her face was drooped, the bones underneath the skin shattered. The pink powder made her look alive and I smiled. I picked up a red lipstick, trying to stop the shake of my hand as I colored in lips that had long since withered to nothing. I made her new lips. Over the years her blue irises had turned a chalky white. I smiled, I just had to find a screwdriver to take out the chalky white ones, and insert the new blue ones.

I whistled while I fixed Mother some new eyes. "Now, don't you look all pretty?" I said, staring at my handiwork.

Using the lipstick I wrote one word on the wall above her head.

E N V Y

———

"What did you find that is a distinctive clue?" the chief asked, as he walked in to the incident room.

I was still on the phone to Mr. Cooper. I placed my hand over the receiver.

"Give me a minute?" I asked, holding the receiver up, not that he could have failed to notice I was on the phone.

"One minute, Curtis." We were back to surnames. He stomped from the room. I noticed Corey look at me.

"Mr. Cooper, can you give me details of how Mr. Webster died?" I asked, resuming my telephone call.

"All I can say was that it was a pretty gruesome murder."

The word 'murder' shuddered through me. "Go on," I encouraged.

"He was found in his home, I can't recall all the details. I'm sure the police would be able to tell you more but he was stabbed, something like fifty times. His tongue was cut out, they didn't find that." It was clear that Mr. Cooper was struggling with the memory.

"Do you happen to know which police force was involved?" I asked.

"The Force," he replied. From memory, The Force was the internal name for the RCMP, or more informally, the Mounties.

"I'm sorry to hear about Mr. Webster, I just needed some details on my case. I'll get in touch with the police to see if they found his killer."

"I can forward you details of your case, you're entitled to any information, and as far as I know, his killer was never found."

We said our farewells with a promise from him to email over what details he had, and I'd let him know what happened with the case on Mr. Webster. I stood and walked over to Corey, explained what I had found out, and asked if he could use his influence to contact the Mounties and see what happened. I needed to speak to the chief. As I walked to the chief's office, I was still undecided on what to say.

Chief waved me in as he saw me approach. I waited a little while for him to invite me to sit. He placed his elbows on his desk, rested his chin on his clasped hands, and stared at me.

"What clue do you have that you haven't told me about?"

I took a deep breath. "The killer knows me."

His eyes widened. "How do you know this?"

"The wall was full of pictures, photographs about me, you know that, right?"

"Yeah."

"Among all of that was a newspaper article, about me, when I was arrested for murder at age sixteen." I didn't think I'd consciously made the decision to come clean until that point.

His arms slid, leaving his jaw hanging open.

"Tell me you just didn't fucking say that," he said. I didn't reply.

"I was innocent, the case fell apart. I had an alibi. The man who killed my father was shot, not by me," I lied.

"And this is on your fucking file, huh?"

"No. I wasn't charged," I repeated.

"Fucking arrested, charged, or not, that should have been disclosed. Jesus, Mich, what the fuck..." At least he'd used my first name.

"All I ever wanted to do was be in law enforcement, since childhood. I can't remember the application, but I'm sure it doesn't ask if I was arrested of a crime, only if I was found guilty."

"Don't try that bullshit on me, I've been in this fucking job too long. You know damn well, if you were ever arrested for anything, even a fucking speeding ticket, it needed to be disclosed." He sighed and ran one hand over the side of his face.

"This article, it was pinned to the wall, yes?"

"It was."

"And you took it? You removed evidence from a scene, without allowing it to be processed. No doubt because you didn't want anyone to find it. Where is it?"

I'd transferred the folded article from my jeans pocket to my pants when I'd changed earlier. I reached in for it and slid it across the desk to him. I watched as he unfolded the paper and read.

"Fuck's sake, Mich. You know I gotta suspend you, right?"

"You can't! We are too far into this investigation, and I'm the key, you fucking know that."

"I know, not only did you fucking lie on your application, you've removed evidence from a scene. Then you've told the fucking press about the stolen evidence." He held up his hand to halt the words about to leave my mouth.

"I'm going to ignore this fucking thing, for the moment, Mich. I actually don't know how to deal with it other than calling in fucking Internal Affairs, and I don't want those pricks all over my station. But you took evidence from a scene..."

"I'll get it processed, document it."

"And say what? It just happened to fucking fall into your pocket. Shit, I'm too old for this. I'm supposed to retire in a couple of months."

"Chief, I'm the key. I'm putting myself out as bait here, I'm going to draw him in. He's fixated on me; all the time that I'm still involved in this investigation, I'm safe. If I'm suspended, I don't have protection. He kills me, then what? Can you live with that?" His mouth moved at a pace his words couldn't keep up with. It was a low blow but I continued. "Suspend me after, I'll totally accept that. But hear me out. That lawyer..." I pointed to the photograph in the article of us on the steps of the police station. "Dead, murdered, had his tongue cut out."

"Get out, we'll deal with this when this case is done, okay?"

I gently nodded, thankful for the temporary reprieve and returned to the incident room.

"Still here?" Dean said, with a smirk.

"For the moment. Now, do we have anything?" I asked him and Corey.

"You're not going to like this." As Corey spoke, the fax machine whirled to life.

He stood and walked over, waiting for the ancient machine to spew the one piece of paper he was waiting for. He slowly returned, placing the piece of paper on the desk. Dean and I stared at it.

"Shit!" I said.

It was a photograph of a man, Mr. Webster to be precise, lying on the floor of what looked like his office. The carpet around him was stained dark with his blood, the white shirt he wore completely red across the chest and stomach. What stopped my breath from leaving my lungs were the letters written in red across his forehead.

W R A T H

"Tim, remind me, interpretation of wrath," I shouted.

"Violence, failure to forgive, love of justice perverted to revenge and spite, according to your friend." He waved Dante's book.

"Love of justice perverted to revenge and spite," I said, looking at the image.

"Justice, because he was a lawyer, revenge because he got you off," Dean whispered. It was all I could do to nod my head.

Four people, three of those were kids, had been brutally murdered because of something I did over twenty years ago. There was absolutely no doubt that was the key to all of this, that image confirmed it. No one would be able to convince me that was coincidence.

"But we're out of sequence," Tim said.

"Huh?" I looked over to him.

"Sloth should be next."

"Or we just shouldn't have discovered this yet," Dean said, quietly.

I stood from the chair. "People, we have another murder," I said.

Corey was back on the phone to whoever he'd obtained the image from; we needed the complete case file. It was going to prove difficult because, if our killer was Canadian, they'd want him back. If he was American, they'd want him for trial, if we can solve it at our end, of course.

Things were about to get messy.

———

As the day wore on we got more and more frustrated, our hourly updates produced no new information, other than the phones hadn't stopped with callers claiming to be our killer. Hours were spent on the phone, trying to determine whether they were genuine or not. However, not one of them could answer the one question we asked, to verify their claims. What was the clue that I had spoken about?

The sun had begun to set and I checked my watch. I was hoping for a preliminary report from Eddie, but I didn't hold out much luck that we'd find any DNA. I began to wonder if our killer had police or forensic knowledge.

"Mich! Pick up the phone," I heard shouted from the corridor.

Dean ran into the room. "It's our man, pick up the phone."

"Fuck, we got a trace going?"

Dean nodded just as I picked up the handset and waited for the call to be connected. He would have been kept holding on the line long enough for our trace team to get started.

"Mich Curtis," I said. I watched the chief run into the room and it silenced.

"That was an interesting article wasn't it?" the voice said.

"What was on it?"

"Oh, Mich, don't insult me with the same question I bet you've asked a hundred times already today," he chuckled.

"You know I need to verify that you really are who you say you are," I said.

"Was it satisfying? Did it feel good to pull that trigger and then walk away?"

I gave a thumbs up—our man was on the phone.

"Not really. Since you know my name, I don't suppose you want to share yours."

His laugh sounded distorted.

"I've got a good idea, when you're actually ready to talk to me, why don't you call back without distorting your voice," I said, and then put the phone down.

"Curtis, what the fuck!" the chief said.

"He'll be back on the phone, trust me."

As the minutes turned into an hour, then another one after, my palms started to sweat. The chief paced, scowling at me periodically.

"Relax, Mich did the right thing. The more disrespected, the more riled, the more our guy will want to talk with him," Corey said.

"You better be right," the chief said.

Before he'd finished his sentence, the phone rang again. I looked up and over to the trace team, who had set up in the corner of the room. When I received a thumbs up, I picked it up.

"That wasn't nice, Mich," he said, his voice clear and concise.

"No, but I'm not interested in having a conversation with a machine."

"Are we having a conversation? How exciting!"

"So, are you going to give me anything?"

"Like what, Mich? You want me to tell you who I am? Where I live, perhaps? Why would I do that?"

"I'll tell you what, how about I call you Sam, does that suit you?"

He hummed for a little while. I was trying to ask as many

questions as possible, hoping that his answers would distract him from the length of time I needed him on the phone.

"Sam will do. I like Sam, maybe that'll be the name I use when I'm done here."

"Why the kids, Sam? Can you give me something to justify that? Something I can console their parents with?"

"Ah, the kids. You got it though, didn't you. Casey, the slut. What a wonderful punishment she had. I took away her ability to fuck, Mich, wasn't that clever of me?"

"Not really, I'd say killing her probably did a more effective job. If you'd have left her alive, I'd have been more impressed."

"You're not mocking me are you? Anyway, Dale. Dale was a particular favorite. Ever run onto a scythe? No, I don't suppose you have. He was a druggie, Mich, no need for those around."

I frantically signaled for a pen and pad. One was slid in front of me. I wrote.

How did he know—druggie?

Corey took the pad and pen from me.

Ask if he got high with Dale, he wrote.

"I bet you had fun with Dale, though, didn't you, Sam? I mean, getting high with a bunch of students is a bit lame."

He chuckled again. "They're the lame ones, they want, they get, they abuse, and they have no control, Mich."

He sighed at the end of his sentence.

"Anyway, I really ought to be going now, work to do, Mich, work to do. We're not finished yet. I mean, we're all sinners, Mich, we all have to pay the penance." With that, he disconnected the call.

"Did we get it?" I shouted across the room, slamming my fist on the desk at the shake of a head.

"Fuck! Why, what was wrong?" Dean asked.

I watched a guy take off his headset. "He had a cell that bounced over twenty fucking countries, that's why. I'm sorry."

It wasn't his fault. It was extremely rare to get an immediate trace on the first call. At least the team could weed out the countries we knew he wasn't in and hopefully speed up the tracking process.

"So we're not only looking for a psycho but a technologically intelligent one, as well," Dean said.

"You can learn how to avoid a trace on YouTube," Corey said.

"He bounced his signal over different satellites and through different countries. He cut the call off before we got to him," our trace guy said.

"But we do have a voice recording, so let's start with that," I said.

We replayed the message, listening for anything we could pick up, an accent, for example, or background noise. There was a very slight echo suggesting he was in an empty building. If I had the resources I did when I was in the FBI, I'd be able to identify the type of wall from that echo. Unfortunately, we didn't have the budget, or the time.

"Right, he didn't react at all to your use of the word 'student'," Corey said.

Something clicked in my mind. "Hold on," I said, reaching for the case file. I flipped through it, noticing the details from the *Sinners* murders had been added. I put them to one side. I pulled out the notes from when I'd interviewed Louis.

"Louis said that he thought Dale bought his drugs from a teacher. Our guy knew Dale took drugs. Are we looking for a teacher?" I said.

Dean grabbed the list of teachers at Montford. He drew a line through the females and although we hadn't made extensive notes, we racked our brains on who would fit the profile, deleting any men over thirty-five. We were left with ten.

"Get me all the details you can on these men," I said, handing the piece of paper to Samantha.

"Is he going to call back?" Dean asked.

"He's going to do something before he does. He's not convinced you have enough respect for him. He wants to show off a little more," Corey said.

"How do you come up with that?" Dean said.

"Mich told him he wasn't impressed with him when he wanted appreciation for what he'd done to Casey. He'll act soon, because he's craving that respect. He wants Mich to be proud of him, congratulate him, even."

"Then we need to triple protection at the Chapmans," I said.

The trap had been set. Corey was absolutely right, because I hadn't agreed with *Sam*, I hadn't been impressed with his work, he would try again. When recognition and appreciation was what he was after, he would keep going until he got it. That was something that had been proven time and time again where serial killers were concerned.

"How close are we to this case being taken over?" I asked Corey.

He rocked his head from side to side, as if contemplating. "They know I'm here, albeit unofficially. Get your chief to make it official, and I can probably handle what needs to be done to stop them taking the case off you."

I nodded.

"You can intervene to that level?" Dean said.

"In an investigation of this magnitude, we, or rather, the FBI, would have been called in. The case would have been referred to NCAVC, and their behavioral analysis unit. Corey ran that unit for a while," I said.

"NCAVC?" Samantha, overhearing us, asked.

"National Center for Analysis of Violent Crime. Pretty interesting place," I replied.

I picked up the phone and dialed Mr. Chapman's cell.

"Mr. Chapman, we have made some developments in the case. I can't disclose what, but I want to up the security at your property," I said after introducing myself.

"Okay, I have to say, Detective, we're going a little stir crazy here. We need to get to the store pretty soon as well."

"How about I get a car to take you?"

"I'm not sure about all this. How long is this going to go on for? We can't live like this indefinitely."

"I appreciate that, but until the risk to your son and Kay, is lowered, I can't recommend anything other than what I am. Stay put; you have armed patrols around the clock. I know it's frustrating. If you want to get out of state, or the country even, I can organize transport for that."

"I think we might have to consider that. Let me talk to the others and I'll give you a call back."

Maybe getting Louis, Kay, and their families out of state, across the country even, was a better idea than imprisoning them in the Chapman home.

Chapter 14

It had been quite exciting but also very insulting speaking with Mich. I expected a little more from him. I expected him to be impressed with my ability to dodge his trace. Did he not realize I knew exactly what he was doing? He had disrespected, underestimated me. Maybe he needed another little gift, another death to have on his conscience. I grabbed my duffle, my bag of tricks, as I liked to call it, and headed for the truck. I'll give them the truck when this one was done.

Louis Chapman. He had done exactly what I'd expected of him. The dumb shit couldn't follow simple orders. Now he'd pay for that. He'd got in contact, emailed a fake account I owned, wanting a hit. He was bored, being confined to his house with armed police officers protecting him didn't seem to stop him from wanting to meet me. Well, young Louis, you just made a big mistake.

I didn't care how he'd get out of his house unnoticed. I'd given him the precise times each patrol performed their circuit, how long each one took, the few minutes in between the changeover that he'd need to use to climb from his bedroom window and cross his yard to the field behind, unnoticed. I'd be waiting for him. He used to *send Dale to score for him, the lazy fuck. He didn't really care for anyone other than himself.*

One of the things that was to my benefit was the minute the townsfolk knew they had a serial killer in their midst, according to the press, they stayed off the streets at night. All I had to do was to ensure I wasn't seen by any cruising patrol cars. I knew where every CCTV was. To drive out of town, I skirted around them using the farm roads as cover. I'd been doing it for a while without detection.

Louis was where I'd instructed him to be. The dumb fuck wasn't even suspicious that he was walking to the passenger door of a blue Ford truck, probably the most wanted vehicle in the state. He climbed in, arrogantly demanded his cocaine, and waved a fistful of dollars in my face. He didn't see the hypodermic needle that pierced his jeans, his flesh, and deposited a large dose of ketamine into his thigh. The shock that registered as the drug spread rapidly through his body, causing paralysis, made me laugh. I tutted as he pissed himself, the smell nearly had me gag.

I smiled at him; it was time to take him to meet Mother.

The voice on the other end of the phone was frantic; high-pitched wailing made it hard to understand Mrs. Chapman as she sobbed her way through telling me Louis was missing.

"Fuck!" I shouted. Dean, Corey, Pete, and the team members that were in the room looked over to me.

"Louis Chapman is missing," I said, holding the cell away from my ear.

"Mrs. Chapman, we're on our way," I said.

I jumped from the chair and Dean, Corey and I ran to the

parking lot. We were at the Chapman house within minutes. It was a large, gated property on the edge of town; farmland surrounded it. Outdoor lights blazed, the police presence had doubled as Dean had called in reinforcements. We pulled to a halt outside the electric gates, waiting for them to slowly open. Mr. Chapman was pacing the front yard as we pulled to a halt in front of his house.

"Tell me what you know," I said, as I exited the car.

"His bedroom window is open. We thought he was in his room, watching the TV or something. He was moaning about being bored. Fuck, Mich, what if..."

"Don't go there just yet, he may turn up," I replied.

My initial thought was that our killer wouldn't be sitting outside waiting in the hope Louis might sneak out of his house. I prayed Louis would return when he'd had his fix of freedom. Dean had already started to coordinate a search, firstly of the grounds and the farmland surrounding it. It was early evening; we would lose natural light in another couple of hours. It was imperative that we covered the immediate area as quickly as possible.

Kay was sitting on the couch; her mother had her arm around her shoulders. She cried, quietly, and I could see her body trying to hold back the panic and the sobs threatening to overwhelm her. I crouched in front of her.

"Kay, did Louis say anything to you?" I asked.

'He's bored, he wanted to get high," she said.

"So, he's gone for drugs?"

"I don't know, I guess so." She tried to catch the sobs before they left her lips.

"Kay, who supplies the drugs?"

"I don't know. I honestly don't know. Louis organizes it; Dale collects...collected. Oh, God, I want to go home. Please, Mom, can we just go home?" She turned to her mother and let her anguish out.

"Have you checked his room for his phone, a laptop, anything? I need to know how he contacted his dealer," I asked, turning back to Mr. Chapman.

"Of course," he snapped back. I forgave him that; I would have hated to be in his position right then.

I watched as tears rolled gently down his cheeks. Mrs. Chapman had wrapped her arms around herself and was rocking gently on a chair. She moaned as if in physical pain.

"Can I see his room?" I asked. Mr. Chapman nodded; I followed him through the living room and up the stairs.

Louis had a room that was about the same square footage as my whole house. I stood, at first, in the middle and let my mind absorb the room. The window was open; a breeze blew dark blue, heavy drapes. The double bed to one side of the room had a duvet that was creased. I guessed Louis had been lying on top before deciding to act like a fucking idiot. Had Mr. Chapman not been in the same room, I think I would have cursed him out loud. If he returned, I was going to drag the prick to the station and have him put in a cell for wasting our time.

Somehow, I got the feeling that wasn't going to happen, though.

I looked through the window, just below was a thin ledge where wood siding ended, meeting tiles. Louis was a big lad; I was surprised that ledge would take his weight, yet we were too high for him to have jumped. I saw Dean leave the house and stare back up to me.

Right at that moment, how Louis had left the house wasn't important. Dean pointed to something just to the side of the window

I was looking out of. For a moment my heart raced a little faster than it already was.

"You have CCTV," I said, as I returned to the center of the room.

"Shit," Mr. Chapman said. He turned from the room and ran down the stairs, through to the kitchen, and then a door into a garage.

I called for Corey and we sat with Mr. Chapman as he scrolled back through the past hour's worth of recording. Louis made no attempt to conceal himself as he was filmed running across the lawn. He jumped, his hands catching the top of the boundary wall and he hauled himself over. At that point he was out of view. Although the image captured part of the field behind, I guessed Louis had kept close to the wall.

"Which way did you go?" I said, more to myself.

"Had to be left. There's a farm road a quarter of a mile that way," I heard Mr. Chapman say.

Within a few seconds, Corey was out of the room and instructing as many officers as he could find to get over that wall, and follow the route Louis had taken. We sent a patrol car to drive along the road and meet up with the foot patrol.

I grabbed one of the armed officers. "What the fuck happened, how did he get out?"

"Mich, we patrol this place exactly as we've scheduled. There are one or two minutes where the yard isn't covered. He had to be timing us, unless you give me more men, there isn't much more we could have done," he said.

I sighed. "I'm sorry, you're right. What the fuck is the kid playing at? He knows damn well he's here, you're here, for his protection."

If Louis Chapman turned up anytime soon, I'd personally be the one to kick his ass.

I walked a little way down the drive. Darkness was about to fall and the sun was dipping over the horizon. Yard lights were switched on, some were subtle, hidden in bushes and lining the drive, some blazed and resembled prison searchlights. Was I being too hard on the kid? It can't have been any fun to be cooped up in this mansion, with its cable TV and endless games consoles. Maybe he was bored of the swimming pool, the gymnasium, or the game room even. Perhaps having staff to prepare meals, or run around after you on a whim, was tiresome. Maybe I was over cranky and in desperate need of a break in this case, or a night's sleep. I'd take whichever one came first.

"Nothing," I heard from behind.

Dean walked toward me holding his cell. I guessed he'd been in contact with the officers that had been sent to investigate the field behind.

"Nothing?"

"Not a fucking thing. Ground is too dry for footprints to be have been left."

"Fuck's sake!" I shouted, pacing as I did.

We organized a search, every patrol car in the vicinity was sent to scour the fucking town.

"Can we get this town locked down?" I asked, as Corey joined us.

"As in, military lockdown?"

"Police, military, I don't care. I don't want anyone to be able to move in or out. Can we do that?"

"Not without some serious legal shit to go through, which will take time. And right now we don't know the prick just didn't take off."

Corey's voice tailed off to a whisper when he realized Mr. Chapman was within earshot.

"Oh, don't worry. If that *prick* turns up, believe me, you'll need the military to separate us!" Mr. Chapman said.

My cell phone vibrated in my hand. I looked at it, 'unknown number' flashed across the screen.

"Shush," I said, showing Corey the screen. I slid the answer button across.

"Mich Curtis."

"Mich, hello, how are you?"

"Who is this?"

"Aw, don't pretend you don't know. You'll hurt my feelings, and if you do that, you know what will happen?"

My heart stopped, a sinking, hollow feeling consumed me. Cold sweat beaded on my forehead, and even though I couldn't see myself, the sorrow and desperation in my eyes must have been clearly obvious. I heard Dean mutter an expletive. I heard Mr. Chapman take a sharp breath in, and then cover his mouth with both his hands, as if one wouldn't be strong enough to contain the sob or cry that wanted to erupt from his body.

"Sam, I'm a little busy right now. What do you want?" I asked, abruptly.

"Don't try to rile me, Mich. I know what you're doing. I know what you learned in the FBI, what your friend, Corey, tells you to do. All that goes out the window, now, do you hear me? I'm in charge; it's my time now. Listen..."

All I could hear were the sobs of another person.

"So you have the TV on? As I said, I'm a little busy right now," I replied.

I heard what appeared to be a low growl. I glanced quickly at Corey. Was I pushing Sam too hard? Corey nodded at me; he gave me a small smile. I took that as indication that I was on the right track.

"Mom," I heard down the phone.

"Hear that, Mich. He's calling for his mother. Do you know how many times I did that very same thing? Except mine never came. Shall I tell you a little story? My mother abandoned me; she chose to give me up to a cunt. A cunt, Mich!"

My hands shook just a little as the venom in his words reached my ears.

"I'm sorry to hear that, Sam. But I need to know who is with you," I replied.

"You fucking know!" he screeched down the phone so loud I was forced to pull it away from my ear.

"I need to speak to him, Sam. I need verification."

There was a pause. "Dad?"

"It's Mich Curtis. Louis, is that you?" I said.

Mr. Chapman lurched toward me; I turned my back as he reached for the cell. I heard the scuffle as he was wrestled away by either Dean or Corey. I pressed the cell to my ear, so Louis wouldn't hear the utter devastation in his father's cries as he was bundled to the ground.

"Yes, he's going to…" I guessed the phone was taken away from Louis before he could finish his sentence.

"See! Now, let's talk man-to-man, Mich."

I sighed. "Let him go, Sam. You've made your point. You can

outsmart me. Why don't we meet? Let's talk face-to-face."

"As much as I'd cherish that prospect, don't take me for a fool. We will meet and you will show me the respect I've been denied for thirty-eight years."

The call was cut off.

"He's thirty-eight years old," I said. Corey had been off by a few years.

Dean picked up his phone, understanding immediately. He spoke to Samantha. He told her to narrow down all those that volunteered for DNA of that age; compare it to those on the city's utility records and land owner rolls, see if she could come up with a list of those who hadn't put themselves forward. He also asked her to inform everyone our killer had Louis.

"Please, I needed to speak to him," Mr. Chapman cried. He was lying on his side, his arms bound behind his back. I watched as Dean crouched to release him.

"Our guy will get off on any emotion, Mr. Chapman..." Corey started.

"It's Chris," he said.

"Chris, our guy will get off on your distress. Mich knows exactly how to speak to him, and what to say. You know he was in the FBI, right? He's dealt with this kind of hostage situation before. You need to let him deal with that. I know you want to speak to your son, but our guy has changed his MO, we need to work with that."

I tried to slow my breathing down. While I held the cell, I sent a text to Eddie.

Babe, call me, please. Our guy has Louis; shit is getting worse out here. I just wanted to hear your voice—ground me, Eddie.

I never used terms of endearment with her; she would screw her nose up, or worse, laugh, when I had in the past. But ice-cold fear ran through me, causing my veins to constrict. My heart had to work twice as hard to keep my circulation going, or so it felt.

"You'll find him, right?" Chris asked. I nodded my head gently, hating that I was affirming something I had no idea to be true.

"Mich!" I heard and spun on my heels to follow the sound.

Dean held his cell in his hand, talking on it as he signaled with his head toward Chris Chapman.

'Chris, let's get in the house," I said, taking him by his elbow and guiding him to the stone steps that led to a front door. I handed him over to an officer.

"Wait," he said, as I turned to head back.

"If there is any news, you'll be the first to hear. All the time I'm here, Chris, I'm not out there. And I need to be out there."

Corey, Dean, and I huddled together.

"We've found a blue Ford, license plate registered in Michigan," Dean said.

We ran for the nearest patrol car and roared back down the drive. An officer was stationary at the gates, which, thankfully, had been switched to manual. He was able to open them quickly.

Dean was still on the phone, relaying instructions to me as I drove. Corey was fumbling around for a seat belt as we cornered so fast; it was amazing all four wheels stayed on the tarmac.

We headed out of town and it was the waving of Dean's arm that alerted me to a dirt track off the highway. I took the turn; thankful the road was empty, as I'd had no time to indicate. We bumped along until a farm came into view. Parked outside was a blue Ford.

With guns drawn, we exited the car. Dean was still on the phone and within seconds a patrol car pulled up behind us. There was no point in trying to hide, if anyone was in the house, they would have already known we'd arrived. Dean and I rushed the front door; I shouldered it, wincing at the impact. The doorframe shattered under my weight. Corey and two officers circled the property.

I paused in the hall, listening for any sounds. I could hear a raspy breath coming from the room to my right. I kicked open the door and the sight in front of me had me skid to a halt. I know I kept my gun steady. I know my body went rigid, but the sound that echoed around the room sounded alien until I ran out of breath from the shout.

As if in slow motion, I watched Dean lower his gun and run to a naked Louis. At first I couldn't determine why the lower half of his body was red. But the smell of blood very quickly kicked my brain into gear. I was, however, still rooted to the spot. Not at the sight of Louis covered in blood, but at the woman sitting in a chair beside him.

I was transfixed. I couldn't move my feet, my heart hammered in my chest and eventually, my hand began to shake. I finally lowered my gun as Corey joined us. He rushed to join Dean on the floor. Louis was barely conscious, I could hear him but his eyes were closed. When I tore my gaze away from her, still not understanding what I was looking at, I watched as Dean scrabbled around the floor for Louis' dress shirt. He ripped a section off holding it to Louis' groin. It was only then the realization hit me; I understood what I was looking at.

The woman in the chair, a very dead woman, had Louis' cock in her mouth. Above her head was a word.

ENVY

a Deadly Sin

Chapter *15*

Sweat beaded on my forehead and ran down my back. The evening was humid, but I wondered if it was anger that caused my pores to open. I wanted to be there. I wanted to see Mich when he discovered my gift. I chuckled. Oh, poor Mother. It was about time the whore got some cock, I guessed. She'd had enough of it in the past, before I'd met her of course. I mean; her whoring ways was how I came to be in existence. So my father continually told me.

I was actually quite surprised to discover how easy it was to saw off a cock. My only disappointment was that Louis hadn't been conscious enough to enjoy the experience. I was coated in his blood, I was sure I'd left bloodied footprints, fingerprints at the house, and I didn't care. Mich would know soon enough who I was.

I continued to run through the woods, knowing the way without the need for a flashlight. I knew every inch of the path I took, every branch that I dodged before it took the skin from my face and left further evidence. Leaves crunched under my feet, animals scuttled to avoid me. Still I kept running. My backpack swung, the straps rubbed the skin on my bare shoulders.

Eventually, I came to my clearing. I fell to my knees and

brushed grass and leaves from a rope handle. As I stood back up, I pulled the trapdoor open. I flicked on my flashlight as I descended the steps, closing the escape hatch behind me. It was only when I was in my place of safety, in my 'cave' that I started to breathe easier.

My cave, I sounded like Batman, didn't I? I laughed. The old bunker should have been filled in, boarded up, a long time ago. I'd discovered it just a few years ago, funnily enough, while on a field trip. I struck a match and lit the gas lamp. A subtle warm glow illuminated my space. I had a metal cot at one end, a small kitchen unit with a camping stove next to it. I set a pan to boil. I'd sit for a moment with a coffee and think. The end was near; the time was soon approaching.

———

"Mich, fuck's sake, help us," I heard.

Dean's words had me spring into action, although my mind was whirling with scattered memories, distorted images, and confusing thoughts. I knelt beside him, pushing my hands over his already soaked ones. We tried to stem the blood, but every time Louis' heart beat, although it had slowed, blood pumped out. His artery had been severed. Corey gave rescue breaths to keep some oxygen circulating, but all the while he bled out, it was a pointless exercise.

I could hear the sound of sirens. If Sam had been in the house when we'd arrived, he'd be long gone by then. But there was fuck all we could have done about that. Saving Louis' life was the priority and we were failing.

"Jesus," I heard. A paramedic had run into the room, his feet slid in the pool of blood as he came to an abrupt halt.

When he gained his composure, he pulled me away. I noticed

the lack of pumping blood as soon as we released pressure on the artery to allow him to take over. We were too late. We were always too late. I sat back down on my heels, not wanting to look at the woman.

Light flooded the room as one of the officers had found the power box under the stairs and flicked the switch to on. A green velour sofa faced an open fireplace. The woman was sitting, although sitting was the wrong word, she was bolted and cable tied to a wooden chair, next to it. An old clunky TV sat in one corner, and I doubted very much it would have been able to pick up a signal. The walls were yellowed with age but I could make out a floral pattern on the paper. It was if the room had been transported out of the 1970's.

I scanned the room; an old memory flooded my mind. We had a sofa just like that when I was a kid. In fact, the more I thought about, I remembered that I'd replaced that sofa less than a decade ago. A picture above the mantel caught my eye. I walked toward it. Again, I remembered something similar in the house when I was kid.

"This room has been set up to look like the living room in my house, when I was a kid," I said, quietly.

"Huh?" Dean turned to look at me.

"When I was a kid, we had a sofa like that. Remember you helped me lug it from the garage? That picture? We had one similar, my mother loved it."

"So he set this house to look likes yours? But yours is one story, this isn't."

"I'm not saying this house, but certainly this room."

I watched the paramedics pack up their cases; there was no

saving Louis. Blood soaked bandages were strewn over the wooden floor. Eddie had been called, and we retreated from the room while we waited for her arrival. Dean and I walked through all the rooms. Some were empty, devoid of any furniture. One held a double bed, neatly made. I opened a closet door to find a rail containing five hung t-shirts, all the same grey color, next to them were five pairs of pants, five pairs of jeans, and five white, pressed shirts. Underneath were two pairs of very clean sneakers. A drawer in the dresser held five pairs of black socks, neatly folded in pairs and five pairs of black shorts, folded in half. I counted every item.

"He sure likes the number five," Dean whispered, more to himself than to me.

"It's all very nondescript," I said. "There's not one item of clothing that would have him stand out. Nothing branded, nothing of color."

"A neat freak," Dean said. I nodded.

The kitchen was spotless. Although there was very little food, just a couple of packets of crackers, a jar of ground coffee, and another of sugar. Like the closet, it was neatly stacked. Another cupboard held one dinner plate, one mug, and one bowl. A drawer held one set of cutlery. The smell of bleach permeated the air.

More vehicles arrived, more people congregated outside. There was a charged atmosphere. This was *Sam's* house. We were standing in his personal space, his home, albeit it was clinically clean and without any form of comfort. I walked out of the house, and for the first time in five years, patted the top pocket of Dean's shirt. He pulled out a packet of Marlboros, lit one, and handed to me. I inhaled deeply, fighting the urge to cough as the smoke irritated my lungs. By that point, I was on the verge of collapse; exhaustion, and the knowledge the Chapmans had to be told we hadn't gotten to Louis quick enough weighed heavily on me.

"Mich," I heard. I turned to see Eddie walk toward me.

She took the cigarette from between my fingers. Instead of throwing it to the ground, as I'd expected her to do, she placed it to her lips and took a long draw.

"There's something you need to see," she said, finally throwing the cigarette down and grinding it out with her leather biker boot.

I followed her back into the living room. She held a small flashlight and as much as I didn't want to get that close, she leaned down and shone it on the letters carved into the cock in the woman's mouth.

S L O T H

"That's the sixth one," I said. Eddie looked at me. "Sloth, that's the sixth sin now."

Although I'd tried not to look too closely at the woman, my gaze fell on a brooch pinned to her dress. I closed my eyes, shaking my head at the confirmation. I know a groan left my lips; I'd heard it.

"Mich?" Eddie's voice only just penetrated the noise that escalated in my head.

I think I fell to my knees, I know I came in contact with something hard. I placed my hands on the floor in front of me; it felt tacky, wet.

"Mich!" A man's voice that time.

"That's my mother," I said, although not entirely sure if I'd said that out loud or not.

I was sitting at a desk in the incident room. Our whiteboards were full of photographs of Sam's house and the bodies. It had been three days since we'd discovered it, in those three days we hadn't heard from Sam at all. I'd expected him to be on the phone, gloating, goading, and explaining at least. The house and surrounding area had been taped off, and the woods surrounding the house were still being processed. It was going to be a long and arduous task.

"What's happening?" I asked, as I saw Dean enter the room.

"It's a match. I don't know what to say," he said.

A sample of her hair had been taken; DNA extracted that matched mine. I had been correct; the decomposed body was my mother's. It was the brooch that finally had me recognize her. Her features had long since distorted to be sure. I remembered my father buying her that, he had been so proud that he'd finally saved enough money to purchase the one of a kind piece of jewelry she'd been admiring for years.

"How?"

"That's something we don't know yet. There's no sign of him, and I'm just waiting on results of DNA found at the house. I should have those later today. I just wanted yours rushed through," he said.

Corey was officially in charge of the investigation; a couple of his colleagues had joined us. I was grateful that he had insisted I stay on. The chief had wanted me removed from the case, 'a conflict of interest,' he'd said.

"You need to go home and get some rest, or at least a shower," Dean said.

I hadn't left the station in three days. I'd caught a couple of hours sleep every now and again, but my hair was a mess and stubble covered my chin. I nodded.

"I'll give you a ride," he added. I nodded again. Sleep deprivation had begun to affect my vision; I wasn't capable of driving.

I followed him from the room and to the passenger side of his car. I slumped into the seat as he started the engine.

"She committed suicide, how the fuck did he have her?" It was a question I'd asked so many times over the past few days.

"I don't know, Mich, I really don't know. Eddie is going to meet us, she wants to talk to you."

I hadn't spoken to her since that day, she'd had two autopsies to perform, the one on my mother, had taken her two days. Louis' death had been easy to record. He'd been shot up with a drug to sedate him, and then his cock had been removed with a rusty wood saw. The saw had been left at the premises. Although there were no fingerprints on it, the house had been a goldmine for evidence.

I didn't speak to Dean as I climbed from his car. I was simply too exhausted for any more conversation and my mind was still whirling with shit. I didn't notice the broken fence, or the overgrown yard, as I walked the path to the front door, I normally always did. The locks had been changed, as per my instructions some days ago. In fact, I couldn't remember which day, but I struggled to find the right key, trying three before the new lock opened. I unhooked the spare from the ring and placed it in the hanging basket by the front door. Eddie never accepted a key from me, leaving it in a place she'd suggested had been our one and only compromise.

I didn't bother to turn on any lights; instead I made my way to my bedroom. I stripped off my clothing as I walked into my bathroom. I stepped into the shower before turning the dial and shivered as cold water hit my skin. It took a moment for it to warm and I stood letting the water cascade over me.

When I felt clean enough, I shut off the shower, wrapped a

towel around my waist and stood in front of the sink. I didn't recognize the person looking back at me from the mirror as I shaved. I brushed my teeth which had furred through lack of care, then headed to bed. I put my cell on the bedside table, making sure it wasn't set to silent, and placed my gun under the pillow.

At first I struggled to sleep. Every time I closed my eyes I saw either my mother or Louis, I saw Casey and Dale, Mr. Webster, Vicky. At some point their images meshed together. In my mind's eye Casey had gold eyes, Mr. Webster was slashed across his stomach instead of stabbed. Louis was impaled on a cross, and my mother was still sitting in the wooden chair.

It was a hand stroking sweat sodden hair from my forehead that had me bolt awake. I grabbed the wrist, twisting it back and away from me before my eyes could focus on Eddie. She was sitting on the edge of the bed. I released my grip and slumped back into the pillows. I sighed.

"Hey," she said. "I just wanted to check up on you."

"I'm fine."

"You're not, and no one would expect you to be."

I watched as she kicked off her boots and slid onto the bed beside me.

"You must be going through hell right now," she whispered.

"Not quite there yet."

"Dean gave you the DNA results?"

"Yeah. That wasn't a surprise. I recognized the brooch," I said, then told her how my mother had come to own it.

"Tell me about Canada, Mich." I looked at her. "Dean told me," she said.

"He shouldn't have." Anger laced my voice. Dean had no right to betray my confidence.

"Why?"

"Because I told him in confidence, that's why."

"But we're..."

"We're what, Eddie? Partners? No, that would imply we had some kind of a relationship beyond fuck buddies." I knew my words were harsh, I heard her sharp intake of breath.

I reached out for her, not caring that she might pull away, stiffen at my touch. She surprised me when she relaxed into my side and we slid down the bed. She rested her hand on my chest.

"I'm sorry," I whispered. She didn't reply.

For a moment we lay in silence. "I watched my father be murdered, Eddie. We went to Canada for a job he'd been contracted to do. I don't know why he was shot. We returned to the U.S. and my mom fell to pieces for a while. One day, I walked into her bedroom and she was dead. She was naked, lying on top of her bed, in this very room. Her eyes were staring at me as I stood at the doorway. I guess I lost it. After a month or so, I hitchhiked back to Canada and stayed with my grandma for a few days. I spent time tracking him down and...

"I should have told the police, I knew the man who'd shot my dad but my mom had begged me not to. I don't know why. I guess she was scared for us. Instead, I killed him. I shot him through the head, lied, and was never charged. The rest you already know."

"What happens now?" she whispered.

"I imagine this will all get out, I could be rearrested and jailed. Or they could decide, since my grandma is now dead, to leave it as a cold case. I don't know, to be honest."

"It will only get out if you want it to, Mich."

I looked over to her. "You know, Corey and Dean know. The chief believes I was innocent and the investigation fell apart."

"Then it stays that way. There's no reason for us to say anything. It was a long time ago, Mich. What good will come of confessing now?"

Her comment surprised me. "Those kids, Eddie, are dead because of me, somehow. How do I carry on, knowing that?"

"You just do, Mich. You just do."

We fell silent for a while. "There was further DNA. Your semen was found on her dress."

For the second time I sat upright, pulling Eddie up with me. "My what...?"

She didn't answer, not needing to. "How?"

"You said you thought someone had broken in here. What if he was here when we..."

"Jesus! I thought I heard a noise, outside the window. I saw someone jogging past; it went out of my mind after that. And then I thought someone had been in here. There was a file on the kitchen table that was open, yet I know I left it closed. It's why I had the locks changed."

"What do you do with the condoms?" she asked.

"I put them in the trash...Shit, you don't think he...he had to, didn't he?"

Sam had to have taken a used condom, which meant he had to know we were having sex, for the semen to be 'fresh' enough to then deposit on the dress.

"What a fucking...sick fuck!" I said.

"I think he had intentions of framing you," Eddie said.

"Maybe, although there's no possible way that would have

stuck. Or…"

I chuckled, bitterly. "No, it had nothing to do with him framing me. He wanted you to find my DNA; he knew you would have to test her to identify her. What better way than to have your results come back and find out we were related?"

"Maybe he didn't know about the brooch, assumed you'd never recognize it, so he wanted to be sure. But then surely everyone knows, because you're a cop, your DNA is on record anyway?"

"Yeah, but he'd also assume we wouldn't run a match using our own, would he?"

My phone began to ring; I looked over to see that Corey was calling me.

"Hi," I said, once I'd answered.

"Time to get your ass back here, my friend. I think I might have something I need you to see," he said.

I told him I'd be there as soon as I dressed. Eddie fixed me a quick mug of coffee as I changed into clean clothes. She drove my car to the station, and I sipped on my black coffee during the journey. I expected her to drop me off but she followed me in.

"Don't you have reports to write up?" I said, regretting my words as her face hardened a little.

"All done, Corey has them," she said.

I nodded and gave her a small smile. I felt out of the loop, I'd have been sent those reports normally. I hated being down the pecking order. We walked in to the incident room together.

"We might have something interesting here," Corey said.

He slid a piece of paper over to me. At the top were the words, *Sinners Case #7823*. It was a list of the three men that had left town immediately after the murders in Millbrook. One name stood out, enough to have me close my eyes, take a sharp breath and curse myself for not looking sooner.

Thomas Jameson

"What is it?" Eddie asked, reading over my shoulder. I pointed to the name.

"That was the name of the man I killed," I said.

"How does that help now?" she asked.

I looked up to Corey. "James Thomas, maybe he shortened and reversed it?" He slowly nodded.

"Who the fuck is James Thomas?" she asked.

"Teacher at Montford. A philosophy teacher, to be exact."

"And missing," Corey added.

Chapter *16*

I didn't like living rough. I had left the 'cave' shortly after the house had been raided. Although I was sure I wouldn't be found, it wasn't a risk I was willing to take until the task was complete. I still wore my 'work clothes.' I missed my neatly pressed t-shirts and pants. I didn't miss the house. It had been fun to recreate the same living room as Mich. It had, for a while, made me closer to him and also gave me the childhood I'd missed out on. I remembered when I'd found the old photograph album. I think Mich must have been renovating his house at the time. He threw away so many childhood memories. He clearly had no pride in the things our mother worked hard for. It showed contempt for his past, as far as I was concerned.

The house on Perry Street had belonged to my father, not that anyone would be able to trace it back to me. He had put it in his daughter's name, another product of an affair. She got that house, Mich got our mother's; I got nothing but years of being beaten. I was nothing to them, a nobody. But I'd shown them, hadn't I? I was a somebody; I was practically famous.

I chuckled as I sat in a diner one town over and watched CNN give an update on the case. I wanted to tell everyone that it was me they were talking about. I wondered how Mich was faring. It must have been a huge shock to come face-to-face with his mother. Oh, how I would have loved to be there.

I decided that I would tell him how I came to own his mother. It was a rather funny story really, but only when the time was right. Only when I was able to look into his eyes and watch him take his last breath. I wanted to steal that from him, like he'd stolen my life. When I was done, I was heading home, back to my real home; back to the only group of people who understood me. I rubbed the tattoo on my forearm. I'd done a good job inking that symbol into my skin. My tattoo was my passport, my initiation into a family that had embraced me for who, what, I was...

A man of God, well, a cult, but we don't need to split hairs, do we?

—————

"How the fuck did we miss this?" I asked, mainly to myself.

"Mich, why would we connect it? We have now, so let's not dwell on the past. I've already spoken to the head of Montford. James, or Thomas, didn't show for work, as of three days ago. He did, however, leave a message that he was sick."

"He left a message?"

"Yep, and I have a copy of it ready for comparison." Corey smiled. This was the fucking breakthrough we needed.

"The house, that was his wasn't it?"

"Yes, leased, but registered to him."

"The furniture had traces of your DNA on it," Eddie said.

"So, somehow he'd gotten the things I threw out? Fuck! How long has he been stalking me?"

"At least a couple of years, I remember when you threw that sofa out, finally. It had been sitting in your garage for years," Dean said.

"He only lived in two rooms, it seemed: the kitchen and the bedroom. The living room was staged, as you know. He had every intention of drawing you to that house," Corey added.

"And the house on Perry Street? What do we know about that?" I asked.

"As I said, it belongs to a woman who lives in Florida, she inherited it from her father. A father she hadn't seen since she was a child. Although the name on the deed isn't Thomas Jameson," Dean said.

"Is there a chance he's is related to her, though?" I asked.

"Possibly," Dean said.

"At least we know who we're looking for," I said, a bubble of excitement burst in my stomach. All traces of tiredness left me. "We need to make contact with him. Call another press conference."

"How do you know he's still around?" Eddie asked.

"Because he isn't done yet. He still has pride, the ultimate sin," I said.

"So which kid does that relate to?" Dean asked.

"None of them."

Corey, Dean, and Eddie looked at me. "It's me, he's coming after me next."

———

For the second time, I stood on the steps of the station, except this time I wore a creased and stained grey t-shirt, crumpled jeans, and dirty sneakers. When silence reigned, I looked directly at the TV camera, having identified CNN and knew they'd play the messaged on a loop.

"Thomas, it's time. Let's end this," I said, then turned and walked back into the station.

Chaos erupted outside. Two officers had to hold back the hoard of reporters that thought they were getting an update; that they were getting more. I heard calls, shouts, and I carried on walking, pulling off Thomas' t-shirt as I did.

I kicked off the sneakers and allowed Pete to bag them up; I threw in the t-shirt and pulled off the jeans. I dressed in my own clothes and we sat and waited.

After three hours I began to get twitchy. Maybe my plan had backfired. I wanted 'Sam' to know that I knew who he really was. I wanted to show him how much I disrespected him by wearing his clothes, not only wearing them but trashing them first. It was clear from the house that the guy had some form of obsessive compulsions that maybe fit in with him being on the autism spectrum. I also wanted to throw down a challenge.

The data team was collecting as much information on him as possible. We had a Social Security number; fake of course. We had a copy of a birth certificate, another fake. The child on the birth certificate had died in infancy. The Social Security number related to a poor soul who had died in a vehicle accident.

"Who is Thomas James then?" Corey asked, as we scanned through paperwork.

"The son of the man I killed, obviously. This is about revenge, I guess."

"Okay, what do we know about Thomas Jameson Sr., then?"

"Owned a carpentry business, part-time logger, jack-of-all-trades by the looks of it. In fact, he owned the company that made the caskets for the local..." I looked up from my notes. "Shit!"

"Funeral home?" Corey asked. I nodded.

"The same funeral home that had my mother," I said.

"But he was in Canada, wasn't he?" Dean asked.

"He didn't *live* in Canada, just traveled there for contracts, same as my dad."

"How long after your father died, did your mother?" Dean asked.

"A year, I think. I can't remember. We left Canada pretty soon after my father died and came back here. I went back to Canada a couple of months after her suicide. I stayed at my grandma's until...Well, you know the rest."

"So at that point, Thomas could have been living here as well?" Dean said.

"His father owned a sawmill, not here though, next town over. He traveled a lot for certain woods to make furniture and caskets, that he sold," Corey read from his notes.

"A mill?" Dean and I looked at each other. "The cross."

Although we had expanded our search to barns or anything we considered a clinical facility, that search had been concentrated in our town and the outskirts. Unfortunately, or maybe it was fortunate, because the FBI was now leading the investigation, there was no protocol needed for them to search the mill. It did mean though, that Dean and I were confined to the station while they did. It was a shame that possessiveness occurred between our neighboring police forces; we didn't always work that well together. Although it was unlikely, had I taken the role of chief, it was something that I would have wanted to eradicate.

"A search is being organized as we speak," Corey said, and I nodded.

"Did he take the DNA test?" I asked.

"Not that I'm aware of, but it doesn't matter, we must have enough evidence of him in that house," Dean said.

Eddie had been to rustle up some coffees; she came back into the room carrying a cardboard tray with four takeout containers. Between her teeth, she held a stack of papers. I took the tray from her.

"Preliminary autopsy reports," she said, as she placed the papers on the desk.

I started to read, scanning through the medical details for Louis until I came to the second one, my mother. I read slower.

I paused over the words, *death to be confirmed.*

"What does that mean? She committed suicide," I said, looking up at her.

"How?" Dean asked.

"She took a load of pills."

"We can't test for that, not now. There are no obvious wounds but I was waiting on a second opinion for something. That report will be updated with exact cause of death," Eddie said.

Eddie very rarely sought a second opinion; she was a qualified forensic pathologist, having ranked top of her class every year she'd been in training, so she'd told me. Something wasn't right.

"A second opinion on what?" I asked. She looked at Corey before she spoke.

"I sent tissue samples to an old friend for clarification on something I discovered. He confirmed my findings, your mother was murdered."

I stared at her, not sure at first what to say. "Murdered? How can you tell after all this time?"

"Your mother had been embalmed, that can prevent decay for decades, Mich. The room she was found in was pretty chilled, didn't you notice? I tested the metabolites in her teeth, that gave me a picture that she was in good health overall, and I found strychnine in her hair."

"In her hair?"

"In the keratin. I found a serious toxin that I believe was the cause of death."

"Why have you not said anything before now?"

"Because I wanted all the information in hand first. Your mother's first autopsy report said cause of death was the result of an overdose of barbiturates. Unless strychnine is suspected, it wouldn't have been looked for. She suffered cardiac arrest, organ failure, all the usual things we'd see in a regular overdose, as well as strychnine poisoning. The coroner reported empty packets of pills, I think an assumption was made, the wrong assumption," she said.

"So what prompted you to look for strychnine?" I asked.

"A small amount was found at Thomas' house," Corey answered.

"I thought it had been banned years ago."

"It was, 1990 I think, but that doesn't mean there isn't a shitload of it around still. I guess if someone had a stock of it, for pest control, they didn't dispose of it just because the government banned it. And, think about it. Thomas Sr. owned a saw mill, I imagine that was running alive with vermin," Corey said.

I slumped back in my chair. As far as the investigation was concerned, I was done. I knew I'd be removed immediately because, if Eddie was right, I couldn't be impartial. Despite knowing Thomas was responsible for the deaths of the kids, a lawyer would immediately jump on the fact that I was the son of a murdered woman. A woman found in Thomas' house, whether he'd murdered her or not. They'd play on that; use that as part of his defense. If there was the slightest opportunity to scream 'planted evidence,' a 'revenge arrest', it would be hurled my way.

"Why do you need a second opinion, Eddie?" I asked.

"Because I know the implications, how that will affect this case, and you. I wanted to be doubly sure," she said.

I sat in silence for a while, staring at the whiteboard. I'd failed all those kids. That fact weighed heavily on my shoulders. I wasn't sure what I could have done differently; I just knew I should have.

I should have caught him; he should have been locked up before now. That wouldn't have stopped the death of my mother. It wouldn't have saved Casey, Dale even, but had I done enough? It was a question I was sure I'd ask myself a lot.

"What now?" I asked. Corey sighed before he spoke.

"Go home, Mich. Sleep, let's catch up tomorrow. We'll have searched the mill by then. I promise you that I'll keep you in the loop, but you know you can't take an active role anymore."

"What happens when he calls me?"

"Then you get your ass back here as soon as possible. He won't talk to anyone other than you, I don't believe."

I stood and nodded. Without a word, I walked from the station, ignoring the call from the chief. I'd let Corey bring him up to speed.

I pushed through the small group of reporters that seemed to have been permanently camped outside. I kept my head low as I walked to my car. Thomas would call, whether on my cell or through the station. It gave me the smallest comfort that I'd still be needed.

I pulled into the driveway and then just sat and looked. My mother had loved that house and I'd neglected it. She'd taken such pride in her little home. Each year she'd repaint the exterior, I'd help of course. She would tend to the garden every Sunday, mowing the lawn, weeding, and fixing the fence if needed. My father would want to help but she'd wave him off. I remembered many a conversation between them. He worked, often leaving us for a week or two while he traveled. Sometimes, we traveled with him. Sometimes, Mom stayed home taking care of me, the house, and making sure he had a home to come back to.

I climbed from the car and pulled up the garage door. I pushed the old mower to the lawn and cut the grass. The sun was low on the horizon by the time I'd finished raking and bagging up the clippings. I couldn't remember the last time I'd mowed the lawn.

I heard the roar of a bike before I saw it. I'd packed the lawnmower away as Eddie pulled into the driveway. She swung her leg over the bike, removed her helmet, and then pulled the strap of a backpack from her shoulder.

"Takeout?" she said, raising the backpack for me to see.

"Sure, why not?"

She followed me into the house and to the kitchen. I grabbed a couple of plates from a cupboard overhead, while she pulled out containers from her backpack. We sat at the table with a couple of beers and Chinese.

"How are you doing?" she asked.

"Okay, I guess. For someone who's just discovered his mother was murdered. Who's off a case. Who's got the blood of six people on his hands."

She laid down her fork. "Oh, Mich, you can't think..."

"I can, and I do. This started with me. And it will end with me."

"What do you mean?"

"I'm going to end this. Thomas wants me, Eddie. Why the fuck he had to kill those kids to do it, I don't know yet, but I will."

She sighed. I laid my fork beside my plate; I had no desire to eat.

"And when this is all done, I'm quitting, moving on."

I wasn't sure when the decision to quit had come to me. I was only thirty-six, I had many years of police work ahead of me, but the appetite for it had gone. The rational part of my brain fought with the irrational. Those murders had come at such a pace, we didn't stand a chance and that, I believed, was Thomas' intention. He'd wanted us in a spin, but no matter what, my confidence in my ability was in tatters.

"What do you mean? You can't quit, Mich. You're a great cop."

"What holds me here, Eddie? Honestly, what do I have to stay for?"

"Us?"

"There is no *us*, you don't want that."

She didn't answer me. She didn't say the words I'd have liked for her to say. Thanks to Thomas, the house I lived in now felt poisoned. Once word got out about my past, my career was probably over, and I was holding on to a relationship that didn't exist.

"Do you want me to leave?" she asked, quietly.

"No, I want you to tell me what holds you back."

She paused before she spoke. "I can't, Mich. We all have secrets, skeletons, we can't share."

"Can't or won't?"

"At what point would you have told me what happened in Canada?" she said, turning the question back on me.

I sighed. "There was nothing to tell, in my mind. The case fell apart."

"You lied, and you got away with it. Big difference."

"I did what I did for the right reasons."

"Maybe my reluctance to commit to you is for the right reasons also," she said, her voice just above a whisper.

We did what we always did, went around in circles. I stood and picked up the plates, dumping the forgotten Chinese in the trash.

"Will you fuck me?" Eddie had spoken so quietly, I'd only just heard her.

I stood with my back to her, resting my hands on the countertop.

"That's your answer to everything, isn't it? Won't talk but you want to fuck. It's as if that distraction, as if offering your body to me, is enough. Do you fuck to forget, Eddie?"

Her sharp intake of breath stopped me from saying anymore.

I knew I was being unfair, whatever it was that held her back had to be tough to deal with. I didn't believe she was satisfied with what we had, not for one minute. I just couldn't help myself wanting to dig deeper, to find the real Eddie, the one I saw just the shortest glimpse of every now and again.

The scrape of her chair had me turn around. I watched as she picked up her backpack from the floor and slung it over one shoulder. She gave me a sad smile as she made to pass by. I followed her. Before she got to the front door, I grabbed the strap of her pack. I pulled her back toward me and wrapped my arms around her chest. I heard, and felt, the sigh that left her body. She leaned back into me.

I kissed the side of her neck, trailing my tongue across her soft skin and inhaled her scent. She turned in my arms, letting the backpack fall to the floor. She wrapped her arms around my neck and kissed me. I parted my lips to allow her in as her hands gripped the hair at the back of my head.

I walked her backward, slamming her against the wall hard enough to feel the breath leave her lungs. She breathed in deep through her nose. I pushed my body up against hers and ground my cock into her. She moaned. I pulled my head back slightly.

"So you want me to help you forget?" I said.

She nodded slowly. "How?" I asked.

"Hard," she whispered.

One thing I had discovered was that Eddie couldn't come unless our fucking was hard, fast, frantic, and rough. Skin would be clawed at or broken by teeth. Sweat would drip from both of us. There would be no sensitivity, no emotion attached at all. She sunk her teeth into the side of my neck, sucking on the skin. I gripped her hair and pulled, hard. I felt my skin break as I yanked her head away.

I turned her away from me, pulling at her hips until she bent over. She placed her palms on the wall and I reached around to unfasten her jeans. I lowered to a crouch, pulling them, and her panties down. She stepped out of them and using my foot, I scooted them away.

I kicked at her ankles until she parted her legs then ran my hand down her ass. I reached under, teasing her clitoris and soaking my fingertips. She let out a small moan. I pushed two fingers inside her roughly, stroking her until she moaned again.

"Harder, Mich," she whispered.

I lowered the zipper of my jeans and pulled out my cock. I wrapped my hand around it, stroking myself as my fingers pumped in and out of her. If she wanted hard, she was about to get it. I pulled my fingers from her and ran them up her ass. She tensed as I pushed one in. I paused at my first knuckle to let her relax a little before adding a second finger. I stretched her and listened as she took a sharp breath in. When I saw the slight nod of her head, I pushed them all the way in.

While my fingers fucked her ass, my other hand worked my cock, sliding up and down, my thumb brushing over the tip. Her moans grew louder. I watched her fingers curl as if trying to dig into the wall. She pushed her ass back toward me, wanting more. I removed my fingers and replaced them with my cock. She screamed out in pleasure. Fucking her ass was one of her favorite things. I wrapped my hand in her hair, forcing her head up, arching her back. I held one hip and gave her what she always demanded—hard and fast.

Sweat ran down my forehead and stung my eyes. I gritted my teeth. White noise filled my head as my orgasm built. I felt my balls draw up, my stomach muscles tighten, as I shot my cum into her ass. It took nearly a minute for my breathing to regulate and I pulled out of her. I watched as my cum dripped from her. I ran my fingers through it, smearing it over her ass.

Before she could speak, I picked her up and carried her to the bedroom. I kicked the door open and lay her on the bed. I slid my jeans off and climbed on beside her. I reached over to the bedside cabinet and grabbed a condom. I wasn't done with her yet, and she wasn't done with me. Before I'd finished rolling the condom down my cock, she straddled me. I felt the stickiness of my cum on her skin each time she lowered herself. She clawed at my stomach as her orgasm built. I watched her chest rise and fall, quicker as she struggled to get her breath. She threw her head back, and for a moment, I thought she was about to cry out my name.

Before she could come, I rolled her off me and onto her back. I wouldn't let her take her orgasm from me; I needed to give it. I placed my hands under her knees, lifting them to her chest and then knelt. I slammed into her, jolting her body up the bed. I fucked her harder than I ever had. Her orgasm ripped through her, tears rolled down the sides of her face, and she screamed.

———————

I dozed, letting the sweat and cum dry on my body. I know I removed the condom and deposited it on the floor beside the bed, but other than that, I hadn't moved after rolling away from Eddie. I could hear her breathing beside me. We hadn't spoken; we hadn't cuddled, or even touched. We just lay side by side, as normal. I felt the bed dip as she sat; she placed a hand on my chest.

"I'm just getting a drink, do you need anything?" she asked. I shook my head.

She padded, naked, to the bedroom door. I watched her pull it partway closed behind her. I closed my eyes, my body finally caving in to the sleep I so desperately needed.

A cold breeze blew over my body; the shiver woke me. I felt disorientated when I opened my eyes. The room was dark but a sliver of light shone through the crack of the bedroom door. I sat up. I was alone. As I swung my legs over the side of the bed, I felt material. Eddie's tank top lay on the floor beside the bed. I switched on the bedside lamp and stood. My head felt fuzzy, having woken suddenly from a deep sleep. I walked from the room calling Eddie as I did. Silence bounced back at me.

Eddie's jeans and panties were still on the floor in the hallway; when I saw them, my heart began to race. A feeling of dread washed over me when I walked into the kitchen and saw the back door open. My foot stepped in something wet but it was too dark to determine what. I reached to the light switch on the wall and flicked it on. I stared at a small puddle of red surrounding my foot. I ran out into the yard.

"Eddie!" I shouted.

I slipped as my wet foot connected with the tiles on the kitchen floor when I returned. I grabbed my phone and called Dean.

"Eddie's gone," I said, as he answered.

"What do you mean, gone?"

"She was here, now she's gone. There's blood, I think, on the floor."

"Did she get a call out, leave to go home?"

"No, her clothes are still here."

"Fuck! I'm on my way."

I then called Corey and told him the same thing. I scrolled through my phone to find the number Thomas had called me from. It had come up as unknown and I cursed as I realized I couldn't call it back. If he had her...I couldn't think that way, but there was no other explanation. She'd hardly leave without her clothes. I ran to the bedroom and dragged on my jeans and then made my way to the front door. Eddie's bike was still in the driveway.

Dean pulled up at the roadside as I was shouting Eddie's name. I'd already run one way up the street.

"Back inside," Dean said, grabbing my arm and walking me to the front door.

"She might be hurt, out here," I said.

"And so might be whoever has her."

"You think..."

"I don't know yet, but come on, inside, Mich."

I let him lead me through the front door. I noticed the one red footprint across the floor tiles. I gathered up Eddie's clothes, not wanting Dean to see her panties.

"Sit," he said, as we got to the kitchen. He carried on walking out into the yard.

I placed Eddie's clothes on the seat beside me.

"Right, tell me everything," Dean said.

"We...she needed a drink, she got out of bed, I remember that. I fell asleep, it was the cold that woke me and now she's gone."

"When did she get out of bed?" he asked, licking the end of his pencil as he spoke.

"I don't know the time. What time is it now?"

He consulted his watch. "One, in the morning."

"Shit. She could have been gone for hours."

"Mich, think. I need some kind of timeframe here."

I took a deep breath. "I got back here, from the station, and mowed the lawn. That must have taken a couple of hours, I guess. Eddie arrived with takeout, we ate, then..."

"No time for embarrassment, Mich," Dean said.

"I'm not embarrassed, okay? We fucked, a couple of times, once in the hall, then in the bedroom. That had to be at least five hours ago. It wasn't dark when she arrived."

Bile rose to my throat. I felt beads of sweat form on my brow and fear ripped through me, causing my stomach to knot and my fists to clench. I heard a car pull up outside, Dean went to the front door and let Corey in.

"Shit," he said, sidestepping the blood on the floor.

"That's mine," I called out.

"Yours?"

"Not mine, I stood in it," I said.

Dean was on the phone, I heard him calling the station and the forensic team.

"What happened?" Corey asked.

I repeated what I'd told Dean. I struggled that time, my heart was racing, and I found it hard to breath and talk at the same time.

"He's got her, I just fucking know it," I said.

No one disputed that. I rose from the seat and walked to the en-suite. I washed the blood from my foot, praying that was his and not Eddie's. She was strong; she would fight. She wasn't someone who could just be taken, I hoped. I grabbed some clothes from the closet and dressed. I was tying my shoelaces when Dean came into the room.

"Forensics are here," he said.

"Good. Now, I don't care what anyone says, I'm involved in this case. Let's go, they'll want me out of the house anyway."

Dean nodded as I walked past. Corey was outside talking to a couple of officers, he'd already organized searches, but I knew they'd be fruitless. After every murder, we'd done the same thing with no results. I was trying not to be despondent, but I needed to think outside the box. I'd failed those kids, mainly because I'd followed a set of rules, textbook 'how to find a murderer' procedures. Thomas didn't work to the same rules, no fucking murderer worked to our rules.

Because I was the most senior detective on the force, my role had always been to coordinate, to sit at a desk and direct the investigation, analyze results, and then take responsibility when it fell apart. I was already being criticized in the press; that was something that just went with the job and normally went straight over my head. If I let every negative comment get to me, I'd never be able to do my job.

Corey posted two officers to keep watch over my house, while we headed for the car. As we drove I called Samuel, the caretaker of Montford High School. I wanted access. Once it had been discovered Thomas James, or James Thomas, as he was known at the school, was the person we were seeking, a team had been sent to speak to the teachers, the principal, and search his classroom. But I needed to do that again. I needed to become him, get inside his mind.

Samuel met us at the gates, he had them open and we pulled into the parking lot. I thanked him as he unlocked the front entrance and was dismayed to note they had no alarm system in operation. Dean, Corey, and I walked to the classroom I'd first met Thomas in. Other than a few papers scattered on the desk, the room was exactly the same as before. Not that I expected it to be any different, I guessed.

I walked to the bookcase and scanned the books. Dean went through the drawers in his desk. I ran my finger along the spines, reading every single title. Nothing sprang out at me and disappointment started to settle in my stomach. I wasn't sure what I expected really, a letter hidden among the books maybe.

"Come on, there's fuck all here," I said, trying to keep the frustration from my voice.

———

We had been back in the station for no more than a half-hour when my cell rang. I stared at it, Corey and Dean looked at me. 'Unknown number' flashed on the screen.

"Don't answer it," Corey said.

"What?"

"Don't fucking answer it." He ran from the room, shouting for one of his FBI team as he did.

"Fuck that," I said, reaching for the phone.

Dean reached for it at the same time. The phone slid from the table and I scrabbled to catch it before it hit the floor. The ringing stopped.

"What the fuck!" I said.

"They'll want to trace it, Mich," Dean said.

"We don't have fucking time for them to get themselves organized. He has Eddie!" My voice had risen to a shout just as the chief, Corey, and his colleague walked back in.

The cell was taken from my hand and placed into a handset, a cord was attached to a laptop, and the cell was placed back on the table.

"He'll ring back, Mich, you know he will," Corey said, gently.

I ignored him and sat watching the cell's digital clock click through the minutes. Eventually, a half-hour later, it rang again. I looked at Corey, on his nod, I answered.

"Thomas?" I said.

"Well done, Mich. I'm surprised it took you that long. What was it? At what point did you find out my name?" he said.

"Do you have Eddie?"

"You're not answering my questions," he replied.

"Fuck your questions, there will be no conversation until I know Eddie is okay."

"Aw, are you worried? She's a pretty woman, isn't she? She smells of you, Mich, of sex. I might have to fuck her to eradicate that."

"You fucking…"

"Now, now. Answer the question."

I took a breath. "You leased the house in your name, you prick!"

"In my name?"

"James Thomas. You transposed your name. Your father was Thomas Jameson.

"Transposed. That's a nice word but why not just use reversed?"

"I answered your fucking question, now where is Eddie?"

"You think I'm just going to give up a location? Really, Mich, you continue to underestimate me."

"I'll find you, you sick cunt!"

"Are you getting angry, Mich? I'm not sure I can deal with such anger."

I had to pull the phone away from my ear a little, so he couldn't hear the deep breaths I was taking to regulate my heart, to control the blind anger that was threatening to overwhelm me.

"Where is she, Thomas? It isn't her you want, is it? So, let's swap. I'll give you me, if you let her go."

"But don't you see, Mich? I have you. Your life is now mine. And as for finding me, that will only happen if I allow it."

"We found your house," I said.

"How, Mich? I drove past every CCTV I could, I think I might have even smiled up at one. I parked that truck in full view of the road, with the lights on, and it still took you a couple of hours to find it."

"Thomas, what do you want me to do?" I asked.

"Mmm, now let me think. Oh, out of time, I'm afraid."

"Wait, Thomas..." My sentence was cut off as the call ended.

I slammed my fist down on the desk. He knew exactly how many minutes he had to talk before our trace was complete.

"It's a voice match, for sure," I heard. I fucking knew who I was talking to; I needed to know where he was.

"What happened with the search at the sawmill?" I asked.

"Turned up nothing. It's still operational; it was sold years ago," Corey said.

So many dead fucking ends! I balled my fists and rubbed them over my eyes.

"Think," I whispered to myself. "Clean that board." Pete leapt from his chair and cleaned one of the whiteboards.

I wrote down everything we knew about him. His father made the caskets, so did that gave him access to the funeral home? But why would he *steal* my mother's body? If he wanted revenge for what I did, why now? Why wait this long?

"You said your mom and dad weren't married, who's surname do you have?" Dean asked, after reading my notes.

"My dad's."

"So maybe that's why it took him some time to track you down."

"But he had my mother's," I said.

"Maybe your mother meant something to him, other than her being just your mother."

I looked at him; he shrugged his shoulders. I stared back at the board just as the sun began to rise.

Chapter 17

I liked Eddie. Even after I'd punched her in the face, she didn't shed a tear. I could see pain flash through her eyes, they watered, but she blinked the tears away. She gritted her teeth, I could see a pulse pound on the side of her neck. I placed my fingers over the pulse, wanting to feel her blood pump from her heart to her brain. She flinched, but didn't make a sound.

"Now, Eddie. There was absolutely no point in stabbing me, was there?" I gripped her chin and stared into her eyes. She closed them.

"Look at me, or I'll staple those eyelids open," I said.

She opened them. "That's better," I said, giving her a smile. "You have pretty eyes, you shouldn't hide them away."

I looked down at my arm; the blood had seeped through the makeshift bandage and dripped to the floor. It was a deep wound, but I felt no pain. I think I was incapable of that. When I'd grabbed Eddie in the kitchen, she'd been standing at the sink filling a glass with water. I'd placed a rag over her mouth to stifle her scream, before jabbing her with a small dose of ketamine. I didn't want her completely out of it. But, the silly woman had picked up a small paring knife. She rammed it into my bicep before she passed out. I didn't particularly care about leaving my blood at the scene. Mich knew my name, and I had no intention of going to jail.

I turned away from her. "Have you ever seen her naked?" I asked Dan. He sat on his stool and shook his head. "Bet you've always wanted to though, haven't you?" He nodded that time.

Oh, how ironic it was, I chuckled. The chief medical examiner sat on a metal stool with her feet and hands bound. Opposite her, sat her assistant. They'd stared at each other, without speaking, for a long while when I'd first brought her in. Her features displayed the shock she felt. I wonder if betrayal ran through her veins. If it did, she'd feel just a miniscule amount of what I felt.

"It's a shame this building was abandoned," I said, as I walked around the room.

I ran my hand over the white tiled walls, although the white was greyer with age. The old coroner's building had been the perfect location for my work with Eddie. What was more amusing was the fact it was just a stone's throw from the police station, albeit not visible anymore. I chuckled and shook my head. I'd watch the police search buildings, not once had they thought to come here. Mich was going to be so pissed when he found that out.

"Not long now, Eddie, then I'll take you home," I said.

———

"What can you remember about Tommy Sr.?" Dean asked.

I shook my head. "Not much, my dad worked on and off for him, over the years. They didn't particularly like each other. I don't know why."

I was getting impatient. I checked my cell regularly, making sure I had enough charge should Thomas call back. I listened to the radio comments from officers out on the streets searching, and all the time I silently prayed. I kept asking myself why. Twenty years was a long time to wait for revenge. Corey had asked for Thomas' name to be run through all the databases the FBI had, which were way more than we had access to. If he'd spent time in prison in the U.S., his fingerprints would be on record and so far Thomas James, even James Thomas, was a fucking ghost.

"We have a hit. Thomas James spent just under ten years in prison in Toronto for sexual assault, battery, and kidnapping of a minor, pretty nasty stuff according to the report," Corey said, as he walked back into the room holding a document.

"Ten years? So, he did his time, came here and took my mother?" I asked.

"That, I can't answer, but it goes some way to answering the *why now* question."

"I'm assuming he got deported on release...the dates don't tie up, Corey." I read through the report. "He was released after my mother died." I closed my eyes for a moment. "He's not working alone."

The room silenced. I stood and walked to the two whiteboards. One contained all the victims; Eddie's name had been added to the bottom. The other had my random thoughts.

"It took Eddie and two of her technicians to lower that cross," I said, pointing to a photograph of Casey. "Dale was a big lad, how easy is it to lift a dead weight into a dumpster? Vicky? Okay, so he could have done what he did alone there, likewise for Louis. But he had help," I said.

I thought about Eddie's team. "Someone ought to get over to the doc's and let her guys know what's happened," I said. She would be expected to turn up for work shortly. Although Eddie wasn't the only medical examiner at the facility, she was in charge.

I paced the room, feeling completely useless as the team went about their work. Some were on the phones, others on laptops. I wanted them all out on the streets but knew Dean would have organized dozens of officers and civilians to do that.

"Do we have all the fingerprint analysis and the DNA testing results?" I asked.

"Just waiting on a few more but I'll chase them up," Dean answered.

Our forensic team had been working around the clock; we'd pushed and pushed for results quickly but with the number of victims, things were stacking up.

"Make sure they prioritize that blood." I needed to know whether that was Eddie's or his.

———

One hour, then two passed and with it, my frustration grew. In all my time being a cop, and my days in the FBI, I'd never had a case that had developed as quick with so few leads. The chief was debating with the FBI on whether to release Thomas' photograph to the media. I could see both points of view. If his picture was shown nationwide, he'd have fewer places to hide. The FBI had different ideas. All the time he had a live victim, and I'd hated those words, he might panic, kill her, and run. He might get off on the attention and play the game for longer. The rumors had already started that he was wanted, to help with inquiries, and I guessed that had started at the school when he'd failed to turn up for lessons. We would neither confirm nor deny.

I sat with my arms crossed on a desk and my head resting on

them. I tried hard not to let the anger consume me and to think rationally. I replayed every scene in my head, hoping for more clues. The house on Perry Street was under guard, no one had been there since we'd left. Thomas' house, if it was where he truly lived was under guard; again, no one had been close. We'd searched every abandoned building in the town; we'd searched occupied ones, too. We had neighboring police forces looking out for him. It was as if he'd gone...

"Underground," I said, and sat upright.

"Huh?" Dean said, sliding a coffee across the table to me.

"Get me a map."

Dean stood and looked toward Pete. I guessed in the age of satellite navigation, we'd ditched the good old paper map. However, after a minute or two a map was spread out over the desk.

"Now someone find out how the fuck we can locate any old bunkers around here," I said.

"Underground!" Dean said.

"It's the only fucking place we haven't looked."

I studied the map, not far from the house Thomas lived in was woodland. Although that area had, and was still, being searched, would we have known if there was a bunker? The house had been thoroughly searched, if there was a basement, we'd have found it.

Pete slid his laptop in front of me. He'd Googled bunkers, although not necessarily ones in our area, so we had a visual on what we needed to be looking for. Some were constructed during the Cold War by the military, others by worried homeowners. There were huge concrete entrances built into hillsides, and there were small, unobtrusive hatches camouflaged in the ground.

"If a person built one, that's not going to be registered

anywhere, but if there's an old military one, it would be on record," Pete said.

"Yeah, on a record we'd have no access to."

"What exactly are we looking for?" Dean asked, as he leaned over my shoulder.

"A clearing, I guess. I can't imagine a bunker, or whatever we want to call it, would be built in the dense trees. They'd need some kind of machinery to dig, access to it. Can we do thermal imagining?" I asked.

"That's going to depend on how deep the bunker is and if anyone's in it," Corey answered. "If you're talking Cold War, nuclear, then I doubt it. The walls would be too thick."

My cell rang, startling me. Corey grabbed it before I could and replaced it on the handset that was connected to the laptop, he then handed it back to me. As before, 'unknown number' flashed on the screen.

"Thomas," I said, as I answered.

He didn't reply, instead I heard a scream, a woman's scream.

"Eddie!" I shouted down the phone.

The scream continued until eventually dying off into sobs.

"Oh, God, Eddie," I shouted again. "Thomas!"

I heard a chuckle but no one spoke. It took me a moment to realize I had tears rolling down my cheeks; they dripped to the table.

"You fucking..." I struggled to speak. All I could hear was her cry: huge wracking sobs. "What the fuck are you doing to her?" My voice became hoarse.

Corey snatched the phone from me and cut off the call. The room fell silent. The chief took the seat beside me and placed a hand on my shoulder. There were no words that could offer any comfort.

In that moment, I knew exactly how the parents of Casey, Dale, Vicky, and Louis felt. I felt sick, my stomach knotted and roiled. I bolted from my chair and raced to the bathroom. I was leaning over the sink retching when the chief walked in. He turned on the faucet and I cupped my hands under the cold water. I splashed it on my face, in my mouth to soothe the burn from acid.

"You and her?" he said, looking at my reflection in the mirror. I nodded.

"How long?" he asked.

"A while, it wasn't serious but..."

"No need to explain. I won't say we'll find her, Mich, because you know I can't promise you that, but we'll do all we can."

He grabbed a paper towel from the dispenser and handed it to me. I held it over my face to soak up the water and tears. I turned off the water and screwed the paper towel into a ball. I threw it at the trash can.

"I'll find her, dead or alive, I'll find her," I said. He nodded and we walked from the bathroom.

"The chuckle didn't match our man," Corey said, as soon as I rejoined them.

"What?"

"The chuckle? I don't think that was our man."

"So he has someone else with him?"

"I think so. We have a recording of Thomas' chuckle; this one was a different tone. Now, the clip is really short but definitely different."

"Fuck! And we can't trace that fucking cell?"

He shook his head. "We know he bought it, it's registered to him, but as for tracing the location...He's either got some serious technological brain, or a cell we've never encountered."

It wasn't difficult to learn how to route a signal, emails, anything that needed a satellite, or the Internet really, via different countries. It annoyed the hell out of most law enforcement agencies to see fucking tutorials on YouTube. But this guy knew exactly how long he could stay on his cell before we'd get close.

"He knows something about forensics, and he knows how to dodge a trace. Let's think on how. He's a fucking schoolteacher. Or..."

"Whoever he's with knows," Dean finished.

"Ex cop?" the chief asked.

"Who knows?" I sighed, tiredness washed over me and I gulped down some cold coffee.

My stomach grumbled. Although Eddie had brought takeout, we hadn't eaten a great deal of it. I wondered how the team was getting on at my house.

"Okay, let's focus on where he could be," I said, returning my attention to the map. "Is there a way we can get an aerial shot of this area?" I asked.

"Google maps," Pete said, tapping away on his laptop.

"Something a little more current," I said, looking at Corey.

"I'll make a call but don't hold your breath," he replied.

It had been known that the FBI, if the right contact had been made, to use drone and satellite imagines collected by the military. It was favor for a favor type thing and strictly off the record. While Corey made a call, I sat next to Pete to see what the Internet threw up.

To my surprise, Google maps showed the house and the surrounding woodland. Although the image was a couple of years old, there was an obvious track through the trees, wide enough for a vehicle, to a clearing. We zoomed in and could see that it was man-made; tree trunks lined the clearing.

"Why was this clearing not noticed when we searched the area?" I asked.

"Because, from the ground, this isn't that noticeable, it's just a gap in the trees, Mich. And I guess we weren't looking for something underground," Dean said. He had valid point.

"I want us there, as soon as," I said.

An undercover team was sent to investigate, initially. Two officers from the K9 team, posing as a couple with a dog, were called upon.

———

Waiting was probably my most hated thing and something I wasn't particularly good at. I wanted to be with the rest of the guys, out on the street, knocking on doors again. I didn't want to be sitting at a desk with a frantic buzz going on around me and watching my cell, waiting for it to ring. I didn't want to listen to conversations, planning, and preparations that I was no part of. As much as I still, technically, had a job, I'd been pushed to the periphery of the investigation. I remembered back to a case I'd worked, many years ago, when a cop's daughter had gone missing. We'd done the same thing, pushed him off the case because he couldn't think rationally, he would react out of emotion and when his daughter's abductor was brought to court, we lost. The father had beaten the shit out of the kid in custody, violated his human rights, and he walked. Sometimes the bad guys win. Sometimes justice was an ass.

Pete was on the phone to the local authorities. We wanted plans for buildings that may have been demolished and that might have had basements still accessible from ground level. We were a small town, but one that had seen it's fair share of development and regeneration over the years. We might have been clutching at straws, but I couldn't shake the feeling that he was hiding underground.

"Oh, fuck. Shit!" I heard. All heads turned toward Pete.

He held the phone to his ear, nodding as he listened and frantically writing on a pad.

"Okay, okay. I need those plans, and now would be good," he said.

Corey walked toward him and Pete tapped the pad with his pen. I sat and stared at them both.

"Where is Tanner Street?" he asked.

"Around the corner, why?"

"The old coroner's office..." Before he could finish his sentence I was up out of my chair.

"Wait! Mich, hold your horses," he said.

"The old coroner's offices had a morgue in the basement," I said.

I'd had the misfortune of visiting the place only once before it was demolished. It was an eerie place, originally built in the early 1960's and resembled a sanatorium with its white tiled walls and sterile rooms. It was deemed to be too small when the coroner at the time had retired, and it was decided a new facility was needed to house the state medical examiner, which would cover a wider area.

"What's there now?" Corey asked.

"A convenience store, not that it's open that often. Can we find out who owns it?" I said, directing my question to Pete.

"Okay, while we're waiting on information about the clearing, let's get over to this building and investigate. Get organized, people" Corey said.

The rush of people around the room, gathering the necessary equipment, protective clothing, and calling the judge for a warrant, had my adrenalin spiking. I grabbed a bulletproof jacket and placed it over my t-shirt, making sure the badge I wore on a silver chain was visible.

"Mich..." Corey started.

"Don't even go there, Corey. I'm going, there's nothing you'll do to stop me."

I checked the clip in my gun and placed it in my hip holster. In the meantime, the plans for the old building, and the new, had been emailed over. Pete projected them to the whiteboard as I was rubbing off my thoughts.

The old building showed a small extension that appeared to have been added as a fire escape from the basement. That small extension wasn't present on the new plans and I prayed it had been left, otherwise it meant accessing the basement, if it was still there, through the store.

One of the team was trying to get hold of the owner for a set of keys, but if necessary we'd break in. It wasn't ideal because we ran the risk of alerting Thomas, if he was there. Raiding a property wasn't something that we'd normally do in the middle of the day, but time wasn't on our side. Thomas worked at a far greater pace than the average serial killer, if there was such a thing, deliberately to keep us in a spin, I believed.

Within a half-hour, the team was ready and we were about to leave the station when Joe, the head of our forensic team, stopped me.

"Mich, I've got something I think you should see," he said.

"Can it wait? We're about to hit the old coroner's office."

He would have already been informed that we might need them should we find anything.

"I don't think so." The tone of his voice sent a chill over my skin.

"What's wrong?" Corey asked, as he walked to stand beside me.

Joe took a deep breath. "The DNA results are all in. You know that was your mother but we found..." He took another breath. "We found further semen on her dress, that didn't belong to you."

"Yeah, come on, Joe, out with it." I'd sort of expected them to find something else.

"The DNA belongs to your guy, Thomas James, but...fuck, Mich. There's no easy way to say this. Thomas James' DNA matches your mother's."

I stared at him, blinking rapidly. "There's got to be a mistake," I said.

He slowly shook his head. "I ran the tests a few times to be sure. Thomas James shares your mother's DNA. There are enough markers to confirm that you and Thomas are half-brothers."

"How...?"

"Mich, you need to stay here," Corey said.

"No fucking way. Joe, I can't process what you're saying right now. I need to go deal with this." I turned away and carried on walking.

Thomas James was my mother's son, my half-brother. How the fuck did that happen? I mean, I know biologically how it could happen, but it had to be a mistake. I'd make them run the tests again when we got back. My head was spinning as we left the station.

"No. Fucking. Way," I muttered to myself, as I climbed into the car beside Dean. He looked over to me.

"Mich, I'm pulling you off the case, immediately," Corey said, holding the car door open before I could close it.

"What's happened?" Dean asked.

"Thomas James is Mich's half-brother."

I shook my head and grabbed for the handle. "No. No, he fucking isn't. It's a mistake, now get in the car."

"Fuck's sake," Corey said, letting go of the door. He opened the rear one and climbed in.

We didn't speak as we drove the short distance to the old coroner's office. We were in an unmarked vehicle and passed another parked outside the front entrance. Its occupants nodded, just the once, as we passed to drive to the rear of the building. We parked a short distance away and for a moment no one spoke.

"Have we gotten hold of the store owner?" I finally asked. Dean shook his head.

"We have someone to break down the door?" I asked, he nodded that time.

"Then let's go," I said.

Using the neighboring buildings as cover, we made our way to the rear of the building. My heart picked up pace when I saw the extension still standing. We scanned the area for any CCTV, and satisfied that there was nothing obvious, we made our way to a metal door, fixed shut with three large padlocks and bolts.

One of the officers used bolt cutters to release the padlocks and on my nod, Dean gently pulled the door open. We were met with a short flight of stairs leading down to a corridor. With guns drawn, we crept down.

We were breaking all protocol but I didn't care. We had a

warrant, and no time to plan a proper raid. Eddie's life was at risk. I refused to entertain the idea that she was already dead.

The corridor was dark and I pulled a small penlight from my pocket. It was enough to light the way without notifying anyone we were coming. The place smelt of damp, of death, with chemical overtones. Halfway along the corridor was a door. We paused before it. Bringing up the rear were two armed officers. I signaled to them to carry on to the only other door, at the end. I raised my hand, using my fingers to count to three. On the third, I kicked open the door at the same time as the other officers kicked open theirs.

I swung my gun, left to right, as I entered the room. It was empty save for a metal table bolted to the floor in the middle. However, there had been evidence of recent use. On the floor were some bloodied rags and in the corner, and an old furnace. I heard my name being called and backed out of the room.

We ran along the corridor and into the second room. I closed my eyes at the sight that greeted me.

Written in red, presumably blood, across the back wall was one word.

P R I D E

Red dripped down the wall from each letter.

In the center of the room was a metal chair, rope was still attached to the legs, the same rope we'd seen used on Casey. On the seat was a piece of paper. I walked over to it. It was a note, written in red ink, I hoped. The font was scratchy, italic looking as if written with an ink pen.

Pride – The ultimate sin, Lucifer's downfall. Love of self, perverted to hatred and contempt to one's neighbor.

"What the fuck does that mean?" Dean asked, looking over my

shoulder.

"Love of self...hatred for anyone else. I don't see how that applies to Eddie," I said.

"Maybe this isn't about her. Maybe it's him, or you," Corey said.

Dean had walked back to the entrance to inform the team of what we'd found. It seemed ironic, and I guessed that was the point, to have held Eddie in the old coroner's office. That had me thinking.

"Casey was found in the school hall, what was it used for?"

"Games, basketball, that kind of thing?" Corey answered.

"Somewhere she'd be doing her cheerleading thing, I imagine. He's leaving them in a very obvious place, according to their sin. Dale was gluttony, an over indulgence of anything. Louis said he liked to show off where his wealth was concerned. Gluttony and a garbage truck make sense. Vicky was greed, she had molten gold poured over her and was left at a jeweler's. So where would you leave pride?"

"Somewhere obvious to you," Dean said.

I couldn't think beyond the fact that he had hurt her. Her screams, her blood, if it was her blood, were all I could think about.

"She has a secret, what if he knows what it is?" I said, quietly.

"What secret?" Corey asked.

"I don't know, she said 'we all have secrets', or something like that."

"Mich, what do you know about her?"

I stared at the wall, at the word whose letters still dripped. "Not much," I whispered.

Eddie never spoke about family; I just assumed she was estranged from them. She never spoke about her past, other than what she had done professionally. My head pounded to the point my eyes started to water, as if I was heading for a migraine.

"They want us out of here," Dean said, noticing forensics had arrived.

"Mich, the blood at your house? It's not hers," Joe said. I nodded.

"Can we talk, when you're done here?" I asked.

"Of course, I'm sure you've got a ton of questions."

I walked out of the room, along the corridor that had been flooded with lights set up and out into the afternoon sun. I stood and looked around, wondering if he was watching me.

"You want me? You fucking come and get me, you prick!" I shouted.

Chapter *18*

If I smoked, now would be the perfect time to light a cigarette. In fact, I tore a piece of paper from a pad and rolled it, held it between my fingers and placed it to my lips while I stared at her.

Post-coital bliss I think it was called. I'd fucked a woman for the very first time, well, a live one. I'd apologized for my clumsiness, I guess I had a lot to learn, but I was sure she'd be able to teach me. My body felt strange, my skin prickled, more so as the sweat dried on my naked frame. I smoothed a piece of hair from her forehead. Her eyes were wide; she stared straight ahead as if the ceiling held her attention more than I should. She blinked slowly when I slapped her cheek.

"Why don't you want to look at me?" I asked her.

She didn't answer. The only noise she'd made were screams when I'd slowly sliced down her biceps with the same knife she'd stuck in mine. I thought it only fair that she felt what a knife wound was like.

It had been fun to watch Mich and his cronies sneak around the old coroner's office. I'd only stayed there long enough to draw enough of Eddie's blood to leave him a message. I would have given him a clue had he not figured it out himself.

I'd been surprised at the length of time it had taken them to figure out I wasn't in the derelict barn on the outskirts of town, nor the abandoned meat packing plant. I wasn't stupid enough to stay above ground when there were so many wonderful 'caves' I could hide in. I liked being underground, the dark and cold comforted me.

My only mistake had been my father's house on Perry Street. It was why I had my fun with those kids. They knew I was there. They tormented me, threatening to expose me, accusing me being of a pervert. Agreeing to supply them with drugs, pandering to their stupidity got them on my side; got me close enough to silence them, some of them. There was still time for the rest.

She moaned, I think she'd been in shock. "Eddie, shall I get you something to drink?" She gently nodded.

Her pretty lips were chapped and I didn't want to kiss chapped lips. I'd need to take care of her. I rose from the floor and walked to a bench. I poured some water from a jug into a plastic glass. When I returned I knelt beside her and placed one hand under her head. I gently lifted it and placed the plastic glass to her lips.

"There, see, that's nice isn't it?" I said, as I poured the liquid. Most of it spilled down the sides of her face, but I watched her sip enough to moisten her lips and mouth.

She was tied to the floor, spread-eagle. Before I stood to replace the glass on the bench, I gave one rope, connecting her wrist to the metal ring bolted to the concrete, a tug. It was secure. I ran my hand over her stomach and it angered me to see her muscles recoil. I dug my fingernails into one of her knife wounds and tore. She screamed out. I smiled. I'd take that reaction; in fact,

I'd take any reaction from her.

———————

We drove back to the station in silence; I was beyond conversation. I had no words to express the fear, the anger, the sadness, that washed over and through me second by second. I felt physically sick, unable to eat or drink anything for fear of throwing up. The acid that bubbled in my stomach burned. When we arrived, we walked into the incident room. I was hoping that plans were underway to search the clearing near Thomas' home.

"Mich, I really can't have you involved anymore, you know that, don't you?" Corey said, as he sat opposite me.

I stared at him, not answering. "If those DNA tests are correct, and the fact that he has your partner, I can't risk any compromise to this case." I nodded my head.

"I can't trust you to not act on emotion and give the state a reason that this won't get to court," he added.

I knew only too well what he meant. The cult I'd investigated had ended up with multiple murders and a couple of suicides. We weren't able to bring anyone to court, and I understood the frustration that Gabriel, a guy I'd grown to like, lived with. When there was no satisfying ending, life was spent going around in circles and not moving forward. But like Gabriel had wanted, my ending of this case would be very different to Corey's.

I decided I needed to know more about Eddie. I might not officially be on the case, but I certainly wasn't going to go home and sit on my ass, doing nothing but wait. I left the station and drove to Eddie's office.

I called ahead, asking if Charles, Eddie's second-in-command was available. Thankfully he had a half-hour before leaving for a meeting.

"Mich, I don't know what to say. Is there any news?" he asked, as I shook his hand.

"We have some leads we're chasing up. Can we talk somewhere private?" I asked. I wasn't up for a conversation in the corridor.

"Of course." I followed Charles to his office, one down from Eddie's.

He gestured to a chair and I sat.

"I'm concerned, Mich, that Eddie won't have her medication with her," he said.

"Her medication?" Charles wasn't, as far as I knew, aware of our 'relationship' so there'd be no reason for me to know of any medication she took.

"She has a heart condition, something she wanted kept private. I knew, of course, but she has to take certain medication daily."

"I didn't know. What do you mean, a heart condition?" I tried to keep my voice even, but I was shocked to the core by his revelation.

"She was diagnosed a couple of years ago with Atrial Fibrillation. It's a condition where the heart beats irregularly. She has to take medication to keep the heart beating normally."

"What happens if she doesn't take her meds?"

"The risk is her heart will go into AFib. If that isn't brought under control quickly, it could result in a stroke or heart failure."

"Fuck! What's the prognosis for someone with this?" I asked.

He sighed. "Most people can live relatively normal lives, but for Eddie, she has a further complication. Her AFib came about because she has congenital heart disease and has had it since childhood."

"She never said," I said, quietly, more to myself.

"She never wanted anyone to know. Her life expectancy isn't as long as it should be."

"That's why she wouldn't..." I cut my sentence short.

"She wouldn't, what?"

"Nothing. I'm trying to get my head around why he would take her. I'd appreciate you keeping this between us for now, the press isn't aware just yet."

"I've told the staff here that she's ill. I'll tell Dan the same when he returns to work."

"Dan?"

"Her technician, he's off work, doing poorly himself."

I knew who Dan was. "How long has been off?"

"A couple of days now. He left a message on the answering machine that he had a bug of some kind. He was a little vague about it, to be honest."

"Vague?"

"It was just a message left but, yeah, vague. I can't explain it, he hasn't had a day off sick since he's been here."

"How long is that?" I asked.

"About two years, I think. Joined us from Canada."

I froze. "Canada, I didn't hear an accent."

"American born but moved up there as a child. I think he came back and forth many times. Anyway, you will keep me informed if you hear anything, won't you? I just don't know what to do to help."

I hadn't heard the last part of what he'd said; I was sending a text message to Dean.

Dan, Eddie's technician called in sick, left a message; it's unusual according to Charles. He also spent time in Canada, might `need checking out.`

His reply came quick.

`    On it, get the recording.`

"Charles, do you still have the voice message Dan left?"

"I don't know, why?"

I deliberated for a moment. "Our killer isn't working alone, and I'm trusting that isn't information you'll share with anyone."

"You think...? No, he's..." Charles seemed shocked at what I'd implicated.

He picked up his telephone and made a call requesting a copy of the recording.

"I'm not saying he's involved, but right now, we have to look at every avenue," I said, when he'd finished his call.

Another thought hit me. "Are there rooms here you don't use?"

"There are a couple of examination rooms, we have more space than we have examiners, at the moment."

"Will you show me the whole facility?" I'd never been beyond reception, Eddie's office, and her examination room.

We left the office, and Charles explained what each room we passed was used for. At the rear of the property were a couple of bays, reserved for the vans bringing in 'visitors.' To one side was a metal door, he took a key and we descended a staircase. Just the act of taking one step at a time down to a basement had my heart racing.

"Nowadays all our records are computerized and we do have a process of uploading all the old records, but, as you can imagine, that's going to take years. So, here we have storage."

"What do you do with the records once you've uploaded them?" I asked.

"They're destroyed, we have a furnace and they're burned. We think that's the safest way."

I froze. Charles stopped walking and turned back to look at me.

"Don't go any further, Charles. We need to get out of here."

His brow furrowed in confusion. I pulled my cell from my pocket.

"You need to get over here. There's a basement, and another furnace," I said, as Corey answered.

"Mich... Oh, forget it, give us five."

"Can this area be accessed from outside, when the facility is closed?" I asked Charles.

"No, unless someone either has a set of keys, and the passcode to disable the alarm, of course. Then there's the pin code pads to access each area and the whole place is covered by CCTV."

Dan did. Dan had all of those things.

Charles and I walked back out. We passed technicians moving bodies from the morgue to examination rooms. Each body was covered with a white cloth. It could be anyone under those cloths, anyone dead *or* alive.

"Does the CCTV extend inside the building," I asked.

"Yes, in reception, the corridors, but not in the examination rooms themselves. Those rooms have their own recording systems, but it's not often that we'll video an autopsy."

I nodded as I thought. "I'll wait outside for my guys to arrive, we need to investigate the basement, Charles. I'd appreciate it if you could keep any staff away for a little while."

"I'm giving permission, Mich, and I'd appreciate if your guys need to remove anything, I know about it first. I have to protect the information that's held in here."

I nodded. "You know about the cases we have, Vicky Bell, for example?"

He looked at me before sighing. "The furnace," he said. I nodded.

"We found a furnace in the old coroner's office, in the basement, but it didn't look like it had been used. We need to find somewhere that would allow our guy to melt gold to the degree he needed. Would that furnace do that? We also know he washed Casey before moving her to the school. Eddie thought we should be looking for somewhere 'clinical'."

Charles slowly closed his eyes. His head rolled forward slightly and he sighed.

"I guess so, I don't know what temperature gold would need to be melted at, to be honest. Do you think...?"

"I don't know, I just know that we are pretty much out of locations in this town, other than here," I said.

"Okay, I'll rearrange my meeting this morning, so I'm available if you need me. I'll be in my office. Please come and find me before you leave."

He shook my hand and walked back toward his office. Charles was due for retirement but in that half-hour he'd aged another ten years. Eddie's disappearance, the thought that their facility could have been used as a crime scene, seemed to weigh heavily on his shoulders.

———

"Bring us up to speed," Corey said, when he and Dean arrived.

I gave him the details I'd learned from Charles. "And he gave us permission to enter?" I nodded.

We didn't necessarily need his permission if we thought we

were entering a crime scene, but it made life a lot easier not waiting on a warrant.

"Is there any point in me asking you to stay here?" Corey asked.

"Nope, lead on," I said, gesturing with my arm for him to descend the stairs to the basement.

I followed behind, Dean brought up the rear. We didn't anticipate meeting anyone, it wasn't an area that the staff of the facility frequented regularly, and I didn't believe Thomas to be dumb enough to hide down there in the day. The basement held three rooms, the first we entered had rows and rows of metal racking that held boxes of notes. Some were yellowed with age and each had the letter of the alphabet and a date range going back years. I pitied the person that had to input all that data.

The second room caused us to come to an abrupt halt. In the center of the room was a metal table and to one side a furnace. What caused us to come to a stop was the cleanliness of the floor. In comparison to the previous room, this had been cleaned, thoroughly. The spike in my heart rate, though, was caused by a bucket and mop that had been left in the corner. A gold smudge could be seen on the handle.

"We've got it," Corey said.

This had to be the room Thomas prepared his victims in. Which gave more credence to Dan being involved. How else could Thomas have gained access?

The third room was set up as an office, what caught my eye was a radio, the frequency set to the same one we'd use in the patrol cars.

"We need all the CCTV around the time Casey and Vicky were murdered," I said. I wasn't sure Dale was killed here.

"How the fuck has someone not noticed this?" Dean said.

I shrugged my shoulders. "I guess the only people down here are the data entry personel, and I imagine they grab a file and take it back upstairs."

"Get someone over to Dan's house, now," Corey said. Dean made his way back to the entrance to make the call.

When a break came in any case, a surge of excitement would normally run through me. It wasn't excitement I felt though. Although it had only been a few hours since Eddie had been taken, it was still fear rippling through me. The closer we got to Thomas, the more dangerous it would be for Eddie. I wandered back to the storage room. The air was stale and heavy with dust, there didn't seem to be any disturbance. It was as I was staring at the boxes that a thought came to me. I wondered if my mother's records had been taken from that room.

By the time I'd joined the others, further officers had arrived. Our forensic team, depleted because some were still working on the evidence we'd already collected, had arrived.

"Mich, outside," Corey said. I followed him back up the stairs. "Okay, the guys at the clearing in the woods think they've found something, about a mile from the house."

"What the fuck are we doing waiting here then?" I asked.

"Because if he has Eddie there, you know damn well we can't go storming in. This is potentially a hostage situation. Second, Dan isn't at his house and it doesn't look like he has been there for a couple of days, he has uncollected mail. If, and it's a big if, he's involved, we aren't going up against just one person."

"What do you mean, if?"

"We don't know that Dan isn't a victim..." He raised his hand to silence my protest.

"It's highly likely he's involved, getting in and out of here would take an insider, we know that. But I'm not fucking this case up, or putting Eddie's life in jeopardy by acting on gut and not procedure."

"So what is going to happen?" I asked.

"There's no point in me telling you to go home, but you are *not* involved, Mich. Do you understand me?"

I smarted; I wasn't a fucking idiot. But I respected the guy, so I nodded.

"We're going to use some surveillance equipment to see what we can find at the new site. A camera has already been set up but we need to know what's underground. There's a metal hatch, very well concealed, which we think might lead down to a bunker. I've got someone trying to find out if it's military or not."

"When, Corey? How quick will you be set up?"

"Hopefully, within another couple of hours. We'll get over there for dusk."

"And if they're there?"

"We'll have to take it as it comes when we get there."

"Make her the priority, please," I said, my voice lowered to a whisper.

"You know I will."

"She has a heart condition, Corey, she needs medication."

"Okay, you know we'll have paramedics there anyway."

One of the things that had helped my decision to leave the FBI had been involvement in a case where the priority had been to catch the bad guy, no matter what; with little regard for the life of the person he held. I sort of understood why, he was a prolific killer who needed taking out, but it didn't sit well with me. Not everyone in a hostage situation made it out. I didn't want Eddie to be a statistic, collateral damage for the greater good.

There was nothing for me to do but to head back to the station, alone. If we were getting close to Thomas, I had to back off; I knew that.

Chapter 19

It was time. The final part of my plan. First I had to dispose of Dan, he'd served his purpose over the years. He had been the only friend I'd ever had, but I didn't trust him to keep quiet. He'd been dumb when he'd called in sick. It seemed I was surrounded by stupid people sometimes.

"How shall we do this, Eddie?" I asked. "Shall I cut his throat? Maybe you could teach me how to perform an autopsy, that would be fun, wouldn't it?"

I liked to see the fear on Dan's face. It was ironic that I'd just administered the ketamine that he supplied to me. I never asked where he'd gotten it, but he sat in the chair I'd bound him to, head lolling and spaced out.

"Yes, an autopsy. Now, I guess I have to lay him down." I kicked the chair from underneath him until he fell face down onto the concrete floor. I untied him, then rolled him over.

"Mmm, Eddie, will he wake up?" Maybe I needed to secure him down.

I walked over to where she lay and stood over her. Her brown eyes looked back at me, she blinked a couple of times.

"Don't," she croaked, her voice was so hoarse. It was the first time she'd spoken.

"Don't? Why?"

"Thomas, please. Just let him go."

"You sound so sexy with that hoarse voice of yours. I can't let him go, no one gets to go."

A single tear rolled down the side of her face. I reached down to catch it on my finger, and then sucked on that finger to taste her.

"What happened to you?" she asked.

"Ah, Eddie, it's a long story, but shall I tell you a secret? Your boyfriend ruined my life. Well, his mother decided he was the more important child. Did you know we are half-brothers? You didn't? How could you not?"

Her eyes had widened in shock at my revelation.

"The whore, our mother, married my father, then left to be with Mich's father, and gave her child up, me. She gave me up to a man who hated to look at me because I resembled everything he couldn't have. My father loved her, the stupid fuck. He pined after her for years and years."

"How is that Mich's fault?" she asked.

"How? How?" I shouted then took a deep breath to calm myself. "She was going to leave his father, come back to us, but then got pregnant again. That baby made her stay. That. Baby."

"But…"

"Shut the fuck up now, you hear me?" I kicked her in the ribs. I didn't want to hear any more from her.

"And then, Eddie, just when I thought my father had moved on with life, just when he started to show me a little respect, your cunt of a boyfriend killed him. Oh, I swore! Oh, I'm so sorry, please, *forgive me?"*

She nodded; she gave me a smile. My smile spread from ear to ear. She had smiled at me!

"Anyway, we need to get rid of Dan, it's important, Eddie."

I walked around my 'cave,' deciding what to do. "How about you show me what to do?" She disappointed me when she shook her head.

"Time is running out!" I shouted.

I dragged Dan to his knees by his hair. He moaned, coming down from the high I'd administered. I grabbed a knife from the bench and yanked his head back. He was kneeling between Eddie's legs, salivating over her exposed pussy I imagined. I drew the knife slowly across his throat and watched as blood spurted over her. She screamed, he gurgled, and I laughed. I let him fall; he lay across her, bleeding out. She writhed, cried, and when he'd bled out over her, I pushed him away and fucked her again. His blood acted as a useful lubricant.

I sat at the station, watching the preparations, listening to the briefing, and scanning the monitor connected to the wireless camera watching the bunker. The only movement had been one of Corey's team planting a listening device to the entrance. They had wanted to find a way to insert a small camera, but when they'd scraped a little of the earth away, they discovered the bunker was concrete lined. Nothing had come back from his military contact so the assumption was made that Thomas, or whoever owned the property, had built the bunker.

"Okay, we're ready to move out," Corey said. I stood and looked at him. "You can ride in the second car. You are an observer only,

Mich," he said, his voice stern.

I climbed into an unmarked car with Pete driving and two officers in the back. They were part of a tactical team, dressed in black and wore balaclavas on their heads, rolled up to their foreheads.

We didn't enter the property via the driveway but from the opposite end. We joined three other vehicles, one being a large surveillance unit. I was told to wait in the unit. The tactical team huddled together to check their equipment before hiking through the woods. They wore cameras attached to their flack jackets so we were able to watch in night vision. They skirted the clearing, dropping to the ground to crawl toward the hatch.

The occupants of the unit were silent as we watched the monitors. One of the team reached forward and gently cleared grass and earth, his camera picked up a metal plate with a rope handle and a bolt, pulled open. He used a snake camera to film the edges of the plate. I could see him watching the feedback on a handheld monitor. He would be looking for hinges, bolts, anything to give him an idea of whether the plate was secured shut from inside. I'd used the snake camera myself. It was a tiny cable with a fisheye lens on the end, perfect for what he wanted to do.

The camera fit between the edges of the hatch and the bracket it sat on. It also picked up another bolt on the underneath. I silently cursed. He'd have to pry open that bolt without being heard.

I could hear my heart beating and the blood rushing past my ears, building as each second, minute, passed, with tension. My palms sweated, the evening was balmy and the unit humid. For obvious reasons there were no windows, and we couldn't have the air conditioner running for fear of making too much noise. I felt a bead of sweat slowly roll down my spine, yet coldness seemed to have seeped into my bones. I shivered.

I watched the guy raise his hand and beckon his colleague forward; they inserted something between the gap to pry the bolt open. Every movement was slow, silent. Eventually, they rose to a crouch and pulled out their guns. It took just another few seconds for a third member of their team to join them.

"Come on," I whispered, as I watched one slowly raise the hatch just a couple of inches.

From the camera, we could see steps leading down into darkness. We had no idea how big the bunker was or what the guys would face when they entered.

"Go," Corey said, speaking through a headset and startling me.

The hatch was flung open and the three guys rushed through with flashlights turned on and guns raised. I held my breath, watching the jolting images that were fed back from their jacket cameras. They descended the stairs and into a square room. The camera focused on a body on the floor. Even with the green hue that was night vision, I could see it wasn't Eddie. My breath was expelled in a rush of relief.

"What do you have?" Corey asked.

"Male, dead for sure. A bench to one side with a cooking stove, gas lamp." The guy reeled off what he could see.

"Is she there?" I asked.

"There's no one else here," came the reply.

"There's a door leading to a corridor," he said and we watched him open it.

We followed him on the monitor as he slowly walked along it, keeping his back to the wall and his gun raised in front of him.

"Fuck!" I heard, as his camera picked up a second set of concrete steps leading to another hatch, which wasn't locked and not fully shut either.

The relief I'd felt just seconds earlier dissipated, frustration, anger, and sadness, washed over me. I collapsed into a chair, placed my elbows on my knees and cupped my face in my hands. I heard vehicle engines being started, headlights cut through the dark, picking out the trees in front of us, searching.

"Fuck!" Corey said, echoing the sentiment. He slammed his fist down on the counter in the unit.

"He's always one fucking step ahead of us," I mumbled.

"Why did we not know about the second hatch?" Corey shouted through his mic.

A breathless reply came back, "We didn't exactly have a great deal of time to scout the area properly, sir."

I could see part of the team fan out toward the woods. Thomas would have Eddie; that had to slow him down but then it depended on how much of a head start he'd had.

"How warm is the body?" I asked.

"Not warm enough," came a reply, coupled with a sigh.

"Can we get some dogs in?"

Before anyone could reply I heard more shouts. "The house!"

Corey and I jumped from the unit and looked toward the house, a light shone through one window. There was an immediate rush to the cars, I'd only just gotten my hand on the door to close it before we fishtailed away, the wheels having no purchase on the ground as we sped toward it.

"You stay in the car, Mich," Corey said, his tone of voice gave no opportunity for argument.

We pulled to a halt at the same time as three other vehicles. I climbed from the car and stood by the door, watching the team fan out around the house. The front door was kicked in and I could hear shouts of 'police' to identify themselves. I paced, clenching and unclenching my fists. Eventually I heard shouts. For a moment I froze.

I ran to the house. I was stopped at the door by a huge son of a bitch who wrapped his arms around me.

"Mich, don't fuck this up," he said.

"Eddie!" I shouted. A laugh echoed back at me.

I was being held to one side when Thomas, with his hands cuffed behind his back, was escorted out.

"Hi, brother," he said, as he passed me. "I've been waiting for you."

"Where is she?"

The only reply I got was a laugh.

"Where the fuck is she, you prick?" I shouted after him.

"She's not here," Corey said, as he left the house.

Thomas was bundled into the back of a vehicle and I watched it drive away.

"He wanted to be caught, why?" I said.

"That's what we need to find out. I've got helicopters coming in with heat sensors to scan the woods, and dogs. If she's here, we'll find her, Mich."

———

By the time we got back to the station Thomas had been arrested and processed. He was placed in a cell, after having removed his clothing and dressing in police issued pants and t-shirt. We were told a doctor had taken a look at his arm, cleaned and dressed it, now he was waiting for questioning.

"Did he say anything?" I asked the officer who had brought him in.

"Not a thing, sat there with a smile on his face."

We watched him on a monitor. He sat on the edge of the bunk with his legs crossed and his hands placed in his lap. Although he didn't stare at the camera, he kept the smile on his face.

"What the fuck are you up to?" I whispered.

"Fucking with your head, that's what," Corey answered. "If he didn't have Eddie somewhere, I'd leave him to stew for a while. He has us by the balls and he knows it."

'He knew we were at that bunker, how?" I asked.

"That's another thing we need to find out. Now, go to the viewing room and let me bring him out."

I left Corey and made my way to the area attached to the interrogation room with one-way glass. The chief was already standing with a mug of coffee in his hand. He offered it to me. I shook my head.

"You doing okay?" he asked.

"Running on adrenalin right now," I said. I hadn't slept in over twenty-four hours.

"You understand why you can't be involved, don't you?"

"Yes, although I have a feeling he'll want to speak to me."

"I don't doubt that, but we have to get as much information as we can from him first."

It took a few minutes before Thomas was escorted into the room. His hands were released from the cuffs but then one was recuffed to the chair that was bolted to the floor. He was offered a drink, which he politely declined. The officer stood at the back of the room and Thomas looked directly at the tinted glass panel in the wall. He smiled. It wasn't a smirk, but a genuine smile as if he hadn't a care in the world. The guy was fucking nuts.

Corey made him wait another five minutes before he and Dean joined him. The temperature had been set specifically to not allow Thomas to get too comfortable. The room was laid out to maximize discomfort and disorientation. Corey took the chair to the side of Thomas, he swiveled it so he was face on and Dean sat opposite.

"I understand you've declined your right to an attorney?" Corey asked, after introducing himself and smiling at Thomas.

"That's correct."

"Can I ask why?"

"You can."

"Why did you decline your right to an attorney?" Corey asked, I wondered how he'd kept the frustration out of his voice.

"Because I don't need one."

"Okay."

Corey started asking Thomas some basic questions: name, date of birth, place of birth, that kind of thing, wanting to gauge his reaction. He asked questions that would require the use of memory, monitoring his body language as he responded. It was all very textbook, and I wanted to bang on the glass. Thomas was anything but textbook.

"Do you know the whereabouts of Eddie Cole?" Corey asked.

"Yes."

"Can you tell me if she is safe and unharmed?"

"She is safe. Define unharmed," he replied.

"He's fucking playing with us," I said, through gritted teeth.

"Have you harmed her in any way? You know exactly what I

mean by that," Corey asked.

Thomas slowly turned his head to face the tinted panel in the wall to his side.

"I fucked her, but I think she liked that," he said, grinning.

Before I could react, the chief had his arms wrapped around my chest. I wanted to smash through the fucking glass and rip his throat out.

"He's goading you, Mich," Chief said.

"Did she give consent, Thomas?" Corey asked.

"She could hardly say no, but you know women, they're up for it no matter what," Thomas replied.

"Does she have access to water?"

Thomas thought for a moment. "Mmm, that's a funny one. She does, but she'll have to work hard to get at it, I would imagine."

Corey opened the file on the desk. He pulled out some photographs.

"Can you tell me about these?" he said, spreading them out.

"What do you need to know?" Thomas asked.

"Why these kids, would be a good start."

"You know what? I think I'd like to speak to Mich."

Thomas sat back in his chair and, once again, stared at the glass. "I know you're there, watching me, listening to me."

"Mich isn't available right now, Thomas."

"Then I guess our interview is over."

"Okay. Interview terminated at..." Corey consulted his watch and formally ended the interview. He gathered up the photographs and slid them back into the folder. He stood and nodded to Dean. Without another word, both walked from the room.

Thomas' arm was released from the chair and he was pulled to a standing position. His wrists were cuffed behind him and he was marched back to his cell. So far, Thomas hadn't done anything we hadn't already expected.

Chief and I left the viewing room and met Corey in the incident room. He was watching the video recording of the 'non-interview' on a laptop. I knew exactly what he was doing. He was watching his body language, studying him, gaining the knowledge he needed when the 'real' interview started.

"You need to think out of the box on this one," I said.

"I know. But I still need to see how he reacts. As much as we're being textbook, Mich, so is he."

Thomas' eyes moved in the direction we anticipated when he had to recall something from memory, when he was telling the truth. No matter how great a criminal, the body's instinctive responses were often hard to disguise. But none of it made any difference if he didn't give the answers we needed. The second stage of the interview would be for Corey to delve into his past, find the reasons, and in doing so, we'd hope he'd involuntary give up some locations.

———

Thomas was brought back from his cell twice more. Each time, he was asked new questions. He answered some, but was vague. The purpose was to wear him down, without violating his rights. He was offered food and a drink, both of which he refused. That pleased me. At some point his natural survival instincts would kick in. He'd become hungry, thirsty; he'd start to become a little desperate. Toward the end of the second interview, Corey brought the conversation back around to the kids.

"We were intrigued with the words you left, Thomas. Obviously we connected them to the seven deadly sins, but what did we miss?"

Corey asked.

"Whose interpretation of the sins were they? Did you figure that out?"

"Dante's, obviously. It was a clever move."

Thomas' smile grew boarder. I knew what Corey was doing; he was giving Thomas a little credit, hoping to build a rapport.

"Let's talk about Casey Long. Why her?" Corey added.

"Ah, lust. She was an obvious candidate. Do you know how many times I watched her fuck men?"

"Was that at Perry Street?" Corey asked, not looking at Thomas as he did.

"She fucked anywhere. In my classroom once, and when I walked in, the whore just stared at me, smirking, mocking me."

"So you killed her?"

"She was a sinner, Mr. Lowe, she needed to be punished."

"But did you need to kill her?"

"Of course, all sinners have to be punished."

I made a mental fist pump, that was our first confession. Corey didn't react but continued with the conversation.

"How well did you know her, Thomas?" Corey asked.

Thomas frowned, as if deliberating on the answer. "Well enough, why?"

"Did you party with her? Maybe do a little coke together."

Thomas laughed. "Party with *her*! Oh, that's so funny. I don't do drugs, Mr. Lowe. Nasty stuff. Of course I gave her a little to...remove her anxiety, I guess. That was nice of me, don't you think?"

"Where?"

Thomas sighed. "Those kids came to my house, regularly. They abused my space. They got scared by a noise, dumb fucks. All ran, except her. Maybe she was too doped up already."

"Your house? Do you mean Perry Street?"

"Well, technically not my house. Yes, Perry Street."

"Can we talk about your wall at Perry Street. It seems you've been tracking Mich for a while," Corey said. He was taking Thomas back and forth between murders, events, and time frames.

"Ah, Mich. Did you know we are brothers?"

"Half-brothers," Corey corrected.

"Whatever, but here's the thing, I will answer any questions you want on those kids, but as for Mich, or the delicious Eddie, you'll need to get Mr. Unavailable Right Now in here."

"Okay, so what was the deal with Dale Stewart?" Corey asked, ignoring Thomas' request.

"He threatened to out me, so I stopped that, quite simple really."

"Out you?"

"Those kids knew about my attic. That house should have been mine; did you know that? I was the first born bastard but I was overlooked by them all."

"You'll need to explain, Thomas."

"My father owned that house, gave it to another product of an affair. I wonder if my father was a serial *affairer*? Is that a word? Can we look it up?"

"Adulterer," Dean corrected.

Thomas laughed. "Caroline got that house, Mich got the mother; I got nothing but abuse."

"So, Dale?" Corey asked, bringing Thomas back on track.

"He was late for work, I guess, didn't anticipate the scythe that he ran into. So, was that an accident? Or murder?"

"Did you swing the scythe into Dale as he ran toward you?"

"Yes."

"Then I'd suggest that was murder." Our second confession. "Where was this, Thomas?"

"He'd just snuck out of Kay's bedroom. Did you know they were fucking? It's shocking, everyone was fucking everyone!" He slowly shook his head as if the thought disgusted him.

"I'm tired now, I think I'd like something to eat, a coffee perhaps, and a break," Thomas said.

I sighed; we had no option but to grant his wishes.

Thomas was led back to his cell and I checked my watch. It was closing on midnight and we were no closer to finding Eddie.

Chapter 20

Corey Lowe thought I was an idiot, I was sure. I understood exactly what he was doing. I'd studied interrogation techniques for weeks. But I had decided to tell the truth, I had nothing to hide, and like I'd said, it was time.

I sat in the cell with a stale cheese sandwich, wrapped in cellophane, and a polystyrene cup of lukewarm, weak coffee. I took my time to nibble at the sandwich and sip the coffee. I smiled and wondered how long it would be before I'd be sitting beside Mich. I felt my cock twitch at the thought. Would they let me pleasure myself while he asked his questions? I chuckled.

So they had two confessions from me, they'd get the others. They'd get everything other than the whereabouts of Eddie. It was all part of the plan, you see. There was no point in just being assumed as the killer, I wanted the fame, the glory. I wanted to see my image all over the media. I got a kick out of that. I was being feted, CNN ran a daily update with 'professionals' talking, analyzing me. I wondered if the police had released my name yet?

The uppers I'd taken just before capture were keeping me going, but I was also aware they'd wear off at some point. Maybe

I should get a little sleep. I lay down on the bunk and closed my eyes, pretending.

Thoughts of Mich ran through my mind, how was he faring? He had to be exhausted; maybe I needed to let him have a break as well. I didn't want him overemotional when we finally met. I'd been building up to this day for years. Telling him the truth, having him recognize me as a brother, it's all I ever wanted.

I wondered how long they'd leave me before they came for me again. I knew the drill, wake me up, interrogate, let me rest, wake me, and so on until I cracked. Except I knew I never would. I'd give them all that they wanted except one thing.

———

I had my head resting on my arms on one of the desks in the incident room. It was quiet, save for the clacking of fingers over keyboards as reports were written up in readiness for the federal prosecutor. I wanted to close my eyes and sleep, but I didn't. My last memories of Eddie were ones of anger, of angst, and frustration. When I thought of her having a heart condition, that anger intensified. I'd put her resistance to a relationship down to being our age difference, but was it? Was it more because her life span was shorter? I didn't want to think anymore, I just wanted her found.

There were helicopters scanning the woods, dogs tracing her scent, men on foot searching each inch of the undergrowth, and yet, so far, there had been no sign of her. I pictured Thomas in my mind, he wasn't the biggest of guys; how had he manhandled her?

"Fuck! Fuck!" I shouted, as I raised my head from my arms.

Dean looked over, "What?"

"You know we said he wasn't acting alone? We thought Dan was his partner, he isn't. Dan's involved, somehow, but it isn't him."

Corey walked over to me. "Think about it. How the fuck did he get out of that bunker with her? He isn't big enough to haul her through fucking woods. He has someone else working with him. Someone other than Dan."

Corey scrubbed his hand over his face; the tiredness he felt was starting to show. Between us we'd been catching a few hours sleep on a cot in one of the offices, and I guessed we were both desperate for a good night's sleep. I had offered him my house to go shower, but he'd opted to use the station's facilities. His shirt was crumpled, he'd lost the tie he'd arrived in some time ago and his pants were creased. Corey had always been the immaculate one. We were starting to come apart at the seams and it showed.

"Why don't you go freshen up?" I said to him.

"I might, I could do with a proper hot shower. You need to, as well."

After letting Dean know we'd be an hour tops, we headed out and to my car.

"How are you holding up?" Corey asked, when we were alone.

I sighed. "This reminds me of our last case, always chasing our fucking tails," I said.

"Yeah. Have you spoken to Gabriel lately?"

"A while ago, I give him an update every now and again. Well, a non-update because nothing changes. He's doing okay, built himself a new house but spends his life looking over his shoulder and protecting his daughter."

The Gabriel case was one that I would never stop working on. Although I'd never voiced my pledge to Gabriel, I wanted to find the people ultimately responsible for the death of his wife. It had been a complicated case, with so many people involved; it had been hard to get to the truth. A cult had destroyed his life, and for the rest of it, he'd live in fear of their return. Of all the victims of the crimes I'd investigated, Gabriel, and he was a victim, was one that settled in my gut and stayed there. His bravery and refusal to give up, to move on with life without knowing who had killed his wife, had resonated within me. I hoped I had the same resolve.

I let Corey shower first and I sat at the kitchen table. I stared at Eddie's clothes that I'd piled on a seat. I picked up her tank and held it to my face. It smelled of her perfume, the same perfume whose name I never knew, that she wore every day. Tears pricked at my eyes. I knew so little about her. I'd been happy to fuck her. I'd been happy to start our *non-relationship*, yet I hadn't taken the time to really get to know her. I mentally corrected myself; she hadn't allowed me to get too close. My memories were clouded with the current situation. I'd been frustrated with her. I'd been planning on walking away, but sitting in my kitchen, in semi-darkness, I realized I loved her. I knew I felt something, and I'd wanted to explore that more. But I fucking loved her, flaws, faults, annoyances, everything that made her the feisty woman she was. I only hoped she was fighting, I prayed she was surviving.

I wiped the backs of my hands over my eyes when I heard the bedroom door scrape open.

"Coffee?" I said, as Corey joined me. He nodded, and I rose to pour him a cup.

I stood and looked around my kitchen, resting my back against the countertop. There was fingerprint dust everywhere, it was going to take some cleaning up, but I couldn't think about that.

"He's not going to give up her location," I whispered.

Corey knew better than to correct me. "Don't give up hope yet, Mich," was all he said.

I took a sip of my coffee. Despite wanting to fight my instinct, I knew, deep down, I was right. I wouldn't give up wanting to know where she was, whether she was dead or alive, but wanting and achieving that were two different things. My mind wandered back to Gabriel. He'd spent nearly a year trying to find answers, and although he didn't get them all, he got enough. That's all I wanted— I just wanted to know enough.

I placed my mug in the sink and silently walked to my bedroom. I stripped out of my clothes and turned on the shower, waiting for it to warm before I stepped in. The last time I'd been in the shower, Eddie had been with me. Although it was only a few days ago, it felt like a lifetime. I pictured her hands on my body, mine on hers. I recalled the expressions on her face and the frustration I'd feel at her lack of emotion. Something hit me. Maybe I was wrong; maybe it had nothing to do with a heart condition that stopped her from committing to a relationship. She liked to fuck, to be fucked, but it was always with a little aggression. What had caused that? What stopped her wanting to make love, to accept a tender embrace without stiffening? A thought started to creep into my mind.

I quickly dressed and found Corey rinsing his cup. I switched off the coffee machine and we locked up the house.

"How easily can you get Eddie's medical records?" I asked, as we drove back to the station.

"It's about as easy as cutting my own arm off with a blunt knife, why?"

"Just something that's niggling me."

"A niggle isn't enough to get a doctor to break his confidence."

234

"Okay, let me rephrase it. How much shit would I be in if I managed to get her medical records?"

Corey turned in his seat to look at me. I kept my gaze on the road ahead.

"Bearing in mind the amount of shit you're already in, I'd say you would just about finish off your career, if you were caught. Mich, what's this all about?"

"Eddie was the one who didn't want to commit to a relationship. She was so closed and emotionally stunted. I thought that might be because of her heart condition but now I don't know."

"And invading her privacy is going to give you answers she clearly didn't want you to know?"

I sighed. "Yes, and no. I don't know. Forget I said anything."

"Mich, don't do anything fucking stupid. You can recover from this Canada thing, but go hacking into computers just to satisfy a niggle, you'll be hung out to dry."

"I'm trying to get to know her, Corey. I fucked her, loads, but I never really knew her. I love her, she didn't love me back, and I wonder why." My voice tailed off to a whisper.

Corey didn't reply, I guess there wasn't much he could say to that.

"How's he doing?" Corey asked, as we approached Dean.

"Still laying on his bunk, hands behind his head, a smirk on his face."

"Okay, let's get him up," Corey said, as he squirted some drops into his eyes.

It was part of the program, Corey looked refreshed, ready for hours of questioning. We'd break Thomas down at some point; we had to.

I took my place behind the one-way glass and waited. Thomas was brought in and the first thing he did was to look at the tinted panel and smile. Although his hands were cuffed behind his back, he pulled one arm to his side and gave a little wave of his hand. He waited for the officer to uncuff him and rubbed his wrists before taking his seat, still with the smirk on his face.

He sat for a full five minutes before Corey joined him.

"Are you comfortable, Thomas?" Corey asked after he'd switched on the recording machine and given the formal speech.

"Do you care?"

"Not really, but I'm duty bound to ask."

"I'd actually like a nice cup of coffee, please. And hot would be good this time."

Corey nodded to the officer beside the door. Another replaced him.

"So, where were we?" Corey said, consulting his notes.

"I'd just confessed to killing Casey and Dale, you thought you'd coerced a confession from me, which isn't true. I'm a little more intelligent that you appear to give me credit for. So, let's get the rest out of the way, quickly, then I can speak to Mich."

Thomas rested back in his chair; he crossed his leg, resting one ankle on this thigh.

"I'll have my coffee first though," he added.

A black coffee was placed in front of him. I knew our officer would have given him high-octane. We wanted his heart racing, we wanted him buzzing, and then we wanted him to crash from exhaustion.

"Vicky Bell. I'm quite proud of that one. Do you know what

greed is? Excessive love of money, Mr. Lowe. I thought it genius that I gave her what she wanted, what she craved. Gold and jewelry. Did you see those earrings?" Thomas shook his head in disgust.

"Did you rape her?" Corey asked.

Thomas looked at him, wide-eyed. "You think I'd rape a child?" It seemed an incredulous question to ask him.

"You raped a minor in Canada, so why not? You raped Eddie and Casey."

"Did I rape Eddie? I said I fucked her. You have no idea if that was consensual or not. And as for Canada, mistaken identity, Mr. Lowe. I paid the price for a fucked up penal system. Mich can testify to how shoddy your counterparts are. And as for Casey? What's the technical term...I did not penetrate her."

"Mistaken identity? How, considering you were convicted of it?"

"I had a shit lawyer, Mr. Lowe. Of course, I dealt with that."

"Webster," I whispered, knowing Corey would have connected that as well.

"Back to Eddie, then. Did she consent? Did she come, Thomas?" Corey asked, ignoring Thomas' plea of innocence.

Corey leaned a little toward him. He stroked his fingers over his lips as if excited to learn the answer. "I mean, she *is* pretty hot," he added.

Thomas leaned forward. I held my breath. "I'll tell Mich just how hot, or not, she was." He rested back in this chair, turned to the tinted panel and smiled.

"Fucking cunt," I whispered.

"Now, the lawyer, what was his name?" Thomas asked.

"Patrick Webster," Corey answered.

"Ah, yeah, Mr. Webster. That was a bit of botched job. I got disturbed so had to settle for a simple stabbing. I'm sorry about that. I thought wrath was a nice sin for him, don't you agree?"

"Why?"

Thomas sighed. "Do you actually get why these people were allocated their sin?"

"Not really. They were just people doing what people do."

Thomas tutted. "Wrath, Mr. Lowe, failure to forgive, love of justice perverted to revenge and spite."

"So how did that apply to Patrick? He was a lawyer doing his job."

"He was a lawyer who helped a murderer get off. He was a lawyer that helped an innocent person lose ten fucking years of his life! He abused his position regularly, lied in court many times. Do you actually know *Patrick*?"

"Not personally."

"Then before you comment, perhaps you should."

"Can you tell me what happened to his tongue?" Corey asked.

"No tongue, can't speak. Really, I'd have thought you'd have understood that!" Thomas was getting agitated.

I watched Corey relax back into his chair, give him a small smile as if to diffuse the situation a little.

I made a note to investigate Mr. Webster further.

Now, Mother…" Thomas chuckled.

"How did you obtain the body, Thomas?" Corey asked.

"Oh, that was easy. The dumb fuck that was Dan helped with that one. You obviously knew he worked at the local funeral home, didn't you?"

"Of course," Corey lied.

"Switching a body in a closed casket funeral is a simple procedure."

"Okay, but why?"

"I wanted to get to know her." Thomas shrugged his shoulders as if stealing a dead body to *get to know it* was the most obvious thing in the world. The guy was madder than I'd originally thought.

"You wanted to get to know a *dead* woman? A woman you murdered!"

"Yes, when Mich finally has the balls to sit where you are, I'll tell him all about *our* mother. And did I murder her? That's quite a bold statement. Maybe math isn't your strongest subject, I wasn't around when our mother died."

"Okay, Mich is at home, asleep I imagine..." Thomas cut him off.

"Really? Oh, Mr. Lowe. If you continue to insult my intelligence, you know this interview will be terminated."

"I apologize. Mich is there; you know he is. So tell him. Tell him who murdered his mother, and how you came to have her," Corey said, looking toward the tinted panel.

"Face-to-face, Mr. Lowe. And she was *our* mother." His voice rose on the word 'our.'

"Can I ask one thing, then? Why envy?"

"Love of ones own good, perverted to a desire to deprive other men of theirs. She deprived me of a mother, of a normal family. Simple. She fucked, she abandoned. She left me to be abused, so I abused her."

"How?"

The look on Thomas' face turned my stomach. "I fucked her."

If I had been in the room, not only would I have heard Corey swallow the bile that I imagined had risen to his throat, but I couldn't have been held back from killing the sick fuck.

"I don't believe you, Thomas. There's no evidence to support that. Your cum was over her dress, as was Mich's, but we know how that got there. I don't believe you're actually capable of *fucking* anyone."

Corey was trying to rile him.

"So I'm lying? Maybe I am, maybe I'm not. Maybe there isn't a shred of truth in anything I've said so far. Maybe I did kill those kids, maybe I didn't. I mean, do you actually have any DNA, on any victim, to support a word I've said?"

"What the fuck..." I whispered as the chief entered the viewing room.

"Maybe I'm just a twisted, sad fuck, who has made all this up for the notoriety. You know you have to back up a confession with some form of evidence, don't you?"

"He's playing with us," I said to the chief.

"I know. He's a clever bastard, for sure."

Corey decided to change tact. "So, Louis Chapman. You gave him sloth, why?"

"Lazy fucker, Louis was. You know he was the one that sent Dale to collect his drugs. He liked to watch Casey get fucked because he was too lazy to do it himself. I used to watch him, watching her. He'd masturbate. Did you know that is a sin? Quite funny that he lost his cock, the tool he used to sin, don't you think?"

"Yet you've masturbated yourself."

"We are all sinners, Mr. Lowe." Thomas leaned forward a little. "Can I call you Corey?"

"If you want to."

"Corey, we are all sinners. You, me, Mich, those kids. Him by the door. We can't actually survive this world without sinning. But we have to be punished for it."

"Who made you judge and jury? God is the only one with the right to punish, isn't he?"

"Are you religious, Corey? Do you believe?"

"I am, and I do."

"Well I do, too, just not your God. You see, religion evolves, gods come and go. My *religion* is powerful; my *religion* will ensure my seat next to my god when the time comes. You, and him, are familiar with *my* religion." He looked straight at me.

My legs buckled, my heart physically stopped in my chest and I had a need to pummel on it, to restart it. The chief was looking at me, his eyebrows furrowed in question as I gasped for breath.

"Mich!" he said.

"I know who he is!" My words were strangled in my throat.

I watched Corey stiffen slightly, his eyes flicked to the one-way glass. Had he picked up on that as well? I prayed he had.

"Why did you kill Dan?" Corey asked.

"Surplus to requirements now. He got me in and out of the morgue, as you probably already know. I wanted to tie up any loose ends. He had no place, he wasn't a *pure blood*, just a servant."

Corey looked at the clock on the wall, he wrote on his pad.

"A pure blood?" he asked, without looking up.

For a moment there was silence. Thomas looked at me, not seeing me, but knowing I was there.

"And that's why you'll never find her, Mich, she's long gone. She's not a Divine Child, though. She was sent here. You, brother, disrupted our activities; you'll pay for that. Or rather, right now, she'll be paying for your sins and her failure."

I ran from the room, kicking open the viewing room door. I heard it splinter as its hinges gave way.

Before anyone could react, I was pushing open the interview room door. Corey rose; the officer by the wall tried to block my entrance. Thomas smiled.

"Pride, Mich. Pride. Lucifer's downfall; the greatest sin of all. Love of self, perverted to hatred and contempt to one's neighbor. You couldn't just let us be, could you?" Thomas said.

"Where the fuck is she?" I slammed my hands down on the desk so hard every piece of paper, every plastic cup and pencil, jumped from it.

He shrugged his shoulders. "Would you trade places with her, Mich?" he asked.

I stared at him. "Yes. Without a shred of doubt I would."

"Even as damaged as she is?"

"Yes."

"Did you know her? Did you know where she came from?" He was talking about her as if she was already in the past tense. "Sit, Mich, this is about to get interesting."

Chapter 21

My heart raced and I took a couple of deep, subtle breaths to calm it. Finally, Mich, my brother, the object of my obsession for years, was sitting in front of me. I felt my cock harden. I ran my tongue over my lower lip to moisten it. He smelled so good. His hair was slightly mussed, his eyes dark with anger. A vein bulged on his forehead as blood pumped hard around his taut body. He held himself rigid as wave after wave of hatred poured from him.

I didn't care that he hated me.

I watched Corey stare at him, as if trying to give some silent communication. But Mich's focus was solely on me. His stare sent an icy shiver up my spine, caused the hairs on my arms to stand to attention. He was intense. I searched his features, wanting to see what was similar, what traits we shared. We had the same colored eyes, but I knew that already. He was more muscular up close. The sleeves of his t-shirt were tight against his biceps, which bulged with pent up aggression.

"How did it feel when you killed my father?" I asked.

I watched him try to regulate his breathing. His nostrils flared with every intake of air. His chest expanded as his lungs filled.

"How did it feel, brother, when you snuck up on him, when you placed the rifle to the back of his head and pulled the trigger? Did his blood, did his bone, splatter over you? Did you lick the hot liquid from your lips?"

I wanted to tap into his basic needs. He was a killer, just like me. "I bet your heart raced; did you get that surge of excitement, of adrenalin? It's like a drug, isn't it? You got the high, didn't you? The rush as you watch someone take their last breath is like nothing on this earth."

He hadn't answered any of my questions and I didn't expect him to. The fact he had bitten down hard on his lower lip had me thinking that he'd wanted to.

I slid my free hand across the desk; our fingertips were a mere fingerbreadth apart. I wanted to touch him. He stared at our hands before raising his gaze back to mine.

"The only time my skin touches yours is when my hands are around your neck, Thomas. And yes, that high as you take your last breath will live with me forever," he said, then straightened up and left the room.

I was fucked, my body crashed as soon as I closed the interview room door behind me. I leaned against the wall and gently slid down. I rested my head on my knees. I wanted to sleep; I wanted to keep going.

The interview room door opened and I looked up as Thomas was led back to his cell. He stared at me, smiled, pleased with what he'd achieved.

"You know she called out your name when I fucked her, Mich," he said, as he was led away.

I shot to my feet, I was two paces away from him and had lost my mind when strong arms wrapped around me, stopping my assault. Thomas laughed.

"Is she alive?" I shouted.

He shrugged his shoulders. "I don't know, is the honest answer. She refused to do what she was tasked, Mich, that's punishable."

His laughter echoed down the corridor as he walked back to his cell.

I couldn't stop the tears from running down my cheeks. I felt my body deflate, the fight leave me, and I slumped against Corey.

"You need to go home, Mich," he said. I didn't have the energy to protest.

"Before you do, someone better get me up to speed." The chief had spoken.

Corey and I followed him to his office. He gestured for us to close his door and he slumped down in his chair.

"What the fuck is going on?" he asked.

Corey and I sat opposite him. I let Corey explain.

"Mich and I investigated a cult that was accused of sexual abuse, incest, murder, you name it, they were involved in it. Divinus Pueri…"

"Divinus what?"

"Divine Child. The founder of the cult was a member of the Catholic Church, Father Samuel. He found a woman and believed her to be an angel, he *mated* with her, produced offspring he believed were of divine, pure blood. It was his passage to his seat next to God, so he thought. We blew the cult open, it had to disband, disperse. We also blew open a covered up investigation within the Catholic Church. They'd known for a long time. Father Samuel ran a convent, he abused the children there, farming them out to families of the cult he set up. Thomas said something that has us thinking he is part of that cult."

Corey looked at me for confirmation. I nodded.

"He also said that *she* refused to do what she was tasked, meaning Eddie. She was part of it too," he added.

"How the fuck have we gone from a serial killer to cults?" The chief shook his head.

"The murders, we think, were done because those kids went to the house on Perry Street, regularly. They must have stumbled across something, or some of them did. He said they threatened to expose him, so he silenced them. Mich, and the situation in Canada, is kind of irrelevant here. This is about us shutting down the cult."

"And did you? Shut it down?" the chief asked.

"By the time we'd gotten to their new destination, some of the elders were dead and the rest had fled. It's a cold case that I work on, in my spare time," I said.

"He accused you of killing his father." I hadn't realized the chief had heard that. "Did you?"

I didn't answer and I guessed that was enough confirmation for him.

"So you lied to me?" Again, I didn't answer.

The chief sighed; he ran one hand through his hair. "You're suspended, Mich. I need your gun and your badge. And you need to leave the station."

"What will you do?" I asked.

"I don't honestly know yet."

The conversation was over. I stood; as I did, I placed a hand on Corey's shoulder. He gave me a nod. I took the gun from my hip holster and released the clip. I laid both on the desk. I pulled the chain I wore around my neck from under my t-shirt and released the badge clipped to it. I laid that alongside the gun. I looked at it. That badge, being a cop, had been my life. I walked from his office and out the station.

A chill ran over me as I stood beside my car. Dawn was about to break, orange streaked across the horizon as the sun fought against the dark sky to rise. I fished in my jean pocket for my keys and unlocked the door. I sat for a while, thinking. Thomas' name had never come up in our investigation of the cult. I didn't believe he'd been a long-term member, maybe he'd found solace in their arms. Maybe he'd found the family he was so desperate for within their sick embrace. He'd certainly found some kindred spirits.

I should have headed straight to bed, my body was shaking with sleep deprivation; my mind had other ideas though. Thoughts cascaded through my head. Everywhere I looked, I saw her: the clothes on the chair, her backpack in the hall. I grabbed the backpack and emptied its contents on the kitchen table. She had a small revolver; I cursed her. It was pretty useless in a backpack. I picked up what looked like a journal. A leather bound book held closed by an elastic strap. My fingers played with the elastic, pinging it against the cover. Should I open it? Normally, as part of an investigation, I would but I wasn't on the team anymore. I should have handed in the backpack. Instead I opened the book. I flicked through page after page of notes, some detailing cases, some forming a diary of sorts but there was nothing personal, nothing useful. There was also no order to it. It was as if she picked a page and wrote. Nothing was dated. Eddie didn't have the neatest of handwriting and I struggled to read some things. I closed the book and placed it to one side.

I knew Dean had visited her house, I wondered if he'd found any more. I decided to send him a text.

Hi, suspended right now but I have Eddie's backpack, there's a notebook in it. Don't know if you found any more at her house.

He replied. I heard, sorry dude. I'll come visit after my shift. Thomas is still in his cell but I'm heading home for an hour.

I pulled the folder with the Gabriel cold case in it toward me. I'd read those notes time and time again, I knew what was written and could recall most of it from memory. I wanted to take myself back to those days. I knew that Corey would try to extract as much information on the cult as possible from Thomas; perhaps in doing so we would learn something new. We. I had to remind myself, there was no *we*.

I guess I would receive some kind of official notification of my suspension at some point. In the meantime, I'd do my own investigating.

I grabbed a pencil and a pad and I wrote. For hours I wrote everything I could remember about the case. I highlighted areas I wanted to come back to. I stopped briefly to refresh my coffee mug. Before I realized, it was midday and my eyes stung, my wrist ached, and my stomach grumbled protesting about the snacks I'd been surviving on for a few days. I was too tired to cook a meal. Instead I headed to the bedroom. I pulled the t-shirt over my head and fell onto the bed.

———

The window rattled in its frame. I bolted upright and listened. The room was dark and I took a glance at my watch. Shit, it was past ten p.m. I'd slept for fucking hours. Someone tapped on the window; I guessed that was the noise that had woken me. I swung my legs from the bed and turned on the bedside lamp. Dean stood outside my bedroom.

"Why didn't you just use the fucking key?" I asked, as I opened the front door. "You nearly gave me a heart attack."

"There is no spare key," he said. I took a look in the hanging plant pot.

"That's how Thomas got in then," I said, mentally kicking myself for not checking before. Now I'd need to get the locks changed, again.

"Coffee?" Dean said, walking straight through to the kitchen.

"Yep. What's happening?" I asked. I hated that I was away from the station, and, more importantly, news.

"We pulled Thomas out for another round of questioning. He refuses to talk about Eddie or the cult. In fact, we think he slipped up by mentioning the cult, an impulsive moment maybe."

"What's your gut telling you?" I asked, as I grabbed my mug from the counter and sat at the table. I cleared a space, pushing all the papers to one side.

"They have her," he replied, bluntly.

My chin dropped to my chest and I sighed. "Tell me about this cult," Dean asked.

I gave him the same details Corey told the chief. "It's recorded as one of the nastiest cults at the FBI. The level of child abuse, incest, fucking inbreeding, is off the scale, Dean. They move around, a lot. The investigation into them is one of the longest on record."

"No one got charged?" he asked.

I shook my head. "By the time we got involved, half of the elders were dead, the victims wouldn't speak out, and they'd moved on again. We spent a year just chasing our tails. We don't know exactly how widespread they are, but they're not just confined to one state."

"And this guy, Gabriel, he was involved?" Dean tapped the edge of the folder.

"Yes. Not in the cult, they killed his wife. I think I might pay him a visit."

"How do you think Eddie was involved?"

"Thomas said she'd refused to do the task set. I need to know if she was born into the cult, kidnapped in as a child, they did that sometimes, or married in even. Somehow she got out, which is a good thing. There is something else, though. Pretty much all the girls, women, were sexually abused. There are some things about Eddie that make sense, now that I think about it."

"Fuck! Her reason to not commit?"

"I thought it might have been her heart condition shortening her life but maybe not."

I didn't want to go into detail. Eddie could only come when our fucking was aggressive, when I took control. She was a loner, didn't court company. I'd been to her house a few times but never overnight, she always opted to stay at mine. Was that because she could have been abused?

"I don't believe Thomas has been a long-term member of the cult, his name doesn't come up anywhere in that file. Well, the name we know him by, of course. And there's no mention anywhere of the cult being in Canada. I wonder if it's a recent thing for him...Shit!"

I grabbed the folder and flicked through. I pulled out a

photograph of one of the elders.

"Check his forearms, look for this," I said, pushing the photograph toward Dean.

"What is it, other than the obvious?"

"Part of their initiation is to carve a cross into the underside of their wrist. They bleed over the girls as they fuck them. If he has that, he's involved for sure. They call the uninitiated, trainees."

"Do any of the others have a tattoo?" Thomas had the strange tattoo on his arm.

"I don't know, you need to ask him about that, but then we hadn't caught up with any other trainees."

Maybe the tattoo was something to do with the cult, it was a symbol; I'd thought it was Celtic when I'd first seen it.

"Okay, I better get going. And you don't need to ask; Corey knows I'm keeping you updated. We're releasing his name tomorrow, the press knows we have someone, his name has, unofficially, been spread around, and they also know you're not on the case anymore, so be prepared."

I walked Dean to the front door. "Thank you," I said. He gave a wave over his shoulder as he headed for his car.

I needed a shower and to eat. I couldn't decide in which order. I headed to the kitchen first and opened the fridge door. It contained very little. I guess a trip to the store in the morning was in order. I grabbed a carton of milk and took a sniff. It would do. I pulled a bowl from the cupboard and filled it with slightly soft cereal. I sat at the kitchen table and ate, drank another cup of coffee, and then headed for a shower. Not before checking every lock, window, and door.

I slid between the cotton sheets and turned onto my side. I could smell Eddie on the pillow she'd rested her head on. When I closed my eyes, I could picture her face. That brief moment after sex when she let her guard down and gave me a heartbreaking smile. A smile that said, maybe, she'd survive, again. A smile that said, maybe, her defenses were coming down, brick by brick, slowly, but coming down all the same. Then the horror of what she could be going through flooded my mind. I'd seen the reports; I knew the abuse the women, the children, in that cult suffered.

A tear leaked from my eye, absorbed by the pillow. "Fight to the death, baby," I whispered.

Knowing what I did, despite how little that was, death would be preferable than a lifetime of abuse for Eddie, I was sure of that.

Chapter 22

My cell was too warm, intentionally I imagined. The uppers were starting to wear off and my body was growing tired. I fought against it. I wondered how Eddie was faring. I'd handed her over as soon as I'd left the bunker, but I missed her. I'd get punished for fucking her, I was sure of that. I liked being punished. I liked the sting of a whip or a belt as it bit into my skin. I remembered the wooden cross and the slap across my ass I'd receive from my father. I especially remembered the 'special' punishments. The times I had to remove my clothes and bend over the back of the sofa. The skin on my ass cheeks tingled as I recalled how he would part them. Despite knowing there was a camera in the room, I slid my hand down the front of my pants and cupped my hardened cock. I fisted myself, gently at first. I smiled. My stomach clenched with need and sweat beaded on my forehead. I bit down hard on my lower lip as a moan traveled from the pit of my stomach, sparked by memories buried deep within me. As I came, I dug my nails into my cock, adding a little sting to the pleasure coursing through my body. I wiped the cum on the threadbare sheet I lay on.

I wouldn't tell them about my father, I wouldn't allow them to use that as a reason for my depravity. Was I depraved? The fact the word had sprung to mind, surprised me. However, I wasn't going to allow my father to take this away from me. What I did, what I'd agreed to when I'd moved back home was all on me. I made the decision to spend two years watching Mich. I made the decision to allow the elders to manipulate me in their quest for revenge. They played on my desire to bring my brother to his knees. They played on the fact that my mother had abandoned me because she wanted to leave the cult. Did she have a choice? I didn't know. Maybe she was forced to give me up to my father, a man so controlling she might not have had a choice. But she didn't fight. She didn't come and get me when she could.

The cult was after two people, they hadn't quite gotten them but they would, soon.

You see, that was one thing that made me chuckle. People thought they were manipulating me but they weren't. I allowed them to believe that for one reason only. I was achieving my goal, knowing I had the backing of something powerful. When this was all over, I had protection.

I had a lawyer lined up; I'd chosen not to call him in because I was enjoying my time in the police cell. I had my own agenda, my own fantasy to fulfil before I got back on the track I'd been told to stay on. I'd deviated, I'd angered, I'd changed the plan, many times. I was in control.

I tried to calculate how many hours I'd been held. They would have to charge me soon, but did they have enough? I'd confessed, I'd confused. I hadn't left a shred of evidence on any of the bodies and that was thanks to Dan and the remarkable medical kit that he carried in his vehicle. Poor Dan. I regretted killing him but, as I *told Corey, he was a loose end that needed tying up. He'd wanted in with the cult, I guess he'd just wanted the opportunity to fuck endlessly. I laughed out loud as I recalled an incident in the morgue. A pretty young girl had been brought in. Well, I say pretty, her face was beaten up as she'd traveled through the windshield of her car. We weren't interested in her face, just her pussy. Dan had insisted any 'play' was after the autopsy, of course. Wise Dan. I'd miss him.*

Sunlight shone through the sheer drapes into the bedroom. I let go of the pillow I'd been hugging in my sleep, my face buried in her scent. My body ached, despite the hours of sleep. I swung my legs to the edge of the bed. My feet connected with the chilly wooden floor. I welcomed the cold; it woke me up. At some point during the night I'd formulated a plan.

I dragged on a clean pair of jeans and a plain white t-shirt. I tucked the silver chain beneath it, missing the feel of my badge. The chain had belonged to my father, he'd worn it every day of his life, and on his death; my mother had given it to me. It once held a small St. Christopher medallion, which had been lost many years ago. Maybe, when this was all over, I'd replace it.

I grabbed the coffee pot and filled it with cold water, ground some beans and set the machine to on. I sat at the kitchen table while I waited. I wanted to get into the mind of Thomas, and to do that I wanted to spend time in his house. I wasn't sure if it was still under guard, I imagined so and could only hope my suspension hadn't been made public.

When the coffee machine gurgled out the last drops of hot coffee, I poured it into a travel mug. I didn't want to waste any more time sitting around. I grabbed my car keys, Eddie's gun, and left the house. The fact I had a visible gun in a holster, I hoped, would give whoever was guarding the house the idea I was still on the case. If not, I'd have to come up with a plausible reason to gain access.

The house came into view as I bumped along the unmaintained driveway. I was thankful not see a police car, although the house was still taped up. Perhaps, whoever should have been there was taking a break; maybe it was shift change. I parked and left my car. I pulled the tape off the door and tested the handle. The door was locked. I made my way around the side of the house and to the backyard. Breaking and entering was probably the least of my current worries as I searched for something to smash the glass in at the back door. I'd been told Thomas had pretty much lived in the kitchen and a bedroom. It was the living room I headed for first.

I stood in the middle of the room, some of the furniture had been removed for analysis, but it was like stepping back in time. I wandered over to the fireplace and stared at the old picture. It had hung over the mantel when my mother was alive. I reached up and pulled it from its hook. I'd hated that picture. I flipped it over and read the inscription. It was a note from my mother to my father, declaring her love and begging his forgiveness. The first time I'd read that I hadn't understood what it meant; now I thought I knew. Had she had an affair? I wasn't sure. She never spoke about my father after he'd died.

I placed the picture on the floor, leaning against the wall. The chair that my mother had been sitting in was gone, but there were four clean squares on a dusty floor where it had once stood. I stared at the space. She had been a good mother to me. Always had a smile ready, a kiss to soothe a bruise. She was kind and gentle. I vaguely remembered her parents, stern and upright, scary and unloving. I was thankful she hadn't taken after them. I couldn't believe she'd willingly give up a child, regardless of how he came to be. She didn't have that in her. The trouble was, there was no one left alive that could answer the question.

I let my mind rest, go blank. My vision softened as I took in the room. I turned, slowly, taking in every detail of a room that was already familiar, yet tainted with evil. The smell of death and decomposition still permeated the air. It was a sweet, sickly smell. The air conditioner had been turned off after my mother had been discovered but the scent of her body lingered.

"Talk to me," I whispered. I wanted the house to give up its secrets.

I walked to the hallway and climbed the stairs. I made a conscious effort to not touch the banisters. Although the property had been processed, I didn't need my prints to be added. There was a basic bathroom, the tiles gleamed and the smell of bleach suggested someone was fastidious with their cleaning. Or someone had used the room to murder in.

I made my way to one bedroom. It wasn't the one Thomas slept in. There was a bedstead and mattress without any covers. The room smelled of dust, as if it had been shut up for some time. I moved on to the next one, his. The bed was pushed against the back wall. It was neatly made; the corners of the bed sheet would have passed inspection in the army, such were the sharpness of the corners. A chest of drawers sat against the opposite corner. Although the drawers were open and the clothes messed up, I knew that before the forensic search, they were perfectly folded. I moved to the closet and picked out a t-shirt, I looked at the tag on the collar. It was a dollar store brand. I had no idea what Thomas earned as a teacher, but I imagined he'd be able to afford to shop anywhere other than a dollar store.

His range of clothing was similar to mine. His sneakers were clean; his shoes polished, and perfectly lined up. I kicked at them, disrupting the regimental line.

I sat on the edge of his bed trying to get a feel of how he lived. He was a neat freak; Corey had that right in his profiling. A shelf held a selection of books, like the one in his classroom, these books were old, worn with the spines cracked and the pages dog-eared. It contradicted his closet somewhat. I guessed he loved his books more than he was bothered about his clothing. I walked across the room and pulled one from the shelf. *Treasure Island* looked like it had been read many times. As I flicked through, I noticed a couple of lines of ink that had been smudged, as if tears had dripped onto the words. Whoever had read the book had been moved by the story.

I sensed a theme; the books were about far away places, adventures. Was he looking for an escape? I refused to feel any empathy for him. I didn't care what his childhood was like; I was only concerned with the present. My fingers ran over a copy of the Bible. I replaced *Treasure Island* and pulled that from the shelf. Like the other books, this had been well-read. Passages were underlined, none of which made sense to me. I pulled my cell from my pocket and sent a text.

Find out if Thomas' father was religious.

Corey didn't answer, I expected he was busy but would pick up the message at some point.

I knew the books would have been searched in case any

documents had been hidden within the pages, which was standard procedure, so I didn't bother to look through any more. Searching for evidence wasn't what I was there for. As much as I tried not to acknowledge it, I wanted to know how similar we were, how much influence my mother's genes had on him. I was a firm believer of the nurture, not nature, theory though. Thomas had been brought up in a completely different way to me. But that niggle persisted.

He'd asked me a question that had stunned me into silence. I hadn't left the interview room because I shouldn't have been there; I'd left to stop answering. The high I got when I saw his father's head explode, under the force of a high-powered rifle, was off the scale. I wasn't as close as Thomas seemed to think I was; I wasn't splattered with his blood, but it did spray into the air. I did get the rush of adrenalin that had my heart race. Maybe killing was in our blood. If I'd have taken a different path in life, I could have well imagined wanting to experience that again.

I left the house with a heavy heart. I hadn't learned anything I didn't, subconsciously, know. Thomas and I were very alike, whether that was by coincidence or not, I had no idea.

I debated whether to walk to the bunker. I knew it had been completely cleared out so I'd gain nothing from standing in an empty space, but it was the last place Eddie had been. I started the mile walk toward it.

The hatch had been completely cleared of earth but contained a new padlock. I stood and looked around; trees surrounded the clearing, the exit hatch just on the boundary. I walked over it. It had been marked with a blue flag. I took the most direct route into the woods. Many footprints and paw prints had made a path. I followed for a little way until it veered off. I knew that path would take me back to a small road. That would have been where Thomas handed over Eddie. I crouched down at the junction and scooped up some soil. I let it run through my fingers as if the earth would somehow connect me to her.

Was it bad of me to pray she was dead? The alternative was just too distressing to imagine. The pain and anguish she had to be going through, especially if she was returning to a lifestyle she'd managed to escape from, was unthinkable. I knew what those bastards were capable of; I'd seen images of maimed women, punished for their disobedience. I'd watched the haunted faces of adults that had grown up in the cult, yet were too frightened to speak out. I'd sat through many an autopsy of a suicide victim who thought death was better than living.

I stood and walked back to the house. I got in my car and drove home, feeling the grit of dirt under my fingertips grate against the steering wheel. Corey's car was in the driveway when I pulled up. He was sitting on the hood, his cell in one hand. He looked up as I closed my door.

"Where have you been?" he asked.

"I'm not on house arrest, am I?" I said, joking.

He rolled his eyes at me. "I went to his house, Corey," I said.

"Why? No, don't tell me any more."

"I wanted to see how similar we were," I said, ignoring his plea.

"And?" he asked, as I opened the front door.

"Unfortunately, I think we are alike."

"Well, you are twenty-five per-cent of each other," he said. I frowned at him.

"It's a gene thing, half-brothers will share twenty-five…forget it. Let's have a coffee."

I set the machine to refill, and while I waited, I washed my hands under the kitchen tap.

"His father was a member of the cult," he said.

"I wondered. His name didn't come up at all though."

"Because Thomas Jameson isn't his father's real name. In fact, Jameson is only one part of a double-barrelled surname."

I took a seat. "Go on."

"Thomas Jameson-Romney."

Corey stared at me, I stared back. "Fake feds," I said. He nodded.

Two of the cult elders had posed as FBI agents when they'd visited Gabriel, one of them was Romney, but it couldn't have been Thomas Sr. He was dead by that point.

"A brother? Son, maybe?"

"Brother. So our Thomas James is actually the grandson of Father Samuel."

"Why has his real surname not come up in any checks?"

"Because, at birth, our Thomas was registered simply as Thomas James. It took some digging, but it seems Tim is not only knowledgeable on the sins but a wizard at genealogy as well."

"Did you check for a scar?" I asked.

"Yes, he doesn't have one. So either he's a trainee, not actually in the cult, or something else."

"Seems odd though, doesn't it? If he's the son of an elder..."

"He doesn't go through initiation. Maybe the tattoo is his passport in," Corey said, verbalizing my thoughts.

We didn't have photographic evidence of Romney. He and Richard Midley had turned up at Gabriel's parents' house, pretending to be investigating the cult that was involved in the devastation of his life. All they were after was information on what he knew.

"Thomas was in this house, Corey. He flipped through that file and it contains Gabriel's address."

"Then maybe you ought to warn him, although they do already know it."

I nodded as I rose to pour our coffee. I remembered that I'd recommended Gabriel leave town; he'd refused. He had a daughter to worry about but believed they were better off among friends. It had been a year since Corey and I had been on that case. Although I'd kept in contact, I hadn't spoken to him in months. He lived just a few hours' drive away; perhaps I'd take a trip over to see him, once we'd gotten a little more information from Thomas. I always knew Gabriel had held back information; maybe he might be able to shed some light on where the cult had moved.

"What happens next?" I asked him, as I handed over a coffee.

"He's been charged on the murders he's confessed to. And..." he paused.

"And, what?"

"Necrophilia."

I spat the coffee I had just taken a mouthful of across the kitchen table. I closed my eyes.

"I'm not sure he actually did it, there's no evidence. It was a statement to shock us, but I charged him with it, regardless."

I'd been there, heard his words when he'd said he'd fucked my mother, but to hear him being charged with it, somehow, made it feel more real.

"I have to warn you, it's not actually a federal offence but, fuck it, I want to throw the book at him."

I felt physically sick. Bile rose to my throat and I took another sip of coffee to wash it down. Acid and hot coffee burned all the way back down to my stomach.

"Can we get the death penalty?" I asked.

Corey shrugged his shoulders. "I'm going to ask the DA to try."

I wasn't necessarily a believer in the death penalty for one reason only. It was quick, and there wasn't any suffering. Take freedom away from Thomas, let the inmates deal with his punishment, incarceration for life was a far harder pill to swallow. I wanted Thomas to suffer.

"He's going to be transferred to the state prison soon. Before that happens, and which is why I'm here, we're not getting anything from him with regards to the cult or Eddie. I can't bring you in, officially, to interview him, but I'm about up for breaking the law right now."

I nodded. "Can I trust you, Mich? Can I trust you not to react?"

I wasn't sure it was a promise I could give, but I nodded anyway. I wanted to sit in front of him. I wanted to ask my questions.

"Do you have to record it?" I asked, quietly.

"You know I do. Whether anything said can be used as evidence, I doubt. I'm waiting on the DA to answer that. I've told him that I think it's imperative that you question him. He wasn't happy, bearing in mind you're suspended right now, but relented."

"Can't I be reinstated, then suspended again?"

"That's what the chief suggested."

"Why does the DA think I've been suspended?"

"Losing it with a suspect, nothing more. He was told there were justifying circumstances but for the sake of the case, you were removed from duty."

I sighed. So the chief hadn't told them about Canada.

"When?" I asked.

"Later today. I want you shaved, clean, and fully awake. You look like shit, I don't want him to see that."

Corey drained his coffee and stood. I walked with him to the front door. Before he climbed into his car he turned to me.

"Two o'clock, okay? And, Mich, you assault him, you'll throw the case right out the window."

I didn't need reminding of that. I nodded, letting him know I understood. I imagined that was exactly what Thomas wanted. Police brutality, no DNA, a forced confession under dubious interrogation methods, his defense would have a field day with that.

I closed the door and cleared away the mugs. I checked my watch. I had a couple of hours to prepare myself. I would be the ultimate professional. I'd remove any trace of emotion. It would be hard, but for the sake of Eddie, for the sake of those kids, my mother, I'd do it.

Chapter 23

The rattle of a bolt as it slid from its metal casing woke me. For a moment, I was disorientated, having not realized I'd fallen asleep. My mind was groggy, my vision blurred. My body clock, thanks to the interrogation through the night, was all over the place. I wouldn't let them know that, of course. I planted a huge smile on my face and opened my eyes. I swung my legs briskly from the bunk and sat. I stretched and gave a fake yawn, rubbing my eyes as if I'd just woken from the best night's sleep.

"Good morning, or is it afternoon?" I said to the officer at the open door. He held a tray with yet another stale sandwich and lukewarm coffee.

"Oh, what delights do we have today?" I asked, reaching for it.

He didn't respond as he handed over the tray. "Mmm, coffee!"

I pretended to inhale the burnt, stale, aroma of coffee. I was sure they were keeping the dregs from the previous day just to give to me.

"Good afternoon, Thomas. Did you sleep well?" I heard. Looking up I saw Corey standing by the door.

"I did. This is surprisingly comfortable."

"Good, we want you well-rested." He smiled at me. "We have a few more questions for you, I'll be along later."

I watched him walk away, the swagger he had annoyed me; he was cocky and I wondered what he was up to. No matter, I'd have the last laugh. It was a shame they had taken my watch, I'd like to know the date. I had a schedule to keep to. I wasn't worried about knowing the time; when the sun rose it was morning, when it set, it was night. I wasn't going anywhere; I didn't care for the time of day.

Waiting was something I was very good at. I'd waited long enough for my time with Mich, another few hours, few days, wouldn't make any difference. I had all the time in the world, really. I placed the uneaten sandwich on the floor but took a couple of sips of coffee. My mouth was dry, my lack of personal hygiene was something that grated on me. I could feel the fur on my teeth as I ran my tongue over them.

I guessed I should have washed my hand; there was a slight tacky feel to it. As if a thin layer of glue had been painted on my skin and then dried. But how great would it feel to shake hands with Corey, or better still, Mich, with cum over my fingers? I sighed. Yep, today was going to be a great day.

I paced the kitchen, watching the clock tick so slowly toward one p.m. To kill some time I took a shower, I stripped the bed linens and put them in to wash, I stood in front of my closet, deliberating between one white cotton shirt and a nearly identical one. I splashed some cologne over my newly shaven chin and cheeks. I selected a shirt, clean jeans, and I dressed. I was at the station by half past one.

"Mich, can I have a word?" I heard, as I walked through

reception.

The chief was standing behind the counter and I met him at the door to his office. The use of my first name had thrown me at first, but then I guessed, I wasn't part of his team, he could afford a little friendliness.

"Take a seat. I'm not happy about this, I don't know if Corey said. In fact, I'm not happy about the whole fucking case being handled in my station by the FBI now, but I have no choice in that."

"Before you say it, I won't do anything to fuck this up," I said, assuming that was his reservation.

"I wasn't about to say that. Here's how I see it. Yes, we got a confession, but we have no evidence. His defense is going to be all over that. You've seen it happen before, at the last minute a confession can be retracted. I need to know where the cross was made, where the scythe is, find me some physical evidence that absolutely ties him to all the murders."

I nodded my head then checked my watch. "I'd better go."

"And, Mich, don't fuck this up."

I walked along the corridor. My palms sweated a little, not because I was anxious, but excited. It was a strange emotion to feel, bearing in mind I'd be sitting opposite a serial killer, one who happened to be my half-brother. I had a plan formed in my mind. I thought Thomas way too intelligent to trap into answering the questions the chief wanted. I needed to play the game he was. I needed to connect with him on a base level. To do that I was about to totally incriminate myself on record. I was about to throw my career out the window and possibly put myself in jail.

I nodded to Corey, who in turn, nodded to an officer. We were ready.

I watched Thomas being walked along the corridor, his step faltered a little when he saw me, then he smiled. I smiled back and gave him a nod. I walked into the interview room with him, forgoing our usual procedure of making the suspect wait.

"Take a seat, Thomas," I said. I carried nothing with me. No file, no pad and pen, nothing. I sat beside him.

At first, I just stared at him. For a moment he stared back but I could see a little uneasiness creep in. I shook my head and chuckled.

"Sorry, I was just seeing how similar we are," I said. "Brothers, huh? Wow."

"You never knew?" he asked. I studied his face and measured my response accordingly.

"No, I wish I had." That answer seemed to satisfy him, he gave a slight nod.

"Tell me about your dad?" I asked.

"Why?" Thomas' shoulders immediately tensed.

"I just wanted to know the man our mother fell in love with, that's all."

He relaxed. "He was a hard man, you wouldn't have liked him. In fact, you kind of did me a favor when you killed him."

I had to decide if he was goading me before I answered. I shrugged my shoulders.

"My dad was a tough one, too. I guess our mom liked that kind of man." I added a sigh.

"Is this an official interview, Mich?" he asked.

I shook my head. "I'm not sure to be honest. It's all a little unprecedented. I've never investigated my brother before," I said, adding a chuckle. "You want the truth? I wanted to get to know you."

I watched him visibly relax. "It's nice to hear you refer to me as your brother," he said, quietly.

"Did you hate our mother?" I asked. I'd made a point of saying *our*.

"For a long time, yes, I did. Is that so bad?"

"No, I think I'd have done the same, especially since you had a hard time with your dad. It's a shame we'll never know why though. I'm not just saying this, but I don't believe she would have given you up unless she was forced to. Did your dad ever say why?"

I leaned forward slightly, relaxing my body.

"They were in love, he said. She wouldn't leave your dad because she feared him, and then she got pregnant with you."

I nodded as if I understood. I'd never witnessed a cross word between my parents and most definitely didn't see any evidence of her fearing him.

"Like I said, he was a tough one," I lied. "It's a shame though, she deserved to be happy."

"Are you really angry that I took her?" he asked. My skin prickled.

"I don't know, is the honest answer. I think I would have liked for her to rest in peace. She had a hard time for a while, which is why I guess she took her life."

He blinked, rapidly. He opened his mouth to speak, but then closed it again.

"How did you end up with her, Thomas?"

He sighed. "She didn't take her own life, Dan killed her. I guess there's no reason for me to hide that. He kept her at the morgue for a while, the old one. But I wanted to care for her, Mich, can you understand that?"

"I think so, but why did Dan kill her?"

He fell silent, gently shrugging his shoulders. "I was so angry with her." His voice had lowered to a whisper.

"So he killed her on your instructions?" He nodded.

"Why, Thomas? I get that you were angry with her, but why not make contact? She might have been pleased to meet you, she might have told you why she had to leave you."

He gently shook his head. For a moment I thought I saw just a fleeting glimpse of remorse and then his face hardened again, the smirk returned. I decided to move on.

"Was your dad a carpenter, as well as a logger?" I asked.

"He was, a master at his craft. He taught me all I know."

"I'd have liked to have learned that skill. I can imagine it's really satisfying to use your hands to craft something. I was impressed with the cross," I said, again adding a chuckle. "I even knew what a dovetail joint was."

He laughed. "One thing my dad always said was, if you're going to do a job, do it well. Took me ages to make that."

"I can just about find a screwdriver. If I move, I'd like a workshop or something. I wonder if I can teach myself some new skills? I need to fix my fence."

"My dad's workshop was like his church. Every tool is perfectly lined up, cleaned after use. I imagined him praying in there," he said, chuckling.

My heart rate increased. He'd used the present tense. We needed to look for a workshop.

"It must have been nice to stand side by side and create something together. I never had that," I said.

"It was. There are times when I miss him, there are times when I hate him so much, I feel sick."

"Why? Why do you hate him so much?"

Thomas' jaw tensed. I could see it work side to side, as if he was forcing it not to open and spill the words I believed he wanted to let loose.

"My dad beat me black and blue once, I remember it like it was yesterday. I'd been playing ball in the yard, kicked it a little too hard and it went clean through the windshield of his truck. I don't think I'd ever seen someone so mad," I said.

"It stops hurting after a while though, doesn't it? I mean, the pain becomes nothing; the broken skin and bones heal. It's the mental cruelty that actually pushed me to become a philosopher, I wanted to understand."

"Why not psychiatry?"

He laughed. "Didn't get the grades. I think philosophy gives you a greater understanding of life in general."

"Does the cult give you comfort?" I asked, changing tact.

"It's the only family I have, well, had, for a long time."

"I've met a few of the elders, I don't think they like me very much," I said.

"No, they don't. But that was before."

"Before what?"

"Before they knew we were related. I have influence, Mich, I can secure your safety," he said, his voice lowered to a whisper.

I leaned further toward him. "I didn't know I was in danger."

"They blame you for having to move on, for losing precious members."

"I guess they would be pretty pissed about that. Do you understand why I did what I did?" I had no idea if he knew the extent of my investigation or not.

"Well, killing off people probably wasn't their best idea. I get why they did, we have to protect the faith."

"You said that the kids were going to expose you, was that because they knew about the attic or the cult?"

He smiled. "The cult, Mich, it's always been about the cult."

"How did they figure it out?"

He leaned back in his chair, away from me. I saw him smirk and the evil glint back in his eyes.

"Look, you've confessed, I'm not trying to get that out of you, I'm genuinely interested. You know me, well enough, I'm curious."

He sighed. "Do you know how much money is made from drugs? Thousands, tens of thousands. It's a very profitable business. Oh, before you get all excited, I'm not a drug dealer. Well, I don't think so. Those fucking kids stumbled across my attic, for sure, but not my wall of art. The other room. For a little while it was used as 'storage.' Instead of doing what they should have, which was to run far away and keep their mouth shut, they decided to blackmail me. They used the room for their 'fuckfest.' They caught me watching, so I supplied them from the 'stock,' and they kept quiet."

"But they kept coming back, I imagine," I said. He nodded. "So the cult makes its money through drugs?"

He didn't answer. He didn't need to. "I've often wondered how it survived, to be honest."

"It's a very powerful organization, Mich. Not one to cross swords with."

"Oh, I've no doubt about that. I bet it feels quite good to be involved in something so powerful? Are they happy with what you've done?"

"Of course, Mich, I am my own man. I make my own decisions,

choices. I'm not some lowly trainee, you know!" His face showed his indignation.

"I wasn't suggesting that, I just wondered," I said, adding a smile. "Did you get initiated or was it a rite of passage?"

"A rite of passage, of course."

"That's what the tattoo is, isn't it?"

He smiled but didn't answer. He angled his arm for me to look at it.

"What is it? It's very intricate."

"It's a twisted cross, can you see? Those there are two scythes, in gold but the color has faded a little."

"What's the meaning behind it?"

"The cross is twisted, it's our version of the religion. The scythes symbolise death and destruction, the way the world is killing itself. Religions kill religions; there's suppression by governments. And the gold? It's one of the greatest, hardest, and ancient metals. Used in Heaven, Mich."

He sat back, pleased with his description.

"I wondered where the scythe came in. I mean, it's a strange weapon of choice. Do you get one? You know, like a gift, or something, when you join?"

He laughed. "You craft your own."

"Wow, so a blacksmith, too."

He nodded. "My father was a very talented man."

"Did you ever meet your grandfather?" I asked.

"Yes. He was a visionary, Mich. He saw the future..."

At that point, Thomas had realized his mistake. Until then he hadn't mentioned his real surname, or the fact that he even knew his birth certificate had been altered.

"Why did your dad drop the Romney? I would have thought he'd have been honoured with that."

"You don't know?" His laughter echoed around the room. Tears coursed down his cheeks and he held his stomach.

I was tempted to look at the tinted panel in the wall; I had no idea what I'd stumbled on.

"Oh, Mich. You really don't know, do you? Romney wasn't my father's birth surname. He adopted it. He added the name of the woman he loved to his own."

I tried not to react. "I don't understand."

"What was your mother's surname, Mich?"

"Simpson."

"No, it wasn't. Your mother was Annie Simpson Romney."

My mother was a Romney! Fuck!

"Why would your father take her name?"

"Because they were married. They were married in our church, Mich."

"But that doesn't answer why your dad would take her surname. Why did she not take his?"

"Because her family were the elders. That's just the way it is."

———

I wanted to take a break. I made the excuse that I needed the bathroom. Thomas was escorted back to his cell with the promise of a hot meal.

"What the fuck!" I said, when I saw Corey exit the viewing room.

"It's bullshit, isn't it?"

"I have no idea. I vaguely remember my grandparents. I think I met them once, when I was young, so my mother couldn't have had anything to do with them. This needs to be checked out. Did she run? Is that why she gave him up, because she wouldn't have been allowed to take him?"

"If what we're being told is true, you know what this means, don't you?" he said, quietly.

I nodded. I had a rite of passage straight to the heart of the cult.

"So how is fake fed Romney related?" My head was spinning trying to work out the *family tree.*

Corey and I walked to the incident room. I grabbed a piece of paper and wrote.

Father Samuel had many sons; Daniel Romney was one of them. I never got to meet him but remembered that Gabriel had described him as being older, maybe ten to fifteen years. Gabriel was about the same age as me. That would make Romney fifty, at the oldest. Was he a younger brother of my mother's? That would make him my uncle, my mother's brother. Shit! And who were the people I assumed to be my grandparents?

Father Samuel fathered children by loads of different women. Some of those women were born into the cult, some brought in from the convent he'd run as children. Others had voluntarily joined.

"I need a coffee," I said. My head had started to pound. I rubbed at my temples, hoping to stave off the headache.

"I don't know how we're going to unravel this," I said.

I looked at Corey. "His father took your mother's name because that gave him the in to the cult he needed. But that doesn't make him an elder, does it? Only the sons of Father Samuel are elders. And their sons. But what about their nephews?" he said.

I shook my head. "I have no idea but I can play on that, I guess. But if I'm a nephew, then so is Thomas, and he said he didn't need to go through initiation. Or it's all bullshit. Some of the elders had that scar, perhaps the scar takes them to another level," The more I thought about it, the more confusing it became.

The cult survived on inbreeding, incest. I shuddered to think just how related we all were.

"I've got some of the guys going through all the property records in the state, looking for anything registered to Thomas James Romney, or variations of the name. Let's see if the workshop comes up. We're also going back to the sawmill. See if there are any old records stored there that might give us some clues."

"What about the daughter, the one who owns the Perry Street property?"

"We had someone talk to her. She never knew her father and was surprised to learn she had been gifted the house in his will. As far as she knew, her mother, a single parent, wasn't aware of who her father was."

"What is she going to do with it?"

"She had it up for sale, some years ago, it never sold, obviously. She said she had all good intentions of fixing it up but couldn't afford to. It was leased for a while. I guess she's just sitting on it for now."

"Do we have anything we can use?" I asked, referring to my 'chat' with Thomas.

"We have the workshop, if we can find that, I think we might find some of the tools he used. If we can get some evidence from that, we're there."

I nodded. I felt exhausted. Holding in the aggression, the need to wrap my hands around Thomas' throat and squeeze the real answers I wanted from him, was taking its toll. I had deliberately avoided talking about Eddie, but with the revelation that my mother had been born into that cult, I might have discovered a way to bring it up.

"Let me take his meal to him," I said.

"I'm not sure..."

"Trust me."

Corey sighed. He nodded and we walked toward his cell. "Don't wear him out, I need to interview him about the *Sinner's* case next."

I caught up with an officer, balancing a tray on one hand, and trying to open the door with the other.

"I'll take that in," I said. He looked to Corey for confirmation. Corey gave him a nod. "Do me a favor? Grab me a coffee as well."

I waited until the second cup was brought back and the cell door was opened.

"Dinner," I said, as I walked in.

Thomas was sitting on his bunk and I placed the tray beside him. I took one of the cups of coffee from the tray and took a sip. I winced.

"It's not the best but I'm glad to see you get the same shit they've been serving up to me. I thought it was some psychological thing," he said, laughing.

"No, the coffee really is shit here."

Although Thomas was relaxed in the interview room, he was virtually horizontal in the cell. He sat with his back resting against the wall and the tray on his lap. I had no idea what slop he'd been served up, some form of ground beef and mashed potatoes. He was clearly hungry as he spooned it quickly into his mouth.

"Daniel Romney is our uncle. Do you know what that means?" I said.

He looked over to me. "I have the same rite of passage as you."

His spoon was suspended between his open mouth and the plastic tray. He slowly lowered it.

"Where do I get the tattoo?" I asked.

"You do it yourself," he replied.

That accounted for the fact we hadn't been able to find a parlor that recognized the tattoo.

"You have no chance of getting in, Mich," he said.

"Why? It's my right. Thomas, I'm out of here, the police, this town, my house. I'm done with it all."

"Bullshit."

I shrugged my shoulders. "You can believe what you want, I mean, you won't know one way or the other."

I saw a very slight twitch at the side of his lips.

"Why do you think I haven't been involved? I'm suspended, Thomas. Soon to lose my job. You asked me a question yesterday, do you remember it?"

He shook his head.

"You asked me what it felt like to kill your father." I shuffled slightly toward him. For the first time, I saw a flash of fear cross his eyes.

"I fucking loved every single second of it. The smell of blood, of brain matter, and bone, Thomas. That stayed with me. The adrenalin that spiked through my body, causing my heart to pound in my chest, the high I got, I want that. You and I aren't that different, it's why I studied you when I walked into that room earlier. I wanted to see a killer's reflection in you."

I heard his soft pants; he had become aroused. His erection strained against the police issue pants he wore.

"It's intoxicating. Taking his life, took my breath away. It wasn't about revenge in the end. I did it, because I could. If I'd have wanted your father dead because he killed mine, I would have killed him long before I did."

"But your mother..."

I shook my head. "It wasn't the death of our mother, Thomas, that prompted what I did. I went back to Canada to visit my father's mother. I tracked your father through the woods, like I'd been taught to track a moose. I trained the sight of that rifle on the back of his head many times. I willed him to turn around, Thomas, to see me, to watch my finger slowly close on the trigger. I wanted to watch the fear in his eyes, I wanted to see the light extinguished."

"Why are you telling me this now?" he asked, his voice husky.

"Because I have nothing to lose. I'll walk out of this station and run. I'll be free but with nowhere to go, no protection. I'll be a wanted man. I've confessed to my sins, Thomas. And it feels fucking great."

I sat up straight, squared my shoulders. "Are they recording this?" he asked, glancing toward the camera in the corner of the room.

"It's visual only, no audio. Why do you think I have my back to it? No lip reading, Thomas." It was a total lie; the room was fitted with a microphone as well.

"Let me tell you about them," he said. "Casey, when she was too high to protest, I moved her from the attic to the morgue. She woke tied to the cross. I would have loved to nail her to it but I knew, when I erected it, they wouldn't hold her up. Dan and I practiced, you see."

"Practiced?"

"We did have access to plenty of 'volunteers'," he said, with a chuckle.

"Okay, go on."

"I fucked her with the cross my father fucked me with. There seemed to be some poetic justice in that. All the things I did, Mich, were all the things I wished I'd done to my father. You got there before I could. Dale, he was running to work, I just stepped around the corner and let him run into my father's scythe. I wished you had been closer to my dad. I wished you had felt the splatter of hot blood and been close enough to see the shock in his eyes, it's like nothing on earth." It was as if he was trying to 'outdo' my crime.

"Then there was Vicky," he sighed with contentment, it seemed. "I don't think I've ever heard such screaming, Mich, it pierced right through my eardrums when I took out her eyes. And the smell of burning, melting flesh." Thomas shuddered, which surprised me. I tried not to react, but my stomach roiled.

"What about Louis?" I asked.

"Don't tell me you weren't angry with him. I mean, you'd gone to all that trouble to protect him. His boredom, his complete disregard for his situation, and for you, Mich, well, that was just plain rude."

I sighed, and nodded, as if in agreement. I made a point to look at the cell door and check my watch, as if I was on a time limit.

"Where did your dad live, Thomas? I think Mom had some photographs of a place; I can't picture it. But I bet they're from the days she met your dad. I'll have to find them and show them to you."

"Sandford, and I'd like to see them," he said, not realizing he'd given me an important piece of information.

"There's something that still bothers me, how did the window get broken?" I asked.

"The window?"

"In the hall, one window was smashed."

"Ah, the window. Dumb fuck that was Dan decided Casey would look better surrounded by light from the window. It didn't hold the weight of the cross, I guess."

I stood and smoothed down my jeans. "I have to go, I shouldn't have stayed this long."

Thomas placed the tray with his long forgotten, congealed meal to one side. He stood, shuffling awkwardly.

"Will you come and see me, when this is all done?" he asked.

"I don't know that the prison will allow that, and like I said, I have to move on now."

Again, his lips twitched ever so slightly. He nodded. "It's a shame really, that it got to this point before we met."

"It is, so much heartache. Can I ask one thing?" I took a step toward him and although it killed me to do so, I placed my hands on his biceps.

I felt him shiver, and my stomach roiled at the thought my touch excited him.

"Where is she, Thomas?"

He closed his eyes and sighed. "I can't tell you that. They'll kill her, Mich, if they think you're coming for her. They'll kill me."

"She is okay?" I whispered.

For the first time, I saw just a hint of compassion in his eyes. "I don't know, Mich. She's alive, or she was when I handed her over. She's a brave, tough woman. She didn't cry much. I guess she knew it was always her fate to return. She left so many years ago, ran away, I believe, like a lot of them do. But we track them down, eventually. They have to return home, Mich, they're needed by the elders."

I made a conscious effort not to squeeze my fingers, to gouge flesh from his arms. I knew exactly how the fucking elders needed the women. Instead, I nodded.

"Take care, Thomas," I said. Then I walked away.

The first thing I did was to walk to the bathroom. I scrubbed my hands like a surgeon would, watching the redness spread as my skin protested. I splashed cold water over my face, cupped my hand under the faucet, and filled my mouth as the need to cleanse the vessel that had delivered the bullshit overwhelmed me.

"There is a building registered to James Romney in Sandford," Corey said, as he pushed through the door.

"Where is Sandford?"

"Couple of hours away, a small town."

I nodded as I looked at my reflection in the mirror. That past couple of hours had taken its toll on me.

"I didn't get the answer I wanted," I said, quietly.

"I know, but you got enough. Mich, he was never going to give up Eddie's location because he can't; I don't believe he actually knows where they are. In time, we will find out, I'm sure of that."

I didn't answer, I wasn't sure Corey was correct. I'd have loved nothing more than to beat the shit out of him, to have caused him so much pain, but then I remembered what he'd said. What could I inflict that would be worse than what his father had done to him?

Did I feel sorry for him? No. I had not one ounce of compassion, or empathy, for him. Whatever happened to him as a child, should have no bearing on how he behaved as an adult. He made a choice to kill those kids; he made a choice to kidnap Eddie. If my mother had been brought up in the cult, there was no guarantee that she wasn't raped, beaten; yet she had grown to be a wonderful human being. I let a tear roll down my cheek as I thought of her.

I wasn't someone who sat by a grave; I mourned her internally. I thought of her often. And I was glad she was dead before she got to meet the monster she'd produced. Nurture, not nature. She would have been devastated to learn how Thomas turned out.

I wiped my face on a paper towel, straightened my shoulders and took a deep breath. At least Corey had a new location to work with. I walked from the bathroom and headed to the chief's office. He was sat behind his desk with his head in his hands. He looked up as I gently tapped on the glass in his office door. He waved me in.

"I'm going to give you two days, Mich. It's the maximum I can do."

I nodded. My confession in that cell wasn't something he'd be able to ignore. My saving grace was that my crime was committed in Canada. I'd need to be arrested in the U.S. then extradited. What the chief was offering me was a chance to avoid jail time. A cop in prison was never a good idea.

"I don't know how successful extradition will be, your grandma is dead, it was twenty fucking years ago, but I have to report it," he added, with a sigh.

"I'll talk to a lawyer," I said.

I held out my hand to the old man I'd worked under for many years. Despite my annoyance at the use of my surname, I had the greatest respect for him. He stood, took my hand in both of his, and just squeezed.

"Good luck, Mich."

I left his office and walked back to the incident room. I stood for a moment, just looking around. Pete was on the phone; Tim was tapping away at his computer. Samantha was running around with a stack of paperwork in her hand. Dean looked up at me.

"Got time for a coffee?" he asked. I nodded.

We walked to the diner opposite the police station, and settled into a booth.

"What happens now?" he asked.

"I don't know, to be honest. I'll talk to a lawyer; see what the chances of rearrest are. The chief gave me two days before he reports me, I guess."

"Two days to do what?"

"Leave. Get a head start, let's see how good you are at tracking me." I added a chuckle.

"I can't imagine anyone taking up the case, Mich, if it came to it."

"You'd have no choice, and it's fine. I walked into that cell knowing what I needed to do. If I could connect with him on a murderer's level, I hoped it might make him open up more. He didn't, and he did."

"How do you feel about him?" It was a strange question for Dean to ask.

"I don't feel a thing for him. I'm beyond hate, I think. I'm numb. I know where Eddie is; I just don't know the location. Want to know something? I hope she's already dead. I know what that cult is capable of."

Dean didn't reply, I guess there were no words to articulate a response to my statement.

Two mugs were placed on the table that separated us, a waitress stood with a pot of coffee. She smiled as she poured. Dean and I sat in silence for a while, we sipped on our coffees, and I looked out the window, watching people go about their business. The news that we had a suspect in custody seemed to have brought the town back to life. For a while, people were scared to venture out. If only people realized, someone in custody, is a long way from someone convicted and in prison. I knew Corey would be meeting with the DA that day, discussing, arguing over what charges could be placed on Thomas. What will secure a conviction and the longest jail term.

"Where will you go?" Dean asked.

"To get Eddie back." No matter what, dead or alive, I would bring her home, one day.

Chapter 24

My emotions were all over the place. I wanted to hate Mich, but I loved him. When he'd touched me, my stomach fluttered. Was that normal? Should I love another man? I sat on the bunk, staring at the cell door for ages after he had left. I could smell his cologne, I wanted to drag the sheet from the bunk's mattress and hold it to my face; I wanted to inhale him. My mind was in a whirl. Thoughts of what I'd done, what could have been had I chosen a different path. I'd spent years and years building up that hate and that had dissolved in seconds. I felt lost without it, hollow. It was all I held onto during the dark days and nights. When I looked at Mich, I saw myself. We shared so many features, the same color eyes; the same shaped nose. I guess we got that from our mother.

His words ran through my mind, over and over. How he felt when he killed my father was similar to how I'd felt killing those kids. I'd meant what I'd said. If he hadn't killed my father first, I would have. For the first time in my life, I felt sorrow. Sorrow for a non-existent childhood. Sorrow for not knowing my mother, other than the odd distant stare at her. And for the first time, I wanted to know why. Why had she given me up? I knew I'd be able to find those answers. I wondered whether I'd share them with Mich or not.

Mich, or rather, Michael Curtis, had the life I never did. I'd harbored such resentment for that, for the longest of time. He'd taken his father's surname. I blinked; he'd taken his father's surname... Didn't that make Mich the bastard child? Was I the legitimate one?

Confusion flooded my brain. Memories became blurred; I suddenly found it hard to distinguish between reality and the fantasy I'd concocted. I stood and banged on the cell door. A small metal panel was slid across.

"I need to see Mich," I said.

"He's not here," came the reply, the panel was slid closed.

I continued to bang until my fists bled.

"I said, he's not here. He's gone," I heard.

All my life I'd been told I was a bastard child, born out of legal wedlock. Or was it that I was just a bastard? My hands began to shake, my body convulsed. I hugged my arms around my waist and sat back on the bunk. I could see a shadow move across the spy hole in the door, someone was watching me. Anger rode over me like a tsunami. I stood and screamed. I upturned the bunk, kicking the mattress across the floor. I pulled out my cock and pissed over it, and up the door. I was losing it.

———

"We're moving him in a couple of hours. Dean's going to ride with them," Corey said, as he walked me to my car.

The local prison had a holding cell available until his appearance in court. They would send a truck to collect him. Corey would continue to interview him, at the prison, right until the last minute.

"And the good news is, we found the workshop," he added.

"What was in there?"

"A scythe, wood, tools, a cross."

"Enough evidence to back up the confession?"

"I think so, I hope the DA will agree. He didn't clean the scythe, Mich," he said, with a smile.

I smiled back, and then nodded. If the blood matched Dale's, at least that was one irrefutable charge. Corey's phone pinged, alerting him to a text. He looked at it, then back at me.

"He's losing it, finally," he said.

I furrowed my brows. "He's freaking out in his cell, screaming out the word *bastard*."

"Reality finally hitting?"

"Or coming down from the high he's been on. Didn't you see his pupils? He had to be doped to the fucking eyeballs."

"I hadn't studied him that hard, pretended to, though."

For a moment there was silence. Corey looked around him. He reached into his pants pocket.

"I want you to take this," he said. He handed over a small black cell. "Untraceable."

I pocketed the cell. "I'll check in, every now and again, when I have something for you," I said.

"You're going after them?"

I nodded. "I have to find her, Corey."

He looked up to the sky and then sighed. He placed his hand on my shoulder and squeezed. Without another word, he walked back into the station. I stood for a moment, watching the world pass me by. For the first time in my life, I was without a job, without a definite plan. I wouldn't even hang around to witness the cremation of my mother, the scattering of her ashes. I'd leave instructions; lock up the house and leave. I started my car and drove slowly home. I stopped at an ATM and cleaned out my checking account.

I pulled off the shirt I'd worn and set about to clean up the house. I washed down all traces of forensics. Why? I wasn't sure. When I was done, I grabbed the Gabriel file and headed to my bedroom. I pulled out a gym bag and packed a few clothes, some toiletries, and the file. I added Eddie's revolver and unlocked my gun cabinet. I added another revolver to the bag, my trusted Glock.

It was as I sat on the bed, I thought. I pictured Thomas in my mind, I heard his words—*When this is all over; will you come and see me?*

A shiver ran over me when I recalled the slight smirk, the tilt to his lips as if he had a secret.

"Fuck!" I screamed and then jumped up. I grabbed the gym bag, my phone, and keys before running for the door. I hadn't bothered to put on a t-shirt.

Thomas wasn't going to jail and he knew it.

I drove at high speed, running every red light, keeping my hand on the horn to encourage the cars in front to move out of my way. I cursed not having a blue light to aid me. I screeched to a halt at the station, and leaving my door open, I ran into reception.

"Thomas, has he gone?" I asked. An officer, looking startled behind the counter, nodded.

I grabbed the clipboard from next to him and ran my eyes down the list.

"Fuck! Fuck!" I shouted. "Call Corey, now!"

Thomas James Romney – vehicle T334 – 1700hrs – Driver

Richard Midley – Escort, Dean Saunders

My body froze on one word. Midley.

Corey came running down the corridor, followed by the chief. I held the clipboard toward him.

"Fuck! Who knew this?" he shouted. The station silenced.

"Want to fill me in?" the chief asked. Corey showed him the clipboard.

"The driver, Richard Midley, he's a cult member. Half-brother of Thomas' uncle."

"How long ago did they leave?" I asked.

"Half-hour, no more," the officer at reception said.

I turned and ran for my car. "Wait up," I heard. Corey ran after me.

We were pulling away before he'd even got his door closed. "Grab a map," I said, waving at the glove box.

I knew the route to the prison but wanted to check any side roads, anywhere a diversion could be taken. Thomas was never going to arrive at prison; it had been part of his plan.

"Take a left," Corey said. I didn't have time to indicate, I swerved in front of a car, and the driver honked his horn in protest.

"This takes us cross-country," he said, looking up from the map.

We were banking on Midley needing somewhere discrete to make an exchange from the truck to another vehicle. I prayed for Dean.

"Why use his real name?" I said, concentrating on the road ahead.

"Huh?"

"Midley, why use his real name?"

"Taunt us, who fucking knows? They think they are above reproach, Mich, there's no fucking logic with any of them. Right here, this takes us out on Route 50."

I spun the steering wheel so violently, the tires screeched and Corey was thrown onto the door. He righted himself and retrieved the map that had fallen to the floor. We were now on the most desolate highway in the U.S. A lonely road: a perfect road for Thomas and Midley.

Ahead I could see a dark grey truck parked on the roadside. My heart hammered in my chest. I pushed my foot further down on the gas trying to gain as much speed as possible.

We pulled up behind and already I could see the rear doors slightly open. I grabbed a gun from my bag. Corey released his from his holster and we slowly climbed from the car, using the doors to shield us. There was no sound. Corey crept along the side of the vehicle; I pulled open the rear door.

I dropped my gun to the floor and raised my hands to my lips, as if in prayer.

My friend, my partner for so many years, was sitting on a hard wooden bench staring back at me. Except his eyes didn't see. A trickle of blood ran down his forehead, along the bridge of his nose and had dripped to his lip and chin. That trickle had come from a bullet hole in the center of his forehead. I wanted to close my eyes, to unsee. I wanted to turn back time and have killed Thomas while I had every chance to. I wanted to do anything other than see Dean dead in the back of that truck.

"Gone," I heard. "Fuck!" Corey said as he came to stand beside me.

"They killed him," I said, as if the sight in front of us wasn't obvious enough.

Chapter 25

I hadn't spoken a word as I was led the rear of the station, still handcuffed, and helped to climb the three metal steps into the back of a prison truck. Dean sat opposite me. I could see the sweat begin to form on his forehead from the heat of the tin can we were locked into.

"Are you comfortable?" I asked, watching him shuffle.

"Yep."

I leaned back against the wall of the truck and closed my eyes.

I'd had Corey, and the officers at the station, believe I was totally exhausted by my meltdown. They had found me sobbing on my knees, remorseful words and lies flowed from my mouth. I was a fucking amazing actor and I wanted to chuckle. I had to keep up the pretense. I was a beaten man; terrified of the next step I was about to embark on. I willed my eyes to let more tears flow.

"I wanted to see Mich, one last time. I wanted to say how sorry I was," I whispered.

"The only thing he needs to hear is where Eddie is," Dean answered.

"If I tell you, will it help my, you know, sentence?"

"I can't promise that, but often, yes it does."

I nodded and closed my eyes as if thinking. "Tell him, Richford."

I watched Dean nod, a smile formed on his face and his eyes sparkled as if he'd just learned the location of the Holy Grail. But like the Holy Grail, he'd never get to find it.

The good thing about the truck was there were no windows in the back, a slotted panel at the top of the wall allowed for a little light and air to filter in, but he had no idea which route we were taking. I suspected that normally there would have been two officers with me, but since my melt down and complete compliance, I guessed they thought they were safe with just Dean. I was also surprised not to have an escort. Did they not view me as a high profile murderer? I wasn't sure whether to be a little insulted about that.

The truck bumped along a little and swerved. I watched Dean bang on the partition between the driver and us. He banged some more when the truck came to a halt. The partition was pulled back.

"We've got a fucking flat," I heard. It was an old line, but effective.

I watched Dean reach for his gun, why, I didn't know. I was cuffed and chained to the fucking bench.

The rear door swung open, and before he could form the words his open mouth suggested were coming, he was dead. He slumped to one side.

Richard climbed into the back of the truck and I smiled up at him. He grabbed the keys from Dean's pocket and released me; I rubbed at my wrists. Before I climbed down from the truck, I straightened Dean up; I wanted him looking toward the door, on *display for whoever found him.*

A car pulled up alongside us, I opened the rear door and slid across the cool leather.

I smiled. "Time to go home," Uncle Richard said.

I couldn't speak; I just stared. Corey was on the phone, pacing. All I could think about was Jo. Dean's wife would be sitting at home, assuming her husband would return at some point. The nearest town was thirty or so miles away, they had nearly an hour start on us, long enough to have gotten there and disappeared.

Corey was calling on every resource we had and begging for more. I heard him ask for aerial support, ground support, the urgency in his voice giving no reason for denial. I took a couple of steps back and sat on the hood of my car. Corey eventually sat beside me. He reached into his pants pocket and pulled out a pack of cigarettes and a lighter. He lit one, then offered it to me. I inhaled, fighting the cough as the smoke hit my lungs, then exhaled slowly. The headrush was instant and I closed my eyes.

"We'll find him," Corey said.

I opened my eyes to look at him. I slowly shook my head. "I don't think you will."

We'd been searching for that cult for years; they were spread out and well hidden. They moved constantly, always a step or two in front of whichever law enforcement agency was on their tail. I'd lost count of the deaths that could be attributed to them, of the families devastated in their quest for an illegal lifestyle. I was one man, but at that moment, when I raised my face to look back into the dead eyes of Dean, I promised him. If it took the rest of my life to do so, I'd find Thomas, Richard, all the elders, and I'd wipe them out.

I'd do it for Dean, for Jo, for the children they would never have together. I'd do it for Eddie, for Corey, for Gabriel even. Mostly, I'd do it for me. I'd become the cult, I'd embrace it, and then I'd wipe it from the face of the earth.

The sound of sirens could be heard, getting louder the closer the vehicles got. I pushed myself from the hood and flicked the cigarette to the ground, grinding it out under my sneaker. I walked to the side of my car and opened the rear door. Reaching in, I grabbed a t-shirt from my bag and dragged it over my head.

Within a few minutes more, one end of the road was sealed off, Corey was directing everyone, and I stood to the side, having no role and feeling completely useless. For a while, no one came and spoke to me. I guess people just didn't know what to say. Some had lost partners in the past and it was those that, as they passed me by, placed a hand on my shoulder, or offered their condolences.

While everyone was busy, taking no notice of me. I slid behind the wheel of my car. I started the engine and ignoring the shouts, pulled away from the roadside. I dodged the two cruisers that had been parked haphazardly across the road and drove. My cell started to ring. I picked it up from the passenger seat, rolled down my window and threw it. I had the phone Corey had given me, it would be the only one I needed. I glanced in my rearview mirror and watched as Corey raised a hand, it wasn't a command to return but a goodbye wave.

––––––

It was dark when I saw the lights of a service station ahead. I was tired, my eyes gritty from the dust kicked up and blown through my open window. I was thirsty and hungry. I pulled in, thankful the store was still open. I refueled the car and headed in. I grabbed a couple of bottles of water, some chips, and a sandwich that looked older than the ones we'd served up to Thomas. I asked for a couple of packs of cigarettes, a lighter, paid, and returned to my car.

I was less than an hour from my destination but night was drawing in. Attached to the service station was a small, rundown motel. I returned to the store, paid for a night and then drove to the parking lot.

The room I'd rented was sparse and very dated. Floral drapes hung rigid with dust, I imagined, over a cracked window. The air conditioner sounded like the engine of a jet but it worked. There was a double bed against one wall and a scratched dresser opposite. I placed my gym bag on top and grabbed some toiletries. The bathroom consisted of a toilet, a small hand sink, and a shower.

The water stuttered, cold and discolored initially. I let it run for a moment before slipping off my clothes. When I stood under the weak jet of water, I closed my eyes. The warmth of my tears as they flowed down my cheeks gave me some comfort from the lukewarm water. I placed my hands against the cracked tiled wall, bowed my head, and sobbed.

I found a scratchy, threadbare towel hung on the back of the bathroom door, and wrapped it around my waist. I didn't care that it didn't look clean. It was as I sat on the edge of the bed that I saw the cell Corey had given me, light up. I picked it up and read a text message.

```
Keep me up to date, Mich. You're not alone
in this. If you need help, you call.
```

I didn't reply, there was no need to. What I did do though was turn the phone off and remove the battery. I'd only reconnect should I have to do what he asked, if I needed help.

I lay down on the bed and shivered as the cold air connected with my wet body. My tears had dried, my mind was empty, and my body was numb. In that moment, I lost all emotion except one. Hatred. It boiled in my stomach creating acid that burned my throat as it traveled up. I swallowed it down. I would not release that acid, no matter how nauseous I became. It was my reminder that I had a job to do, a mission to complete, and I wouldn't rest until I had.

At some point I must have closed my eyes. It was daylight when I opened them again.

———

I dressed quickly, gulped down a bottle of water and took one bite from the sandwich I hadn't eaten the night before. It hurt my throat to swallow the stale bread. I threw the remainder in the trash and left the room.

I found a diner on the outskirts of town and ordered breakfast. The strong, hot black coffee was welcome and gave me the kick I needed to think. I didn't have a plan; I knew where I needed to start, and how I wanted it to end. But the middle part was the tricky bit.

I ate my eggs and toast and drank my coffee. I watched the diner begin to fill and listened to normality. There was no chatter about murders, police inefficiency, deciding who the killer was, here. None of the usual whispered conversations I'd overhear back home. A small pang hit me in the gut when I thought of home. I'd find an Internet café, if the town had one, and send instructions on what to do with my mother. I hadn't had time to leave details. I'd wire some money to the funeral home from my savings account and leave them to deal with it all. Whether I'd ever get back home was something I didn't want to think about.

I wasn't sure if I was on the run or not. Corey knew where I was heading, and I trusted him to keep quiet. But if it meant losing his job, he'd tell, and I wouldn't blame him for that.

I finished up my breakfast and a second cup of coffee before I looked at my watch. I didn't want to arrive too early. After leaving some money on the table, I made my way back to my car. I'd trade it in for a something a little more suitable, once I knew where I was heading.

I took a slow drive through the town reminiscing on the last time I'd been there. The hardware store still had the hatstand beside the door. Outside the grocery store were two women with strollers, laughing and chatting, enjoying their morning. I passed the small school; the children were waiting to be led to class and their excited chatter floated through the window. I'd grown to love the town and my time there had been too short. It wasn't dissimilar to my own, and it's not like I could say without the serial killer, because it'd had its problems. Unlike mine, here was a small community that came together, that respected their sheriff and law enforcement. I carried on through and out the other side.

A half-hour later, I came to a dusty track on my left. At first I came to a halt, not entirely sure I was doing the right thing. To turn up, unexpected, might prove a problem. I had no choice, though. I shifted gears and slowly drove toward the wooden house. The last time I'd been here, the house was a few feet closer to the barn. It had been knocked down and a new one built. As I parked and exited the car, I admired the craftsmanship.

A deck ran the length of the two-story house. I spotted an old rocking chair and chuckled. Prop a shotgun beside it, add an old, bearded man in a checkered shirt and with a pipe, and we could have been in a clichéd movie. Before I made a move toward the house, the front door opened. A young boy walked out, he paused, looking at me. He called out behind him and was soon joined by a young girl. I knew who she was. The two children looked so alike it was uncanny. Both blond, both with big blue eyes. Taylor resembled her mother, Sierra, and each time I met her, the resemblance was more so. She looked at me with her head cocked to one side, she recognized me, but I guess she wasn't sure from where.

"Daddy," she called over her shoulder.

I stood in the yard and waited.

Gabriel came to the door; he hesitated before ushering the kids inside. He closed the door behind him. I watched as he shook a cigarette from the pack he drew from his shirt pocket, he offered one to me. I walked toward him and took it.

"Gabriel," I said, as he raised his lighter for me.

"Mich, long time no see," he said.

I took a long draw of the cigarette, again resisting the urge to cough my guts up.

"Take a seat," he said, walking to a collection of sofas on the deck. "Coffee?"

"Coffee would be good."

He called through the front door before sitting.

"So?" he said, leaning toward me.

I sighed. "Taylor's growing up fast," I said.

"She is, looks like her mother more every day."

"Who's the boy?"

"My son, not biological, of course." He was a little evasive, but then, that was Gabriel all over.

I chuckled. A woman leaving the house with a tray in her hands interrupted me from any further conversation. It held two mugs, a pot of coffee and a jug of creamer. She placed it on the small coffee table between us.

"Vicky, this is Mich. He's with…" He turned to me. "Are you still with the FBI?"

I shook my head. "No, I'm technically unemployed right now."

"It's a pleasure to meet you, Mich," she said, extending her hand to me. "I'll be inside if you need me." She smiled at Gabriel before leaving us.

"Vicky, huh?"

"My wife, that was her son you saw."

"You remarried, I'm pleased for you."

"I never thought I would, but you know, second chances and all that."

I poured two mugs of coffee and picked one up. I took a sip. I watched Gabriel exhale his smoke, lifting his face to the sky as he did so.

"This isn't a social call, Gabriel," I said.

"I didn't think it would be."

"I need your help."

He picked up his mug and rested back in his chair. At the same time Vicky ushered the two kids, dressed in their school uniforms, from the door. Both kids ran to Gabriel. He raised his arm, keeping the cigarette away as he kissed them before they were bundled into a truck.

He stared at me. "What do you need, Mich?"

"I don't know where to start."

"The beginning is always a good place."

"It's going to be a long story."

"I have all the time in the world right now."

I started with Canada.

———

We'd been talking for hours; at some point we'd moved into the kitchen to refresh the coffee pot. Vicky hadn't returned and Gabriel told me she'd gone on to work, she was the local vet. Although Gabriel had interrupted a couple of times to ask a question, he'd mainly stayed quiet and listened. The only break in our conversation came when Sam, a ranch hand, came into the kitchen. He silently filled his travel mug then disappeared again.

"And now I'm here. I'm going for her, Gabriel. I'm going for them all."

"You know for sure Eddie was brought up in the cult?" he asked.

"I don't, I only have what Thomas told me."

I watched him rise and walk to a pine dresser that stood proud in the kitchen. He leaned down and opened a cupboard, retrieving a metal box. I watched as he opened a drawer and pulled out a small key. He unlocked the box and placed it on the table.

"If Eddie was brought up in the convent, she'd be in here."

"How did you get this?" I asked, looking at the box. He shrugged his shoulders, not willing to give up that information just yet.

He pulled out some papers, photographs, journals, and we started to read through. Some of what I read sickened me. Some of it was familiar. Gabriel slid a photograph toward me.

"Could you pick her out from this?" he asked. I looked at a picture of a group of children. I shook my head.

"No. But here's a document with the name Edwina Cole. The date of birth makes this Eddie the same age."

"You know Eddie, or even Cole, isn't likely to be her real name, don't you?"

I nodded. Gabriel had found after, way after her death, his wife, Sierra, was in fact called Savannah. He refused to acknowledge that name and always referred to her by the name she'd wanted him to know her as.

I scanned through the document. It said that an Edwina Cole had been brought into the convent on the death of her mother, father unknown. She had been *fostered* out to a family in Angus, which was where the cult initially started. There was a brief description of her, same colored hair and eyes, but no photograph. Confirmation came on the second page. It gave details of her education, the university I knew she'd attended. Someone had kept track of her.

"This is her," I said, laying the document back down on the table.

I ran my hands over my face.

"Are you sure?"

"Yes, it lists her schools, university," I pointed to the page. "Gabe, do you know where they are?" I asked, hating the pleading that had crept into my voice.

He raised his face to the ceiling.

"It's taken me a long time to stop looking over my shoulder, Mich. To not hold my breath every time my daughter, or my son, leave this house. For a long time, I wouldn't let them out of my sight. I still sleep with a gun under my pillow, with bolts on every door and window because I know they'll be back. One day, they'll come back to finish what they couldn't."

He stood and refilled our mugs with coffee. He kept his back to me while he spoke.

"And I'll be waiting and more than ready. If you want my help, Mich, I'm yours but it's my way. And there's no police involvement, not ever."

He turned toward me. "There's something else I have to say, before you make your decision," I said.

He raised his mug to his lips, staring at me over the rim. He had changed, in the couple of years that I'd known him; he had hardened. Gone was the man who grieved for his deceased wife. Gone was the man who wanted nothing more than to protect his daughter. Instead, standing in front of me at that moment, was a man who had murder in his eyes. Whose blood pumped fast around his body, causing a vein on the side of neck to pulse. A man determined to seek revenge.

"My mother was the sister of Daniel Romney. Remember him? Fake fed."

A slow smile crept to his face as he lowered his mug. "Fake fed, you ribbed me, if I remember, for falling for them."

"I did. I'm sorry."

"Don't be. You've just given me the best news, Mich. We have the perfect way in."

Chapter 26

My face hurt, one eye was half closed from the punch I'd received. I had been stripped naked and tied to a post in the courtyard. The elders had surrounded me, children were forced to sit in perfectly neat rows in front of me. I was on show, entertainment, a warning to those that defied. I was whipped until the skin on my back hung in ribbons and the pain was just piercing, ice-cold. And I loved every second of it. My cock was rigid, pulsing with every swish of the birch branch. I wanted to come. I wanted to shoot my load over the pole I was facing. I didn't get the chance though. I passed out on the fortieth whip.

I'd woken in darkness. I ached; my whole body ached. I was lying on a cold, damp earth floor, a basement somewhere. One ankle was chained to a metal ring on the floor. I'd expected punishment when I'd returned. I'd welcomed it. I didn't shed one tear; I think I was incapable of that. I'd proved my worth by taking the beating dished out by my uncles, the elders.

What was I punished for? I'd ruined Eddie by fucking her. She wasn't a divine child, her mother was a worthless whore who had been killed off, so I was told, but she was valuable. I wasn't supposed to harm her, just deliver her home. She hadn't done her duty, she hadn't brought Mich home, not that he realized where home was. She was the bait, not that she wanted to be, of course. She had defied and refused to continue her task, she had refused to return.

I heard a sob and opened my one functioning eyelid. In the gloom I saw her, sitting on the floor opposite me. She was still naked. It was a thing the elders liked to do: strip us bare, take away any material that shielded us, expose us. They wanted to remind me that, in this basement, on this dirty cold floor, naked, with vermin scurrying around, I was equal to Eddie. I was nothing.

Her legs were drawn to her chest, her arms clasped around them. I could see her ass, her pussy, and she didn't seem to care. Her body was filthy. I would have washed her, I would have cared for her, and I wondered why she was here.

"You continued to defy?" I asked.

She looked up at me. She looked primitive. Her hair was a tangled mess, dirt was smudged over her face, her hands were filthy, her fingers clearly broken. She growled, like an animal. I crawled toward her, as far as the chain would allow me.

She bared her teeth and I watched every muscle on her body tense. If she could, she would have pounced, she would have torn me limb from limb. She was like a caged animal; she'd regressed beyond the point humans walked on two legs. They'd broken her.

I scuttled back to a safe distance. "Eddie," I said, gently. She didn't acknowledge her name.

"Edwina," I repeated. At that, her growl grew louder. I felt the tremors hit my chest and the sound reverberate through me.

"He'll come, Eddie. I guarantee he'll come, one day." Her eyes were wild, flicking from side to side.

"Mich will come for you, Eddie, I promise," I lied. I had no idea if he would or wouldn't.

The sound of his name seemed to calm her, her lips softened to cover her teeth, her shoulders relaxed a little.

"Mich will come, Eddie."

Whether she'd be alive when he did, I had no idea. All I knew was the creature sitting before me was a far cry from the one I'd taken from his house. I had no idea what they'd done to her, I could only guess at the constant rape and abuse. I could only guess at the mindfuck they'd put her through, the drugs they would have pumped into her system.

Maybe she'd be better off dead.

The End

About the *Author*

Tracie Podger currently lives in Kent, UK with her husband and a rather obnoxious cat called George. She's a Padi Scuba Diving Instructor with a passion for writing. Tracie has been fortunate to have dived some of the wonderful oceans of the world where she can indulge in another hobby, underwater photography. She likes getting up close and personal with sharks.

Tracie likes to write in different genres. Her Fallen Angel series and its accompanying books are mafia romance and full of suspense. A Virtual Affair is contemporary romance, and Gabriel and A Deadly Sin are thriller/suspense. The Facilitator is erotic romance.

Available from Amazon, iBooks, Kobo & Nook

Fallen Angel, Part 1

Fallen Angel, Part 2

Fallen Angel, Part 3

Fallen Angel, Part 4

The Fallen Angel Box Set

Evelyn - A Novella – To accompany the Fallen Angel Series

Rocco – A Novella – To accompany the Fallen Angel Series

Robert – To accompany the Fallen Angel Series

Travis – To accompany the Fallen Angel Series

A Virtual Affair – A standalone

Gabriel – A standalone

The Facilitator – A standalone

A Deadly Sin – A standalone

Lightning Source UK Ltd.
Milton Keynes UK
UKOW05f2053300317

297943UK00001B/10/P